Pı

LESLEY A. DIEHL

MUD BOG MURDER

"The new Eve Appel Mystery is here and it is absolutely terrific[....] A great mystery that is all about a fun cast combined with an excellent plot, readers will be thrilled with this one."
—Mary Lignor for *Suspense Magazine*

5 Stars: "*Mud Bog Murder* is rich with heart, strength of character, and independence. A must-read for any lover of mystery!"
—Liz Konkel for *Readers' Favorite Reviews*

"Cozy mysteries have established themselves as a thriving mystery subgenre. While there's plenty of suspense and plenty of investigatory action, the cozies have a warm feeling. Often humorous and usually uplifting, they are on the other side of noir. While the queen of this category is Nancy J. Cohen (who even wrote a how-to book about this subgenre), Lesley A. Diehl is a contender.... These plot interests combine with other features to provide a multi-faceted reading experience. Richly drawn characters like Eve and her grandmother can be at once endearing and irritating. Darrel is a perfectly despicable bad boy. Grandfather Egret has wisdom, patience and courage. Ms. Diehl examines several relationships in rewarding depth. She also provides an entertaining overview of the cultural climate in rural Florida's small, inland communities—this one within shopping distance of West Palm Beach, where Eve and

Madeleine get those upper-class cast-offs to market back in Sable Bay. Read it and smile."
—Phil Jason for the *Florida Weekly*

"The charming, fun mystery kept me sifting through the clues and snorting at some outrageous scenes …. This is the fourth book in the series, but you can read this one without having read the other three. I did. The author drops in some tidbits about previous events and some character insight without barely a hiccup in the story's flow. I hope you give this book a go. I pinkie swear you'll have fun."
—*FU Only Knew, Laura's Ramblins and Reviews*

A SPORTING MURDER

5 Stars: "A fantastic foray into the genre of cozy mysteries, and I simply loved it! In this engaging and extremely entertaining novel, we are introduced to Eve Appel, a delightful and spunky protagonist…. *A Sporting Murder* is fun, funny, fast-paced and exciting, with several twists and turns that I didn't see coming…. I absolutely loved this book. Any reader who enjoys mysteries, suspense, action, or just a great read would love this book, and I highly recommend it."
—Tracy A. Fischer for *Readers' Favorite Reviews*

"Settle in for a nerve-wracking mystery set in the rural Florida. Lesley A. Diehl's *A Sporting Murder* may include women from West Palm Beach, but the characters and murderous activities are right out of old Florida…. character-driven and action-packed."
—*Lesa's Book Critiques*

"An entertaining mix of characters, an engaging setting, and two unsolved murders that baffle the reader until their resolution at the end of the novel. Her intrepid amateur sleuth

Eve Appel is reminiscent of Janet Evanovich's Stephanie Plum, with her lively sense of humor, her unresolved love life, and her uncanny ability to get into—and out of—trouble."
—Michael J. McCann, *The Overnight Bestseller*

"Diehl gives us characters with strength and humor. Eve is a great mix of intelligence, charm and minx, and exhibits the tendency to butt in where it may not be comfortable. She also has a few friends in low places that are there for her regardless of what she needs…. If you enjoy mystery, romance and a little bit of crazy you will enjoy *A Sporting Murder*."
—Leslie Wright, *Blog Critics*

DEAD IN THE WATER

"A well crafted cozy mystery that has action, adventure and detective work involved through a few interesting and fun characters to read about. While reading the book I got intrigued enough by Eve and her list of quirky friends that I'd like to read more books in the series. Especially about Eve's Indian friend."
—Mystery Sequels

"There is action galore. The plot becomes more convoluted as new developments take place just as answers seem evident. Each twist is followed by a further twist, the action is continuous, and Eve is suitably confused…. Recommended."
—Michael F. Hennessey, *I Love a Mystery*

"A laugh-out-loud cozy with just the right balance of suspense, plot twists, romance, and airboat rides."
—Sharon Potts, author of *South Beach Cinderella*

"Lesley Diehl has outdone herself with *Dead in the Water*. She still has her carefully drawn characters you enjoy knowing and the sense of humor that makes you laugh out loud. But in *Dead in the Water*, Diehl has developed her most involved plot. With murder, kidnapping, the mob and alligators, you won't want to put the book down. This second Eve Appel Mystery is a must-read."

—James R. Callan, author of *Cleansed by Fire* and *A Ton of Gold*

"Like the biblical Eve, Eve Appel, the main character in Lesley Diehl's *Dead In The Water* is an impulsive, curious, and determined woman who doesn't always live by the rules. Those characteristics place her in extremely dangerous situations and add to the intriguing plot in this second book in the series."

—Patricia Gligor, author of *Mixed Messages*, U*nfinished Business*, and, *Desperate Deeds.*

A SECONDHAND MURDER

"Lesley A Diehl is a very clever writer. Most of the time I can figure out the murderer in a book but this one kept me guessing right until the end. The characters all have one thing in common, trying to solve the murder …. *A Secondhand Murder* is a cozy mystery, and is part of a series called An Eve Appel Mystery. Hopefully all the other ones will be just as good as this one."

—Sharon Salituro, *Fresh Fiction Reviews*

"Fun from Page one!…. Not only is *A Secondhand Murder* filled to the brim with entertaining characters, but the mystery contained in its pages is also well crafted. Everyone, even Eve, seemed to have some sort of secret. I enjoyed peeling back all the layers of this story as I tried to figure out what was related to the murder and what wasn't. I absolutely enjoyed reading *A Secondhand Murder*. The web of murder and deceit is well spun, but the characters Ms. Diehl has created are truly the

shining stars of this book. Anyone looking for a laugh out loud, fast paced mystery would do well to pick up *A Secondhand Murder* today."
—*Long and Short Reviews*

"A full cast of zany and dangerous characters makes this cozy mystery a fun read. With laugh out loud scenes and some scary moments, this book is so hard to put down and when the end did come, I found myself wondering what madcap adventure awaits the reader in the next book. I loved it!!"
—Kathleen Kelly, *Celtic Lady's Reviews*

"I'll have to personally recommend this book to all of my friends who love cozies. It's a great mystery, with a little suspense, a little romance, some slapstick, and most of all, characters who feel like family."
—Ryder Islington, author of *Ultimate Justice*

"Author Lesley A. Diehl blends humor and suspense into a delightful tale of intrigue. Diehl has created likable, realistic characters that will have you laughing as you try to guess who the killer is. *A Secondhand Murder* flows at a steady pace with some interesting twists along the way. The setting is inviting and the story will draw you in."
—Mason Canyon, *Thoughts in Progress Blog*

"An extremely fun and wickedly entertaining cozy mystery. The quirky characters and the complex entanglements each of them have with the deceased and the protagonist is the best part of the book. The author creates a well-plotted, light-hearted mystery that has some really good laugh out loud scenes. Cozy mystery lovers will thoroughly enjoy *A Secondhand Murder;* it is an outstanding read from beginning to end."
—Robin T. for *Manic Readers*

"Humor, adventure, mystery and romance are all blended together to make this a fun few hours of reading. The book kept me guessing until the end—I kept changing my mind about who the killer was and I guessed wrong. LOL—This was a good thing. I enjoyed this one."
—Yvonne, *Socrates Book Review*

"[*A Secondhand Murder*] will delight you. It has a little bit of everything that you want in a murder/mystery, complete with romance!"
—Mary Bearden, *Mary's Cup of Tea*

"I am absolutely in love with this story. Lesley Diehl has created such a fun character in Eve Appel! She was funny, sassy and smart. She's a great protagonist. The story has a great mystery and there's so many different things going on that I was definitely surprised by the ending. I love a good mystery dashed with humor."
—*Brooke Blogs*

"I really enjoyed the page turning action that even involved getting help from a Mob boss. The story was complex but very easy to follow. The quirky characters including Eve lead the reader through lots of excitement…. I wholeheartedly recommend this cozy for all cozy mystery readers."
—Carol McKinney, *Carol's Reviews*

"There were so many characters that I really enjoyed everyone from Eve's crazy ex-husband Jerry to Alex the Private Investigator to her grandmother and grandfather. They all had their quirks that I loved. Definitely a great new refreshing series that I can't wait to read more of when the author writes more!"
—*Community Bookstop Blog*

Old Bones Never Die

Old Bones Never Die

An Eve Appel Mystery

—

LESLEY A. DIEHL

CAMEL
PRESS

Seattle, WA

CAMEL PRESS

Camel Press
PO Box 70515
Seattle, WA 98127

For more information go to: www.Camelpress.com
www.lesleyadiehl.com

Cover design by Sabrina Sun

Old Bones Never Die
Copyright © 2017 by Lesley A. Diehl

ISBN: 978-1-60381-317-4 (Trade Paper)
ISBN: 978-1-60381-318-1 (eBook)

Library of Congress Control Number: 2016961011

Printed in the United States of America

To Minnie Appel Diehl, my grandmother.

The idea for Eve Appel and Eve's last name came from my paternal grandmother, who was the queen of recycling and gave me a passion for used items. In my grandmother's memory, I gifted this appetite to Eve Appel. Somehow my grandmother foresaw that the world is a greener place when we reuse what we can and preserve what is here. Thanks for the foresight, Granny.

Also by the author from Camel Press:

A Secondhand Murder

Dead in the Water

A Sporting Murder

Mud Bog Murder

Short Stories in the Series:

"The Little Redheaded Girl is my Friend"

"Thieves and Gators Run at the Mention of her Name"

"Gator Aid"

PROLOGUE

———

THE MORNING AIR was cold, but once the sun rose over the levee, its heat penetrated the construction site and brought with it the humidity of south central Florida. The backhoe operator paused to remove his sweatshirt and push his thick, black hair away from his face, then moved the levers of the machine forward so that the mouth of the bucket opened, showing its large metal teeth. Another move of the lever lowered the bucket. The teeth bit into the black dirt of the Big Lake basin.

The operator felt the assessing gaze of the foreman, who stood at the side of the pit, his hardhat pushed back on his forehead. New to the job, Walter Egret was skilled, but he knew he'd been hired by the company against the foreman's wishes. As a Miccosukee, his work would be scrutinized more closely than that of others employed by Coastal Development Company and its construction arm, Gator Way. The foreman's constant surveillance bothered him, but not as much as the feeling that someone else watched him from the cover of the sabal palms that stood at the edge of the property. He'd felt a shadowy presence there for several days. It was probably nothing, but today he would take a walk over to the trees during his lunch break.

This land now being readied for a sportsman's retreat had once belonged to his people, but legal maneuvering by slick lawyers deeded it away from the tribe into the developers' hands. Walter didn't like to think about that too much. Being a backhoe operator was a job, a way for him to support his three boys. He dumped the bucket of dirt and maneuvered the machine back to bite the earth again. This time the bucket picked up debris lighter colored than the soil. *Probably some buried tree limbs*, he thought, halting the rise of the bucket. *Huh. Looked like bones from some animal, maybe a cow. Lotta bones.*

"Hey, dump that back in the hole. What the hell have we got?" shouted the foreman.

Walter did as he was told and deposited the bucket load back in the area he'd dug. He shut down the backhoe, and both he and the foreman jumped into the hole to take a closer look.

"Oh, damn," said the foreman, "look at that." He pointed at a round object, dull and gray, lying in the dirt. "I think we've got ourselves a burial ground. I gotta make a call."

The foreman climbed out of the hole and walked away, his cell in his hand.

Walter continued to stare at the object. A skull. Those were human bones. Maybe the bones of one of his people. Bending over to get a closer look, he saw a metal object buried in the loose dirt. He pulled it out, brushing the soil off what turned out to be a heavy gold chain. At the end of the chain swung a pocket watch. It looked like one he dimly remembered seeing when he was a child.

"Get the hell out of there. Don't move anything." The foreman's face was red and shiny with sweat, not from exertion but something else—fear, maybe? "You find something?"

Walter's fist closed around the watch. "No. Just more bones."

"Yeah. Well, we got to shut down and notify the authorities. That damn Indian grave stuff."

"The Native American Graves Protection and Repatriation Act," Walter said.

The foreman shot him an angry look. "Real wiseass, aren't you? Well, I don't know when we can begin work again, so you're out of a job for now." His words seemed to suggest it was Walter's fault the job had to be halted.

The foreman hesitated, then added, as if embarrassed by his earlier accusatory tone, "Well, you seem to know your way around machinery, so you'll probably hear from us." He grunted a goodbye and turned toward his pickup truck, which stood parked near the palm tree grove. "You go on, now. I'll wait here for the authorities." Walter watched him climb into his truck and start it up. He knew the foreman would sit there in air-conditioned luxury until someone showed up.

As he began his five-mile walk home, Walter envied the man the cool air. His old Ford truck wouldn't start this morning, so he'd had to walk to work, and he was spectacularly unsuccessful at thumbing a ride. No one wanted to pick up a Miccosukee in work clothes and beat-up work boots unless it was some other tribe member. The morning's walk hadn't been so bad because it was cool. Now the midday sun beat down on his head. He pulled a strip of leather from his pocket and tied his long hair back. Once well away from the construction site, he stopped and took the watch from his pocket. It was battered and scraped; a long gash on the back told him one of the bucket's teeth had gouged it. He wiped away the dirt on his jeans to reveal a plumed wading bird etched on the cover face. He tried to pry open the case, but wasn't successful. He knew that if he did, he'd find an inscription inside. He was certain this was the watch his mother had given his father as a birthday present.

Finally, the mystery was solved. He'd found his father. After so much time. Grandfather was right. The swamp had returned him. He had to call Sammy. Sammy would want to know, and Sammy would know what to do.

He had no cellphone, but he couldn't wait until he got home

to call. He'd have to stop at the Dusty Boot, a biker's bar up the road a mile, and use the phone there. He quickened his pace despite the heat. Once in the cool darkness of the bar, he grabbed a stool and asked for a coke. Remembering he'd left his lunch in the backhoe, he ordered a ham sandwich.

There was no payphone in the bar, so while he waited for his sandwich to arrive, he asked the bartender if he could borrow the house phone.

"It's really important. A local call."

The bartender, a woman with teased blonde hair, a spaghetti strap top, and two full sleeves of tattoos hesitated, but once she'd looked around the empty bar, she shoved the phone his way. "I ain't supposed to let ya, so be quick and don't tell no one."

The call connected to Grandfather and Sammy's answering machine.

"Sammy? I need to see you tonight. I found Father's watch on a body we unearthed at the construction site today. I think the body is Father's."

The bartender brought Walter his sandwich, which he ate slowly, savoring every bite of the dry white bread and fatty ham concoction. Walter was happy. Now he knew what had happened to his father. Now he could bring Father home to rest.

THE CAR HIT Walter Egret a mile down the road from the Dusty Boot. Two men stepped out of the black SUV and approached the body.

"Do it," the man in the suit said to the other.

The other man, short, ferret-faced, and dressed in jeans and a tee-shirt, searched the body. "Not much money, no cellphone, cheap wallet, and this." He held up the pocket watch.

"Nothing we should worry about, I guess. Leave it all. We want this to look like an accident." The man in the suit got back into the car. He didn't see the other man pocket the watch.

The driver spoke into his cell. "We cleaned everything up here. We'll finish it later."

CHAPTER 1

———

"No turtle bites. Darn. I've been wanting to try them since I moved here, but every time I order them, this place is out." I perused the menu, looking for some other exotic, genuine Florida swamp delicacy to try. Actually, almost everything seems unusual to me. I'm Eve Appel, and sometimes I wonder if I belong here. I'm originally from Connecticut, but I moved to rural Florida several years ago to get away from Jerry Taylor, my husband at that time, and to start a business. Along with my best friend, Madeleine, I own a consignment shop here in Sabal Bay, a small city sitting on the edge of what Floridians call the Big Lake—Lake Okeechobee.

To be clear, we now own *two* shops. One is stationary, housed in a newly renovated store in a small strip mall at the edge of town; the other has wheels, a large recreational vehicle converted to hold our merchandise. The big rig shop happened by accident when we were forced to move out of our original location. It was the brainstorm of my dear friend, mob boss Nappi Napolitani. He's not merely "connected," he's creative, too.

I was seated across the table from my friend Frida Martinez, a local police detective. She had the day off, so I invited her for lunch at the restaurant near the bridge crossing the Kissimmee River, where it flowed into Big Lake. Before you get all excited picturing blue water, long stretches of sand, and gentle southern breezes, this lake is for fishing only. The water is brown, it's shallow, and the alligators rule. No one except the very stupid, inebriated, or drug-addled swim in it.

Frida ran a hand through her dark hair and gave me a smile of sympathy. "Unfortunately, it's today or never for the turtle. This place is scheduled to close this weekend. That sportsmen's resort complex is breaking ground as we sit here, and the restaurant will be replaced by something finer. That's according to the article in this morning's paper."

"Sabal Bay doesn't really seem like the place for 'fine dining.' Aren't we more of a barbecue, pizza, and wings sort of town? I can't see a sportsman just in from cleaning his catch, scales still clinging to his vest, eager to be seated at a table with a linen tablecloth so he can order foie gras."

Frida chuckled and nodded. The waitress approached again.

"I'll just have a burger, medium, with fries," she said.

"Me too."

The waitress gave us the look of disappointment I recognized from earlier, when we ordered the turtle. "We're out of burgers. And fries."

"What *do* you have?" I asked, hoping against all odds it would be something I wanted to eat. If I waited much longer for lunch, I'd chew on an old cow hide. I was that hungry.

"We have barbecue."

"Oh good. I'll have that. How about you, Frida?"

"We only have one serving left," the waitress said.

"I don't understand why you even opened your doors today," I said.

More diplomatic than I—and who isn't?—Frida said, "We'll split the order. And cole slaw. You do have that, don't you?"

"Some," the waitress said. She turned quickly away and headed to the kitchen.

"I guess it was stupid to think this place would have much to offer just before closing its doors." Frida sighed. "But the view is great."

We both turned our heads to look out the windows, which provided a view across the mouth of the river. Boats flew down the waterway into the lake while others sat at anchor, lines over the side, fishing for whatever the water offered here—bass, speck, and catfish.

The doors to the outside porch were open, and earlier we had heard heavy machinery working the construction site just south of the restaurant. Both of us sat back and let the scenery envelop us.

It was more than wanting to have a chat over food with an old friend that made me ask Frida to lunch. I wanted to pick her brain about something Alex, my ex-boyfriend and a private investigator, had said to me. Our relationship had shifted gears, and where it had once been made up of a lot of lust, now we were friends, no benefits. I still respected his opinion on criminal matters.

I was about to steer the conversation around to my questions when Frida's cell rang. She answered, but said little, then disconnected.

"I know I'm off for the day, but there's been some problem over at the construction site. My boss knew I'd be here for lunch, so he thought maybe I'd take a look since my assistant Linc Tooney is out with the flu this week. Why don't you stay here while I run over there to see what's up? You have my share of our lunch order."

The announcement that there was some official police affair made me lose my appetite—not because I was nauseated, but because the only thing I loved more than barbecue was poking my nose into crime scenes. Murder was the main crime that inspired my nosiness.

"Couldn't I come along? I promise to stay out of the way."

Frida gave me a skeptical look. She knew my promises about keeping out of her cases were worth about as much as a Confederate dollar, at least back in the days when Confederate money had no value to collectors.

"Please? I mean we did come out here in your car. How am I supposed to get back to the shop? You owe me."

"I owe you a ride, not the right to pry into police business." Frida hesitated. "But I suppose if I say no, you'll just tag along and annoy everyone until you cause some kind of an incident."

"Oh, goodie."

The waitress approached our table and said, "I guess that serving of barbecue was already spoken for." She nodded at the only other table occupied in the entire restaurant.

That settled that. It was our fate not to eat, but to do crime stuff instead. My PI friend Alex Montgomery told me I had a nose for crime—not that he liked that trait in me—but he admitted I was pretty good at sleuthing out clues. That was why I'd asked Frida to have lunch today. I needed another opinion about how good I was at this detecting business. Alex had even suggested I might want to go after my PI's license, as if I had time to do professional detecting with two consignment shops to run and Madeleine about to give birth to twins.

Oh, did I forget to say that? Yep. My tiny best friend had found her soul mate, married him, and they were about to become parents. Any minute now, I suspected. She looked like an overstuffed piñata.

"Well?" said Frida. "Are you coming or what?"

I tossed a tip on the table. The waitress looked grateful until she saw the amount was only a few bucks; then she shook her head and muttered something about how badly women tip.

"We'd tip better if we got food!" I yelled back at her as we rushed out the door.

A BULLDOZER SAT at the edge of an area scarred by earth-moving machinery and scraped clear of trees and grass. The debris removed from the site was piled up near the edge of the road. More than just bushes, trees, rocks, and dirt had been mercilessly disturbed and shoved to one side; I saw the wing of a white heron lying under one of the downed live oak trees. A breeze caught the feathers and moved them as if the bird were still alive and trying to lift itself from the rubble. Nothing escaped the machinery of development.

No one was around, but as Frida and I approached, a man in a hard hat jumped out of a pickup parked near a stand of sabal palms not yet destroyed by the work.

"You the cops?" he asked.

Frida pulled out her badge and introduced herself. "And this is, uh, Eve Appel, who is observing today."

He nodded at Frida and said to me, "You must be on some kind of a criminal justice internship, huh? You look kind of old for a college student."

"I am," I said.

For a moment, my remark puzzled him, but he shrugged and turned back to Frida. "Let me show you what we've got here."

He led the way to where the ground had been dug down several feet and leveled to begin setting forms to pour cement for the foundation of a building. He took us to the edge of the hole and pointed into the middle of the area.

"See there? We dug up a skull."

I could just make out a domed grayish object and a few longer ones near it.

"You the one who was operating the machine?" Frida asked.

"Nope. I'm the foreman. I sent the operator home. Nothing for him to do now. I also phoned my boss and told him what we found. You know what this means, don't you?" From the tone of his voice, he was clearly frustrated and angered at having to stop his work. "Damn nuisance."

"What's he mean?" I asked.

Frida explained, "This land used to belong to the Miccosukees, but the courts deeded it to the state, and the state sold it to the development corporation. Since it once belonged to the tribe, finding a body means it could be a tribe member buried here. The tribe might want to reclaim it for reburial in accordance with the Native American Graves Protection and Repatriation Act."

"That damn foolishness," the foreman said.

"Any body found on any piece of property requires investigation by the police; you know that."

He grunted in reply.

"I'll need the name of the backhoe operator. You should have kept him here, so I could talk with him. Have you informed the state authorities yet?"

"Nope. Not my responsibility. My bosses might have."

Frida looked perturbed at the foreman's obstructionist attitude. "I'll call in case your bosses forgot." She stepped away from the site and made a call. I leaned over the area.

"The bones don't look that old," I said.

"You some kind of an expert—an archaeologist, maybe?" the foreman asked.

"No, but you can see pieces of fabric, maybe the person's clothing near the bones."

He grunted again and walked back toward his truck.

Gosh, it was tempting to get closer for a better look at those bones.

I felt hot breath on my neck. "Don't you dare, Eve," said Frida. "You stay here. I want to take a closer look." She stepped gingerly into the depression, drew on a pair of latex gloves and leaned over the skull. "I'd better not move or touch anything until we get the state authorities and our forensic team out here for a look."

I tried to stretch my neck out farther to examine it more closely and would have pitched forward if someone hadn't grabbed my arm and pulled me back.

"Who ...?" I said.

"Danny Cypress. I'm the lawyer for Coastal Development and Gator Way. Sorry to frighten you, but I was certain you were going to pitch forward into the good soil of our area and spoil your beautiful boots. We wouldn't want that, now, would we?"

I looked into black eyes and a broad smile. "You're Miccosukee, aren't you?"

"Yes, ma'am, but only half on my father's side. Maybe you've heard of him. He's a rancher around here. Name's also Danny."

"I'm not from around here," I said. His hand was still on my arm, and the physical contact was beginning to make me feel uncomfortable.

"I didn't think so. You don't dress like any woman I know in Sabal Bay. What's your name?'

"Eve Appel." I moved away from him, forcing him to drop his hand from my arm.

"You must be from the state then."

"No. I'm with the detective." I nodded toward Frida, still carefully moving around the bones.

"So ... cop, then." His tone turned less friendly.

"She's a friend," Frida said. "How are you doing, Mr. Cypress? I heard you'd taken a job with the company developing the sportsmen's complex." Her words were respectful but had an edge. She appeared wary of Danny Cypress, and I wondered why.

"I gather you contacted the appropriate authorities?" he said.

"Just now. I assumed the company might drag its feet."

"Now, why would we do that? We like to stay within the law, and we respect the tribe's right to their dead. I mean, if this body even belongs to the tribe. And that will take some time to establish, won't it?"

"Well, since you're so eager for the company to obey the law, would you like to notify the tribal elders? With your contacts, you probably know them better than I do."

"I do, but I don't think it's my place to make that call. I work for the company, despite my Miccosukee heritage."

"Let's keep everything above board. No conflict of interest, right?"

"Right."

Wow, what a tense conversation this was.

"Oh, and by the way, the state won't be sending anyone out here until tomorrow. I'll have to wait until then to see what evidence I can gather. I'll be posting a guard here until they arrive."

A police cruiser pulled past the palms and drove up to the bulldozer. "Well, here the guard is now. Time for everyone to leave." Frida said "everyone," but her remark was directed at Danny Cypress.

"She doesn't trust me," said the lawyer to me, loud enough for Frida to hear.

"Right," she said.

Frida and I watched the foreman as well as Danny Cypress leave. Both of their vehicles—the foreman's truck and the lawyer's black Escalade—had the development corporation's name and logo on the driver's door: "Gator Way" and a picture of an alligator with a huge grin on his face. I looked over at the heron's feathers in the pile of debris and couldn't think of a more incongruous image for this company.

"I wish I could get into that area with my forensics team. I'd like to take a closer look at those bones and collect evidence to take back to the lab." Frida turned the cruiser into the parking area in front of the consignment shop.

"Yeah, I know just what you mean."

"I'll bet you do. I shouldn't have allowed you near the place today, but I didn't know what to do with you. All I did was set free the snooping monster inside you."

Restless, I wiggled around on the seat. "That's something I wanted to talk to you about today."

"Turning over a new leaf? Is it that you'll stay out of police business because you have enough stuff of your own to do? What is it with you, Eve? It seems you have the need to multitask more than any person I've met. Don't those two shops take up enough of your time? Maybe I should talk to your Miccosukee lover Sammy about filling your life with more stuff like canoe rides in the moonlight, or would you like to take over his airboat business too?"

She was kidding, but her words held a kernel of truth. I seemed to have endless energy. And the most curious mind. That was what finally drove Alex and me apart, my insistence that I could do the job he did—follow leads, interview people, ferret out clues. He agreed I could do these things and well. He just didn't like my presence in his cases. Frida felt much the same way.

As for Sammy, my snoopy nature didn't bother him. He accepted it as part of who I was. He and I had something going on, but we hadn't yet decided what it was. I'd felt nothing like it for any other man. There was an odd tension between us, a sensual feeling, as if the air was filled with a longing almost fluid in nature, like a mist. We seemed to breathe each other in, as if there was no space between our bodies or our souls.

Frida broke into my thoughts of Sammy and surprised me by her comment, an echo of something Alex had said. "Maybe you should consider working with Crusty McNabb, apprentice yourself to him. With Alex gone to Miami, this area has only one private detective. I know Crusty could use the help, and his office is about next door to your shop."

I was aghast at Frida's words. "You're kidding, right?" Why would she suggest such a thing? And then I knew. "You figure if I have cases of my own, I'll be too busy to help with yours."

Frida smiled. "I think the word we want here is 'interfere' with my cases."

"I've been a big help. You know that."

Frida leaned her head into the headrest. "You have, but

if you're hell-bent on fighting crime, you could use some discipline, not enough to destroy your creative, intuitive side, mind you, just enough professional training to hone your skills. I'm only saying this to make my life easier."

I gave her a look filled with hurt. "You find me a nuisance."

Frida reached out and touched my arm. "Sometimes. And sometimes you are positively brilliant. I want you to find your calling. Maybe it isn't selling secondhand designer fashions fulltime. Maybe it's a combination of things."

"Okay. I'll give it some thought. Would you help me? I'll have to carry a weapon—I mean other than my sassy attitude and my stiletto heels."

My meaning seemed to finally hit Frida. Her normally café au lait skin blanched. "A gun? Oh God. You'll be carrying a gun. I hadn't thought of that."

I had, and I thought I liked the thought, but before I could tell Frida how I felt, I caught sight of Grandy, my grandmother who was tending the store today, waving to me from the front window.

"Gotta run. Something's up. We'll get together and talk more about guns and stuff."

Frida gave me a tentative smile as I jumped out of the car and ran into the store.

"DAVID JUST CALLED. Madeleine's gone into labor." Grandy sounded excited and looked as if she couldn't be any happier if she was Madeleine's grandmother. Instead she was mine, the woman who raised me and who was responsible for the nosy, impulsive gal I turned out to be. She grabbed me and hugged my skinny frame to her shorter, chubbier one. Her white curls bounced as if with joy.

My heart seemed to momentarily stop beating, then take up a faster rhythm. Finally, Madeleine, who had spent the last two months in bed, could look forward to the imminent arrival of her babies.

"I'll bet she's overjoyed. I am," I said to Grandy.

"I can't figure what's gotten into David. He was with his first wife when she delivered, but he's totally fallen apart with Madeleine."

"She's having twins, and she's tiny. He doesn't know how tough she is."

"I think we should close up the rig for the day and pop off to the hospital," said Grandy.

"They probably won't let us in to see her."

"I'm not worried about her. We need to be there for David. He's supposed to be her labor coach, but he didn't sound like he could coach Jell-O out of a mold."

I thought about that image. "All you need to do is upend the mold and then dump it. Not difficult at all."

"That's what I mean. You want to drive or me?" she asked.

"Me." We jumped into my Mustang convertible, and I sped out of the parking lot and onto the road.

At the hospital, we found David in the maternity ward waiting room.

"This can't be good," said Grandy, as she dashed over to his side.

"Aren't you supposed to be in there, coaching her?" I asked.

"They kicked me out. Something about one of the babies being in distress."

CHAPTER 2

———

GRANDY PUT HER arms around David and walked him over to the waiting room couch. "That's not unusual with twins, and she is small. Didn't they tell you about the possibility of having to do a C-section?"

"Oh, right."

Grandy seemed to know just what to say and do to help him. David brightened up, and he seemed less distraught.

I stood by helplessly, almost as upset as David. Madeleine and I had been best friends since elementary school. With the death of my parents in a boating accident when I was nine, she and Grandy were the only family I had. Madeleine had to be all right. She just had to.

Grandy caught my panic out of the corner of her eye. "Eve, honey, why don't you get David here a cup of coffee from the cafeteria. I think it's still open."

"I really don't want—" said David.

"Oh, yes you do," Grandy insisted.

I stood, unmoving.

"Get going. *Now*, Eve!" Grandy said.

I knew that tone of voice. Grandy's orders were not to be

disobeyed. I ran out the doors and down the hallway. I had no idea where the cafeteria was located, but I ran into a cleaner—actually, I ran him over—and asked him.

"Turn right across from the elevators." He pointed, righting his bucket of soapy water.

By the time I got back with the coffee, I was out of breath, and David was calmer. Leave it to my Grandy to know how to handle us both. Thank God for the Grandys in our lives.

"Any word on Madeleine?" I asked.

Both Grandy and David shook their heads.

We waited. And waited.

"Should I try to find someone?" I asked.

"I'll go," said Grandy. She grabbed me to her and whispered in my ear, "Keep him relaxed, would you?"

I guess I'd graduated from the role of hysteric to that of calming influence, but I didn't have Grandy's know-how with stressed-out husbands.

"How do I do that?"

"Talk to him."

"Great idea. About what?"

"Anything but babies, pregnancy, delivery, hospitals, C-sections. You know. Nothing Madeleine-related." She gave me an encouraging pat on my shoulder and left.

The only thing David and I had in common was Madeleine. Now what?

David owned a game ranch, and although he now had Sammy operate it part-time because David had an aversion to guns—odd, huh?—he still knew more about hunting and weapons than most of the cowboys around here. All I grasped of firearms was they made loud noises, fired bullets, and when aimed with some accuracy, could kill. If I wanted to go into the PI business, I needed to know more. So I talked to him about guns.

If David figured out what I was up to, trying to take his mind off Madeleine and the babies, he didn't let on. We played the game, and it made us both feel better.

Grandy appeared several minutes later when I was just about to run out of questions and David was starting to fidget and glance anxiously out the door into the hallway. Behind her trailed the woman I knew was Madeleine's obstetrician.

"Sorry I couldn't get in touch earlier, but we were kind of busy," she said.

"A C-section, right?" said David.

"Nope. That little gal of yours just kind of popped both of them out like lifesavers from a roll. One of the shortest labors and delivery times I've ever seen with twins." The doctor grinned.

"But David said one of the babies was in distress," I said.

The doctor's grin widened, and she leaned close to me. "Madeleine saw how agitated he was, so she asked me to make up a story to get him out of there. I agreed. She was doing just fine, but I was worried he'd upset her."

The doctor turned back to David. "You want to see her and the twins now?"

David nodded and followed the doctor down the hall. Grandy and I were right behind him.

Madeleine sat up in bed, the picture of maternal beauty, a tiny baby on each arm. The smile on her face could light up the entire city of Sabal Bay. Of course, she looked as if she had run a marathon, her skin red and sweaty, her hair lying in damp ringlets over her ears.

We all rushed over and planted kisses on her and oohed and aahed over the babies. One baby was small and had Madeleine's red hair while the other was a dark-haired bruiser with David's coloring.

"So what are they?" I asked.

"They're babies, Eve," Madeleine said, a twinkle in her eye.

"I know that. I mean boy, girl, boys, girls. What?"

"A boy and a girl," Madeleine said.

"Perfect," Grandy added.

David reached for the bigger of the two. "Daddy's big boy," he said.

"That's the girl," Madeleine said. "That's Eve. And the boy is David Junior."

I hardly knew what to say. Eve was not one of the names we'd talked about, but obviously, from the expression on David's face, he and Madeleine had.

I took a deep breath, but it didn't help. I began to blubber and cry, and Grandy had to lead me out of the room because I'd upset the babies. Both were howling.

"A fine aunt you'll make. They'll never ask you to babysit." Grandy handed me a tissue.

I blubbered some more, soaking it through.

My cell rang.

Continuing to sob with happiness, I handed the phone to Grandy. "Can you answer it?"

She said hello and listened for a moment, then held the phone against her chest. "Get ahold of yourself. It's Sammy, and there's trouble of some kind."

GRANDY AND I left an exhausted Madeleine and an equally wrung-out but happy David and headed down the highway toward Sammy and Grandfather Egret's house and airboat business. With Sammy working David's game ranch, the airboat business was being operated by Grandfather Egret, who booked reservations and sold tickets while Sammy's two nephews piloted the boat. Sammy was eager for David to find a permanent foreman for the ranch; he wanted to get back to the airboat tours. And everyone wanted him back there. His tall, dark, good looks and knowledge of the swamp were as much a draw for the tours as the life found in the swamps. My ex, Jerry, had stepped in at one point to help out on the tours, but tourists expected a member of the tribe, not some pasty white guy from up North.

Sammy wouldn't tell me on the phone what was happening. He only said he and Grandfather could use my help in a criminal matter. He knew I couldn't ignore that kind of request.

I pulled my car into the now deserted parking area next to the airboat chickee where Grandfather sold tickets for the tours. Grady and I climbed out and hurried down the path to the Egrets' place, a traditional Florida swamp house made of hand-hewn lumber and set on stilts. A light shone through the open door onto the porch, which ran the length of the front of the house. Grandfather Egret sat in his rocking chair, puffing on his pipe. Sammy paced up and down the porch. He ran to greet me and pulled me close, enveloping me with warmth like the sun of a Florida summer. Each time Sammy and I got together, the heat between us could start a bonfire. From our first meeting, it had always been like this, though we had ignored it as long as we could.

"We just had a visit from a state trooper. My half-brother Walter was found on the side of the road that runs out to the Kissimmee bridge. Someone hit him and then drove off."

"Is he …?" I asked.

"Dead."

Grandfather removed the pipe from his mouth and nodded. "The body has been removed to the medical examiner's office for autopsy."

Headlights from a car pulling into the airboat parking lot shone onto the side of the house.

"It's me," Frida called. "I was told a trooper notified you about Walter."

She approached the house, stepped past me onto the porch, and stooped to give Grandfather a peck on the cheek. Reaching out to touch Sammy, she said, "I'm so sorry. But we'll get the guy. I was just at the scene."

"Eve and I are leaving to go out there," Sammy said.

We were?

"It's too dark now to see anything," Frida said. "We've covered the area pretty thoroughly." Her tone was reassuring and held a note of official finality.

"I need to see the spot for myself," Sammy insisted, his voice anguished. "We were more than half-brothers. We were brothers and close friends. And he's left behind three boys. You know his wife died several years ago?"

Frida shook her head. "I didn't."

"Cancer took her," Grandfather said.

I was puzzled as to why Grandfather didn't try to dissuade Sammy and me from visiting the site of the accident. To anyone who didn't know the old man well, he appeared to be handling the death of one of his grandsons calmly, thoughtfully. I, on the other hand, could tell from the faraway look in his eyes and the slow, rhythmical puffing on his now unlit pipe that something was bothering him. Sammy's urgent agitation to visit the scene and his insistence I go with him was a signal he wanted some kind of action taken. But what? And why?

"Well, I just thought I'd let you know the police are on the case." Frida's reassurance came not out of official duty but because she was sensitive to the tribe's concern that police authorities tended to trivialize criminal acts against tribal members.

"You look beat," I said to Frida. "You haven't had much of a day off." I knew Sammy didn't want Frida to accompany us to the site, so I gave her an excuse to go home. It was more than an excuse. She needed the rest. Her shoulders slumped with fatigue, and her face appeared to have suddenly developed more lines than I'd noticed before.

A puzzled look crossed Sammy's face.

"Eve can tell you all about it," Frida said, and waved goodbye as she trudged to her car.

"She's right, you know," I said to Sammy. "We won't be able to see anything in the dark. Besides, the cops will have covered the scene better than we can."

"They were looking in general," Sammy said. "I know

specifically what I'm looking for." He pushed me gently toward my car. "Grandy can stay here and entertain Grandfather. We'll fill everyone in when we get back."

"What's going on, Sammy? You and Grandfather have something up your sleeves. What is it?"

"I need your eyes to help me out. You're always good at figuring out murder stuff."

"Well, technically, it's manslaughter, but sure, I'd be glad to help. But why now … when it's more likely the poor light won't help us find what you're looking for?"

"I think you might be wrong. I think the cops might be wrong. We'll see when we get there."

Before I started the car, Sammy reached up to turn on the overhead light. "The state trooper gave me this." He handed me a tattered wallet. I opened it to find Walter Egret's driver's license, a picture of three boys with wide grins on their faces, two dollars, and a bill dated yesterday for a truck's generator cable.

"Oh, and twenty-three cents in change. That's all they found on him."

"You think somebody stole his credit cards, is that it?"

Sammy let out a short bark of a laugh. "You should know us better than that, Eve. When have you known any of us to have credit cards? Well, maybe some of our richer tribal members, but not the Egret family."

"But you think something is missing that should be there, so you figure someone robbed him as well as ran him down." I started the engine and drove out to the road.

Sammy nodded.

"What are we looking for and why do you think Walter had it with him?'

"We're looking for my father's pocket watch."

I knew Sammy and Walter had different mothers and that their father had left Sammy's mother soon after Sammy was born. He hadn't been heard from since. Sammy's mother was his second wife. She was white while Walter's mother and the mother of Walter's brothers was Miccosukee. She had died giving birth to Walter's youngest brother. Sammy's mother Renata had told me that she and Sammy's father had made a poor marriage and that she had left Sammy in Grandfather Egret's care, but Sammy's father had simply disappeared with no word to anyone.

"My father carried a pocket watch, gold with an egret etched on the watch cover. Walter remembered it from when he was a kid. Father would take it out and let my half-brothers play with it. It was an unusual watch. Grandfather described it to me."

"So he gave it to Walter, and Walter always carried it with him?" I was still confused about the watch.

"No, Eve. The watch disappeared along with my father, but Walter called me just after noon today, very excited. He told me he had found the watch on a body unearthed at the construction site near where the river enters the lake. He thinks the body found there was our father's."

"Walter had the watch on him?"

"I think so."

I thought about this. "Then he must have taken it from the construction site."

Sammy nodded. "The watch is gone, Eve. What does that make you think?"

"Maybe you're jumping to conclusions. He could have left the watch somewhere or with someone for safekeeping. Or, if he had it on him, someone stole it from him after he was hit."

"Or it's more likely Walter took the watch off the body, someone saw him take it, and he was run down for it. That's my explanation. The cops won't be interested in pursuing this. They could have taken the watch."

I could hear Sammy's voice shake with indignation and his reasoning take an illogical turn. "Let's slow down a bit. We don't have all the facts."

Sammy gave a small snort. "Okay, but I need to see for myself."

"I know you don't trust the police because they don't always deal with tribal members fairly, but what reason would any of them have for taking the watch?"

Sammy shrugged. Old feelings of distrust didn't fade easily.

"Look. We'll search the area to see if we find the watch. If not, then we need to find out if Walter took it from the site, and if he did, did he leave it somewhere before he was hit."

I slowed the car and pulled over to the side of the road where the vegetation had been crushed and the ground was churned up with tire tracks. I took out the flashlight I always carry in my car, and Sammy pulled another torch out of his jacket pocket.

"Yep, this is it." I swept the area with my light. "I even think I see …." I stopped talking. The dark stains on the pavement looked like blood. Sammy saw them too.

Suddenly our world was illuminated by a set of car headlights. Instead of passing us, the car pulled onto the shoulder. I shielded my eyes against the glare to try to identify the individual.

"It's me, Frida." She turned off the headlights, got out, and strode toward us, flipping on her flashlight.

"I thought you went home because you were tired," I said.

"No, you thought I was tired and told me I should go home. I wondered about that. You provided me with a very convenient excuse for not accompanying you out here, and I fell for it. Now, will somebody tell me just what is going on here?" Frida gave me a dark look.

Sammy stepped forward. "Don't blame this one on Eve. I didn't want you at the scene because I had something to hide from you, but maybe it's better if you know."

He told Frida the story of the phone call from his stepbrother.

"We think he took the watch off the body found in the construction area," I said.

"He was the backhoe operator?" asked Frida.

Sammy nodded.

"I had a lot of questions for him, and now it seems I can't ask them. Interesting, but that doesn't mean he was run down for the watch. Why would someone do that? You know, it could just be a hit-and-run, and the driver jumped out to take a look at what they did, found the watch and nabbed it. It's probably in some pawn shop right now."

Sammy looked skeptical. "It doesn't bother you that the person who got closest to that body at the construction site is now dead?"

"Sure, but like I said ..." Frida began.

I'd said little while Sammy and Frida talked through the hit-and-run. "Murder or not," I said now, "that leaves other questions unanswered." They both turned toward me. "Who killed Sammy and Walter's father and dumped him out there? And why?"

CHAPTER 3

——

Frida remained skeptical about the watch. "I believe Walter called you, but you and your brothers have searched for years to find clues about your father's disappearance. Nothing has shown up. And you haven't seen the watch Walter claimed he found. Maybe it belonged to someone else."

"Walter knew our father's watch. The etching on the cover is unique. No one else had a watch like that," Sammy insisted.

"Still …" Frida began.

"I don't know why I told you. You're just like all the others. You think Walter would make up that story? That I would?" Sammy's black eyes snapped with anger.

"No, I don't," Frida said softly.

"You know her better than that, Sammy."

He cast down his eyes in defeat, the fire gone. "I thought we'd finally get some answers. That's why I had to come out here."

"You go home and grieve for your brother. Let me work this scene."

Sammy nodded and headed for my car. Drawing me to one side, Frida said, "I've got this hit-and-run to cover and the body at the construction site. Linc is still sick, and there's no one at

the station to cover for him. I need to listen to the recording
of that phone call from Walter. And if you want to be of help,
Eve, get a detailed description of the watch and the etching on
its cover face. Maybe Sammy or Grandfather can draw you a
picture of it. Then you can hit all the pawn shops in this area."

My feet almost broke into a happy dance, I was so delighted
that Frida wanted my help.

"And keep your mouth shut about anything to do with this
case or the one at the construction site. I know Sammy will be
discreet out of distrust of the cops if nothing else, but you?"

I made the zipping motion across my mouth.

"Maybe it would be a good idea to take Sammy with you
when you look at the pawn shops. And be sure to tell him not
to erase that message from Walter. I want to hear it." She got
back into her car and pulled away.

"What was that all about?" Sammy asked, eyes narrowed
with suspicion.

"You and I have been deputized." I stomped on the accelerator.
"Giddy up," I said to my Mustang as if it was a horse not a car.
I was absolutely giddy at the thought of the assignment Frida
had given me … uh, us.

"You are something, Eve." Sammy leaned over and gave me
a quick kiss.

I DROPPED SAMMY at his house and gave a wave to Grandfather,
who still sat on the porch with Grandy. He remained motionless
while mosquitoes buzzed around his head in the light. Grandy
extracted a small canister from her purse and sprayed her arms
and legs, swatting the hungry insects away as she sprayed her
hands and spread the concoction onto her face.

"Doesn't he mind getting bitten?" I asked Sammy as he got
out of the car.

He cocked his head and squinted at me. "The mosquitoes?
He never gets bitten."

Sammy retreated down the path to the house and waved

goodbye from the porch. Grandy kissed both Egrets and headed to the car.

"Find out anything?" she asked, climbing into the passenger's seat.

"Not what Sammy was looking for." I started to explain about Walter's call, but she interrupted me.

"Grandfather told me about it. It makes Walter's death look very suspicious, don't you think?"

I'd gotten my snoopy nature from Grandy. Maybe I was cloned from her, and my mother had nothing to do with my birth.

"I think so. Frida stopped by and was not as convinced, although she did give me an assignment." I related the details of deputy duties to Grandy.

"That should make you happy." She patted my hand.

"I'll be sure to include you where I can," I assured her. There was nothing Grandy liked more than joining in a caper. Well, she loved her husband Max more—most of the time anyway.

Grandy smacked her lips in satisfaction. "Oh, good. You know how I hate being left out."

I settled back into the seat with a deep sigh as I shifted into gear and backed out of the parking area. I was tired, discouraged, and regretting how little time Sammy and I had to be together alone. His work schedule, my work schedule. We were lucky to be able to steal away into the swamps in his canoe to our secret getaway, an old shack we'd discovered when lost in the swamp. Recently, it had become the place we went to find each other and make love. It probably wouldn't sound romantic to most—a chorus of swamp creatures and the solo roar of a bull alligator provided the soundtrack for our passion—but we liked it. I never felt afraid when I was in the swamp with Sammy. It almost felt like it was my home as well as his.

Our stomachs growled in unison. I looked at my watch, then at Grandy. Past time for dinner.

"Did you call Max and tell him what we were doing?" I asked.

Max had recently suffered a heart attack. Because of it, he and Grandy had cut back on their fishing charter business out of Key Largo and had hired another captain to take over their boat for several months. They had moved up here and were living in my spare bedroom until they decided what their future plans were. Max was adjusting to life on the range rather than life on a boat, but I knew he was itching to get back to the Keys. Despite his almost daily fishing in the waters of the Big Lake, it was, according to him, "brown water and small fish." He was right. The water was the color of strong tea, and no speck, catfish, or bass could match the size of hefty mahi-mahi or mangrove snapper from the ocean waters around Key Largo.

Grandy held up her cellphone. "I called when I was with Grandfather Egret. Max had just come in from a day on the lake with Captain Mike and has a mess of bass for us. I told him I'd ask if you felt like bass tonight. If not, he can clean them anyway, and we'll have them tomorrow."

I thought about a nice bass filet, but the picture of it on a plate faded, replaced by another, tastier image.

"I think I'd like a big platter of ribs, slaw, and double fries."

"God, Eve, with your dining tastes, if Max and I stay here much longer, we'll both be as plump as overstuffed turkeys. Mark my words. Someday all this eating will catch up with you."

I hoped not, because along with a stiff double Scotch, food was my remedy for the blues. And I felt pretty blue about Sammy and Grandfather having to deal with Walter's death. That family had enough sorrow with the murder of a nephew several years ago, killed by kidnappers intent upon taking him to a game reserve to be used as prey, the death of Walter's wife from cancer (although it was many years ago), and the disappearance of Sammy's father. Now there was Walter. I thought about those three boys of his. Now they had no mother. Who would take care of them? I sighed again.

"Okay, I know you. You're feeling bad about Walter and the Egrets and especially about the kids, so I guess we need to get some ribs into you before you slip into a severe depression."

Grandy, like Grandfather Egret, was tuned into me like a shortwave radio operator and could read my mind. It was spooky, like I had no privacy, yet there was a kind of comfort and safety in it too.

WHEN WE WALKED into the Burnt Biscuit, my favorite place for ribs, who should be at the bar but my old pal Nappi Napolitani? I hadn't seen him for several weeks. I rushed up and threw myself into his arms. He hugged me back with enthusiasm, then turned to Grandy with his usual greeting for her: he kissed her hand. With his impeccable manners and dapper appearance, Nappi acted more like a Connecticut blueblood than a mob guy. I'd met him years back, right after my divorce from Jerry. Jerry had been dating Nappi's daughter, and thinking she was pregnant, was eager to get my name on the divorce papers. A guy doesn't delay marrying a gal he gets in the family way if his prospective father-in-law is "connected"—as in Family with a capital goodfellas F. As it turned out, she wasn't pregnant, and she wasn't all that eager to marry Jerry anyway—I could relate—but I got rid of Jerry and Jerry got a legitimate job becoming Nappi's gofer. Well, maybe not "legitimate" in the legal sense, but it was steady work, something Jerry had never been able to pull off while we were married. Nappi had been a good friend, often coming to my aid or that of my friends and family.

"Evie, honey." Jerry peeked out from behind Nappi.

"I'm not your honey, and don't call me Evie."

"Rumor has it that you're thinking of going into the private investigating business," Nappi said with a wicked grin on his face.

"How did …?" I began.

"The grapevine. Oh, not the usual Sabal Bay rumor mill. I'm an old friend of Crusty McNabb. He said you paid him a visit."

Grandy shot me a concerned look.

Oh damn. I hadn't wanted any of my friends or Grandy to know what I was up to, not yet anyway. I knew Frida would keep my confidence, but I didn't want Madeleine or Grandy to worry I wouldn't be able to keep up with my responsibilities at the consignment shop, if I decided to go the PI route. And that was still a big if.

"Just paying him a visit. He's in a space near our consignment shop. Being neighborly." I turned my face away from everyone, feigning interest in the Brahman bull head that hung on the back wall of the bar and hoping no one could tell I was lying. Well, it was close to the truth. I did like to meet my business neighbors.

I fooled no one. Grandy snorted in disbelief.

Nappi caught the look on my face. "Sorry, Eve. I thought Grandy would be the first to know."

"I knew you had something up your sleeve. Grandfather and I were talking about it tonight." She gave me one of her I-know-you-too-well looks.

"Do I not have any secrets?"

"Sure. No one knows where you and Sammy go to be alone," said Grandy. Nappi nodded, as did Jerry.

"Okay. It's something I'm thinking about, something Alex suggested to me." I signaled to the bartender. "I don't want to talk about it. And it's no one's business where Sammy and I meet. Or *if* we meet. I need a rib fix and a drink."

Max joined us at the bar. "I've got a table."

"How's the fishing?" asked Nappi. Max smiled, about to launch into one of his long fish tales.

"Join us. This sounds like a story that requires sitting," Grandy said to Nappi. "And you too, Jerry."

We took our drinks to the table Max had reserved. Grandy and I caught everyone up on Madeleine and David's babies.

We toasted the new arrivals and then all tucked into our food, which had just arrived. The wait staff at the Biscuit knew us all well enough that ribs arrived without us having to order.

"We should all go visit her tomorrow. Do you think she'll still be in the hospital?" asked Nappi.

"We'll call first," Grandy suggested.

Talk then turned to the body found at the construction site and to the hit-and-run of Walter Egret.

"You sound as if you don't think it was a simple hit-and-run," said Nappi.

I couldn't tell them about the phone call to Sammy, so I merely nodded. "Frida will sort it out."

"Or someone will," said Grandy with a wink at Nappi.

As we finished our meals, the sounds of Karaoke drifted from the bar into the dining room. I caught a familiar voice singing an old country ballad. "My friend Antoine's at the microphone. I'd like to listen for a minute, then get on home. This had been a long day."

"And you're opening the store tomorrow," Grandy reminded me. "Unless you have other, uh, things to do."

"I'll open if you step in for a few hours later."

Even if Sammy wasn't free to accompany me, I planned to get started on surveying the pawn shops for the watch. This was the first time Frida had asked for my help, and I wanted to show her I could get results.

"The weekend's coming up. Are we opening the rig here at the flea market or taking it over to the flea market on the coast?" Like me, Grandy loved to drive the huge RV, our shop on wheels, over to the coast. She said piloting it successfully down the narrow road to the weekend flea market at Stuart made her feel like the captain of an ocean liner. She drove well, which is more than I could say for Madeleine, but then, she was at a disadvantage, having to place something behind her to reach the wheel and adjust the seat so her feet would reach the pedals.

"We don't have enough merchandise to cover both stores. Maybe you'd like to make a run with me to some of our clientele in West Palm to see if they have any items for us," I suggested to Grandy. We not only took in merchandise from wealthy matrons from West Palm, but we also offered them a pick-up service at no charge. "Shelley can open the store on Saturday."

Shelley McCleary was the daughter of one of our former customers—the victim of a murder just last year. Shelley possessed great artistic talent, especially in the dress designer category, and we had hired her to do the shop's tailoring. Not only did our place sell used designer clothing, but we offered alterations, something few other secondhand shops did. Shelley attended a fashion institute in West Palm at night and worked in the shop some weekdays and most Saturdays. She was responsible as well as skilled, and she loved selling and suggesting ways she could make an outfit look better on a customer. Someday she might join us as a partner in the business.

We all listened to Antoine for several songs. When he was finished, I went over to say hello and was joined by his boss, Jay Cassidy.

"Eve," he said, greeting me with a tip of his hat.

Jay and I had been friends since I settled in Sabal Bay. We didn't always see eye to eye on community issues, but we managed to keep the relationship going despite our disagreements. Madeleine and I, concerned about the preservation of wildlife and the loss of habitat, had challenged his view of land usage, which ran more to grazing cattle, sugar cane planting, and any development project that would bring in more tourists. He thought we were insensitive to the issues of economic development in the area. No one was persuaded to the contrary, but we kept our arguments friendly.

"Dance, Eve?" Jay asked.

"Not tonight. I'm beat. Did you hear Madeleine had her babies today?"

"I did. I had some flowers delivered to her room. I'd visit tomorrow, but I have to go to the polo field in Port Mayaca. I'm on the planning committee, and we're going to have a gala around Christmas this year. You should come."

I noticed the look in Jay's eyes and guessed the next thing out of his mouth would be an invitation to attend the event as his date. Despite the fact that he considered me a nosey damn Yankee, he was also a bit sweet on me. I guess he'd heard Alex and I were no longer a couple.

"I'll see if Sammy's interested in doing a bit of dancing. Thanks, Jay."

A dark look erased his earlier flirtatious manner. "Right." He turned on his heel and left.

"You knew he was going to ask you to the dance, didn't you?" asked Grandy. "I think you damaged his ego."

"He'll survive. He never holds on to negative feelings long. That's what I like about him."

Everyone said goodnight outside the restaurant. Grandy got into Max's car and followed me to my place.

"Anyone want coffee?" asked Grandy when we got home.

"Nope. Only bed." I walked into my room and flopped onto the bed with all my clothes on, including my shoes. The next thing I knew, I was jostled out of a deep sleep by Grandy shaking me.

"Didn't you hear the phone ring? It's right by your head." She handed me the headset phone from the living room.

" 'Lo," I muttered into the receiver.

"It's Frida. The body's gone."

"Huh?"

"Someone hit the guard I stationed at the construction site over the head, tied him up, and took the bones. I hope to hell Sammy and the tribe had nothing to do with this."

Frida did not sound happy.

CHAPTER 4

———

FRIDA DIDN'T ASK for my help, but she'd told me earlier Linc Tooney was out with the flu, so of course she could use some assistance. Whether I was her choice for temporary partner or not, I determined her situation called for intervention—snoopy Eve intervention. I was out the door and in my convertible in seconds, heading to the construction site. Under other circumstances, Frida would have problems accepting my assistance—maybe she'd even reject it and shove it aside—but then, I argued to myself, why did she call me and let me know about the body? Clearly a call for help. I knew better than to discuss her call with anyone else, not even Grandy and certainly not Sammy.

Frida had called in the county sheriff's department for backup, and the lights from her cruiser and those of the county cars lit up the construction area like daylight. An ambulance was at the scene, and one of the paramedics was attending to a uniformed officer, obviously the one who had been assigned to guard the scene. Frida spotted me and left off talking to the officer.

"I have mixed feelings about you being here, but …" she began.

"But you need to run all of this by someone with good instincts for snooping, and that's me. Girl snoop."

"Don't step there, Eve." Frida pulled me back from where the crime scene techs were working. "We're trying to lift tire tracks."

I nodded, and without being told, walked a wider perimeter around the construction area, shining my light at the ground.

"I've got a cigarette butt," I called to her.

Frida directed one of the techs to it. "Bag it, but I'm certain it's Henry's." She nodded at the officer whose head was being bandaged by the paramedic. "He thinks no one knows he smokes on the job. But I do."

I knew it, too. I'd run into him at the police station numerous times. I have the nose of a bloodhound, so I smelled smoke despite his use of menthol cough drops.

"Any footprints?" I asked.

"Too many," Frida replied. "I'm certain there are footprints from when we were here earlier today. And the prints would include those of the foreman, the backhoe operator, yours, mine, Danny Cypress and any others who were on the site this morning. Half of the county likes to come out here to see how the construction is coming. Big money for this area. The promise of jobs." Frida shook her head. "This is a disaster—one I'll get blamed for, I'm sure. I should have put more than one guard here, but we are so short of people. Budget cuts and all." She rubbed her eyes.

"Anything I can do to help …."

Frida raised her head to gaze across the site and into the grove of sabal palms standing near the road. "Let's take a look over there." She motioned for me to follow.

I caught the first rays of the sun hovering at the east edge of the lake as we walked toward the trees. Daylight would help our search of the area. The amount of time that had elapsed since the attack on Henry would not.

"This is the only area the machinery hasn't yet destroyed," I said, picking my way across the dirt piles to the palm grove.

Despite it being untouched by the construction, the area wasn't easy to walk through. Dead palm fronds covered the ground and vegetation grew thick under the trees.

"Watch your step," Frida said.

I nodded. "No point in turning an ankle."

"I meant look out for snakes. And it's swampy in here. You can never tell if a gator might be snoozing under one of these fallen logs."

Yuck and Yikes.

But nothing moved as we made our way through the shadowed area and approached the other side, nearer the road.

"Someone's been in here," Frida said. "There're signs a person sat on this moss-covered log. It's matted down and there are indentations in the ground in front."

"As if someone was here, out of sight, watching the construction."

"Someone hidden who could have seen Walter take something from the body," said Frida. "Someone who might not have liked Walter removing the watch, if it was the watch. If Walter did remove something."

"If so, then there should be vehicle tracks where the individual parked his car or truck out there." I pointed to the other side of the trees, the side near the road. "No one in the construction area would have spotted a vehicle parked here. The palms obscure the view."

It was a good place to park a vehicle if you needed it to be hidden from the backhoe operator and the foreman, and because the dirt track was located in a depression, it couldn't have been seen from the road leading to the site.

Frida shrugged. "The construction workers could have parked here, not just someone wanting to hide their presence. We'll take molds anyway."

I nodded my head in agreement.

The sun seemed to suddenly pop up over the water, its reflection flooding the shoreline with brilliant light.

"Another screaming hot day." Frida lifted her heavy hair off her shoulders and twisted it into a knot at the back of her neck. "I think that about does it for this crime scene."

"Anything else I can do, I'm—"

"It was great to have a second pair of eyes, but if my boss knew you were here, he'd …."

I put my finger in front of my lips.

"Or any of your friends," Frida warned.

We headed back toward the construction site as the ambulance drove out onto the main road and another car followed by several older pickups pulled in.

"Here comes trouble," Frida said.

"What?"

"The people from the state, and of course, some friends of yours."

"I'm not sure I follow."

"Representatives from the tribe, wanting to know if the remains found here yesterday are one of theirs. They will not react well when I tell them I lost the body." Frida pulled back her shoulders and stepped forward, looking much like a prisoner feigning courage on the way to execution. This was one thing I could not help her with. She had to face them alone, and her guilt over her failure felt as palpable to me as the humidity that descended upon the desecrated burial site.

"ARE YOU GOING to tell me what that phone call was all about?" asked Grandy when I returned to the house. "You rushed out of here like a shore bird being pursued by a hungry alligator."

I couldn't tell Grandy much. I'd promised Frida, but I could repeat what I knew the newspapers would pick up on for this weekend's local edition.

"That body had been taken," I said.

Grandy's eyes held a speculative gleam. "And just why were you privy to the early edition of that information?"

"Frida wanted to share." I held up my finger to signal silence. "That's all I'm allowed to say."

Grandy shook her head. "The last person I'd want traipsing around my crime scene would be you, Eve."

"Any why would you say that?"

"Because there would be no end to your continued interference into the case, now, would there?"

I couldn't help myself. "Maybe that's the point."

Grandy made a noise like a cross between a snort and a tsk, but changed the subject. "Are we going to visit the babies today?"

I checked my watch. "We have just enough time to pop in for a minute and then to the shop."

THE BABIES WERE thriving, as was Madeleine. David still looked as if he was in shock. His hair needed combing and his clothes looked as if he'd slept in them, which he probably had. The Egrets, Grandfather and Sammy, were just leaving when we stuck out heads into Madeleine's room. As he walked past me, Sammy put his arm around my waist and pulled me close.

"We need to talk," he whispered in my ear. "We know about the body being stolen. I've waited years to find him, and now someone has taken him away."

Sammy obviously believed the body at the construction site was his father's because of the watch Walter allegedly took.

"Are you working the ranch this afternoon?" I asked.

He shook his head. "David said he has no clients scheduled today."

"How would you like to visit some pawn shops?"

"How does that bring back my father's bones?" asked Sammy.

"It doesn't, not directly, but if we can find the watch and who pawned it, we might get a lead on Walter's killer. That could lead us to more information about the body." Okay, so it was a tenuous link, but it was all I could think of to say.

Sammy was losing patience. I could tell by the way he gave a kick at the floor with the toe of his boot. "Who else's body could it be?"

"Please, Sammy. Let's just do this. One step at a time." I hugged his arm and looked up into his deep brown eyes.

"Okay."

I knew he wasn't happy about the task, but it would keep him away from the more immediate issue of who took the body and why. The tribe would be all over the police on that one. Best to keep Sammy out of it for now.

Grandfather touched my shoulder gently as he and Sammy left the room.

"What was that all about?" asked Madeleine.

I realized for the first time that she didn't know about the body, Walter, the theft or the implications of all of it for the tribe and especially the Egrets. Should I tell her? I glanced at Grandy. Reading my mind as usual, she shook her head.

I crossed the room and kissed my best friend on the cheek. Madeleine reached up and threw her arms around my neck. "What do you think about the names for the babies? I was too tired to ask you last night. It's okay with you to name little Eve, Eve, isn't it? You seemed so upset when I told you about the name last night."

"Of course. I'm just thrilled about it. You took me by surprise, that's all." Thank goodness Madeleine was too preoccupied with the twins to pursue much going on outside the mommy and baby world.

A nurse entered the room. "So, Mrs. Wilson, are you ready to go home with your twins?"

David's face grew a whiter shade of overwhelmed. "Now? It's only been a day. Now?"

Madeleine reached out and grabbed her husband by the hand. "Get ahold of yourself, honey. You didn't think I'd move in here, did you?"

"I don't think I'm ready for this," David said and steadied himself against the wall.

"You should have told me that earlier, before I got pregnant. It's not like we can send them back and ask for a refund." Madeleine winked at me.

"I know that. It's all taken me by surprise." David straightened his shoulders, cleared his throat and tried to look fatherly.

"Nine months of pregnancy, and he's surprised." Madeleine chuckled.

ONCE AT THE shop, Grandy and I opened the doors to several customers waiting there.

"Sorry we're late today, but we stopped by the hospital to see Madeleine and the twins. She delivered yesterday," I announced to the women. Regulars in our shop, they knew Madeleine and me well. We talked for several minutes about Madeleine and the babies.

As I was ringing up a sale for one of the women, the bell announcing another arrival tinkled and Shelley, our seamstress, walked in. She overheard the baby talk.

"Isn't that great news," she said. "I stayed up late last night to get these ready for her." She reached into a bag she was carrying and pulled out several articles of clothing.

"What's all this?" I asked. The items looked familiar—at least the materials looked as if I should recognize them—but after a few minutes I realized what she held in her arms. The several dresses, blouses, and skirts were items we had taken in on consignment a few weeks ago, but now they were almost unidentifiable. In her clever way, Shelley had transformed the clothing to produce several beautiful outfits of a petite size—Madeleine size.

"I figured Madeleine would be fairly sick of wearing those maternity clothes, so I made her some new—well, almost new—outfits. What do you think?"

I hugged Shelley and said, "That is *so* thoughtful. She's going to love these. And she'll need them, since she's going home today."

Shelley looked so proud of what she'd accomplished and so pleased that I thought her work was just the right gift for Madeleine. She blushed and looked around the store for a moment. "I should make up a sign letting all our customers know about the babies. What did she name them?"

Everyone in town knew Madeleine was having twins, but no one, not even the expectant parents, had known the sexes before the births. We'd generated lists of possible names over the months of the pregnancy.

Now it was my turn to blush. "Uh, the boy is David Jr. and the girl is uhm …." A lump formed in my throat. I couldn't speak.

"Eve. They named her Eve," said Grandy. "And Eve here is still choked up about it."

Shelley looked up from under the counter where she was looking for paper to make the sign about the births. "You, Eve, choked up? I don't think I've ever seen you like this."

"Yeah, well, you have your best friend name a kid after you and then see how cool and collected you are." I sniffed and wiped wetness off my cheeks. "Besides, I'm getting over it now. This is just my allergies acting up."

Grandy and Shelley exchanged looks. "Sure," they both said together.

The three of us waited on customers for the rest of the morning, then I scuttled out for sub sandwiches at noon. After we finished our meal, I reminded Grandy that she had promised to mind the store while I ran my errand.

"Exactly what was it you were going to do?" asked Grandy. "Maybe I could help. Shelley can mind the shop. Right, Shelley?"

Shelley nodded. "I'd be happy to. I can do my homework assignment for tonight's class between customers."

"I'm sure you'd be a big help, but this is something I promised to do for Frida and not tell anybody about it. Sorry."

Grandy looked hurt.

"But," I held up an index finger before she could say anything more, "I'm certain I will be calling on you in the future. Count on it."

Grandy fairly beamed with anticipation.

I walked into the backroom to make a private call to Sammy.

He answered on the first ring. "That you, Eve? I thought about what you said, and you're right. This is the first step in finding out about my father and Walter's death."

"I have one stop to make before I pick you up."

"Don't take too long. I'm anxious to get going."

I ended the call, grabbed my purse and said goodbye to Grandy, who was busy showing an evening gown to a customer. Good. I didn't head out to my car, but walked out the front door and turned right. Two doors down was Crusty McNabb's detective agency. I'd been in his place several times before, but when he handed me an application form to fill out the last time I was there, I bolted for the door as if he'd asked me to change my hairdo. This time I wouldn't be a chicken. I'd bite the bullet and apply for an apprenticeship. Really, how hard could it be to become a private detective?

Before I could step into his storefront office, my cell rang. The caller ID was Alex's.

I answered, and before he could say anything, I breathlessly blurted out my plans to see Crusty. "Hi, Alex. Funny you should call because I'm just now entering Crusty McNabb's office. I'm going to do what you suggested. I'm going to become a PI. Great, huh?'

"Eve, it is Jim Clancy. Remember me? Alex and I worked some cases down here in Miami."

Something wasn't right. Why was Jim calling me?

"Yes, I remember you, and I know you and Alex are in Miami

now on a case. What's up?" As I said the words, a shudder ran through my body, and the hand holding the phone shook.

"Alex has been shot. He's dead."

CHAPTER 5

———

CRUSTY McNABB'S FACE came into focus, then Grandy's.
"Where am I?" I looked around the small space and didn't recognize it. The last thing I remembered was the call from Alex's partner, the call that said ….

"You're in Mr. McNabb's office, Eve. He saw you slam into his front window, then he rushed out and carried you in here. You fainted."

I was slumped in a chair, my cell still in my hand. A voice could be heard coming from it. Grandy took it and listened, then said, "Okay," and ended the call.

"Alex is …" I said.

"I know, dear. I'm so sorry. You just lean back and relax. I called Max, and he's coming to take you home so you can rest."

"I don't want to rest. I want to know what happened. It must be a mistake. Alex can't be dead. He can't." I felt like I wanted to cry or rant or shout, anything to take away my feelings of helplessness and loss.

"Sweetie, look. I'll call back and find out more if you promise me you'll go home with Max. Here he is now. Shelley and I will take care of the store, don't you worry."

I grabbed the cellphone from Grandy and dialed Alex's number. Jim answered.

"Tell me it's not true. Tell me it's a mistake. It's someone else who was shot." I tried to stifle a sob, but it worked its way up my throat, and I could feel tears spill from my eyes and down my cheeks. I scrubbed them away with my hand.

"Eve, is there someone there with you?"

"Just tell me what happened!" I yelled into the phone.

Grandy grabbed the phone out of my hand once more. "This is Eve's grandmother. I'm putting her back on. It's better you let her know everything. Then I'll be taking her home."

She handed the phone back to me and said to McNabb, "Let's give her some privacy." Grandy and McNabb walked toward the door. "I'll be right out here if you need me."

I nodded and said, "Jim?"

"This will be hard for you to hear."

"I want to know all of it."

"Are you sure?"

I swallowed and cleared my throat. "I can handle it. Alex would want me to be able to deal with this."

"Alex was in a seedy part of the city to meet a client, an African-American woman whose son had been shot by some gang members. She wasn't happy with how the cops were handling the case, so she decided to hire Alex to look into it. We had just wrapped up another contract, so Alex was free to take on clients. But I told Alex not to get involved with this one. Where gangs are involved, the possibility of a good outcome is almost nil, and it's dangerous to insert yourself into a gang matter. But you know how Alex is … was. He had talked to the woman over the phone and felt she deserved better than what the cops were doing for her, so he agreed to meet with her at her house. He had just pulled up in front of her place when a car drove by and someone shot him. Dead. The only good thing about this is that the cops were staking out the neighborhood and were on the scene immediately. They picked up the car with the shooter."

Yep, that was Alex. The tough PI with a big heart.

"The guy who shot him is a kid, only thirteen years old. The gang got wind of the mother hiring a PI, and they sent this child out to kill him."

"Why did the woman hire Alex? Why not someone local?"

"Alex had taken a number of cases here, and he had a reputation for getting things done. Alex was a great PI, Eve, but then, you knew that."

I did know that. And his reputation for doing his work well got him killed. My mind wandered back to my earlier thoughts about how becoming a PI couldn't be all that difficult. It was more difficult than I imagined. Sometimes it could get you killed, even if you did it right. I rethought my intention to apprentice myself to McNabb. I wasn't scared, but I had doubts I could ever be as good as Alex. What was I thinking? Me, a PI?

"I'm coming down there," I said to Jim.

"There's no point, Eve. What can you do here?"

"When's the kid's arraignment?"

There was a moment's hesitation from Jim. "Uh, not until tomorrow morning. Why?"

"I want to see the guy who killed Alex, just to look him in the eye and see if he's really a cold-blooded killer or just a kid scared of what the gang would do to him if he didn't do their bidding."

"I don't see what difference it would make, Eve."

"I'm doing this for Alex. I want to be his eyes. I want to know the soul of the person who killed him. He didn't get the chance to do that, so I'm doing it for him."

"Just so you know, Eve. The cops contacted his family, and they're coming here to bring his body home to, uh, where was he from?"

I didn't know. I'd known him for almost four years. We'd danced together, laughed together, made love, but I had no idea where his family lived. In fact, I didn't know he had family. Were his parents still living? Did he have siblings? I knew so little about a man who at one time I thought I loved.

"Jim, could you do me a favor and find out about his family? I didn't know them at all, so …."

"Will do, Eve. I'll be at the arraignment tomorrow, and I'll see you there."

He gave me directions and ended the call.

I got up from the chair, and on shaky legs, headed out of the office.

"I can drive myself home, Max. I need to pack a bag and head out for Miami."

Grandy grabbed my arm. "No you don't, honey. Not unless you tell me what you're up to. And then, Max and I will be coming with you."

"Don't be silly. I can take care of myself. I …" I stopped midsentence, grabbed Grandy's shoulder and collapsed in sobs.

"Right," I heard her say.

"Oh, Grandy. How could this happen? Alex was … he was …."

"Your good friend, your lover, and someone you sent away for the good of both of you. Oh, I know what you're thinking, Eve. You're about to blame yourself for this. Don't be silly. Being apart had nothing to do with his death. Both of you agreed, you know."

I nodded. Grandy read me again. In some fractured sense of logic, I was going to blame myself. "I know, I know, but it's so hard."

"It's going to be hard for some time, my dear," Grandy said, hugging me to her.

G<small>RANDY LET ME</small> drive myself home, but she and Max followed close behind. As I turned the corner to my street, I saw Sammy's truck parked in front of my house, Sammy standing on my front porch.

When did Grandy have time to call Sammy, I wondered. But of course she hadn't. Sammy somehow knew.

I got out of my car and ran into Sammy's arms. "Alex is dead."

"Let's go in," said Grandy. "I'll make us all a cup of tea."

SAMMY STEERED ME to the couch, sat me down, and then held me. I felt cold and shivery, as if I were coming down with the flu, but when Sammy got up to get me a blanket, I pulled him back to me. "Don't leave." I moved closer to him.

His arms never left me that night, until Grandy told him to go home and let me get some sleep. How could I sleep? It was as if some important piece of me had been ripped away. I grabbed onto Sammy and refused to let him go.

Grandy had talked me out of rushing down to Miami, promising that she and Max would drive me there in time for the arraignment.

Sammy cupped my chin and looked me in the eye. "You know I would come with you tomorrow, but I think this is something you need to do without me. Grandy and Max will be with you, and I'll be waiting here for you, Eve. You know that, don't you?"

I nodded.

When I lost my parents, I grieved as a child would, becoming rebellious, keeping the hurt inside, finally emerging from my pain with the help of Grandy's love. Now I was an adult, suddenly faced with the reality that people I cared for could be taken from me and never return. I would have to face that truth. My parents were not coming back. Alex wasn't coming back. Sammy grew up with no father, yet he was not bitter, nor did he give any indication he felt cheated in this life.

There are no do-overs with death. Death had knocked on my door twice with news of someone I loved. My parents' death made me the tough, resilient person I was. Alex's made me aware of how precious loving someone was, how losing that person made you feel as if something inside you was gone. Alex and I had made the hard choice, the right choice to leave each other. I was beginning to understand what a gift he had given me when he said I should be a PI. He would never have encouraged me if we had clung to each other. Now I had to get my life right. If I didn't, I'd never be a whole person. His death made two things clear: I would pursue becoming a PI because it was a statement I needed to make about myself, for myself. It was the recognition that snoopy Eve, curious Eve was also intelligent, probing, motivated Eve. The second revelation was that I could be me and reach out for what I knew I wanted: Sammy. Funny how becoming a complete person meant being wrapped up in loving someone else.

I looked up into Sammy's face and knew I was gazing into the eyes of a man who loved me unconditionally. And that was how I needed to love him in return.

"I love you," I said fiercely.

"I know," he replied. "Don't be gone long."

"I won't, not ever."

Despite my newly found sense of how to move through this grief, every time I awoke that night, I sobbed into my pillow as if sassy, stoic Eve had saved up a lifetime of tears for just this moment. This was about loss—gut-wrenching loss—and there was no shortcut through it.

I refused to eat anything the next morning, and Grandy in her wisdom did not give me that line about "eating to keep up my strength." I drank half a cup of coffee and then we were on our way. Grandy held my hand the entire trip. Max drove and expertly navigated the streets of Miami to the courthouse. Sad as I was, I also knew I was the luckiest person in the world. I had family who understood what I was doing and a man I loved who never questioned my judgment in wanting to come here.

The room was filled with people. I assumed they were the family and friends of those charged with crimes and scheduled to appear before the judge today. Jim, Alex's partner here in Miami, met us on the steps of the courthouse, and we walked in together. He kept looking at me as if he expected me to faint or scream or do something crazy, but I was numb at this point. We took a seat in the back of the room and watched other prisoners come before the judge. Then a scrawny boy, wearing gangsta pants and hair in dreadlocks, was led in.

"That's him," Jim said.

The name Jerome Singer was called, and the boy stood up with his court-appointed attorney, who was busily digging around in his briefcase, apparently not listening to the question the judge asked of his client.

"Mr. Saxon," said the judge, "can you spare us a moment?"

The young attorney had the decency to blush. He looked up and said, "We plead 'not guilty,' your honor."

The prosecuting attorney arose. "We're asking for no bail and for Mr. Singer to be tried as an adult."

Singer's attorney said nothing.

"I know this is your first case," said the judge, directing his comments to the defense attorney, "but let me help you out here. How about requesting bail to be set at some lesser sum? Not that I'd agree, but why give your client reason this early in the case to claim your defense was inadequate and ask for a new trial?"

Singer's attorney again blushed and said, "Right, your honor. Request half a million dollars bail."

As if this child or his family could raise anything like that.

The judge said nothing for a moment, directing his attention to the papers in front of him.

"Mr. Singer, it looks to me as if you've never been in trouble before. Is that true?"

The young man raised his gaze from the floor to the judge. "Yes. Never."

"Hmm." The judge looked through the papers, then out at the boy.

"Request to try as an adult denied. Mr. Singer will be taken to an adolescent facility until his case comes before the court."

"But your honor," said the prosecutor, "Singer killed a man, shot him dead in the street."

"I'm well aware of that. I'm also aware of the circumstances. He's never been in trouble before, he attends school, and I want to keep him there. And out of the hands of the gang who recruited him for this job." The judge banged his gavel. "Next case."

"You're out of your mind. What kind of judge are you to let this here killer off?" The voice came from a woman standing behind us. Her face was red and streaked with tears. No one needed to tell me this infuriated and distraught woman was Alex's mother. A balding man, portly and dressed in a suit one size too small, his chubby wrists poking several inches out of the sleeves, put his arm around the woman and shushed her.

"Order in this court or you will be removed," directed the judge.

The woman pressed her head into her companion's shoulder, and he led her out the door. I was torn between following her to offer my sympathies and doing what I said I was here to do: get a closer look at the young man responsible for killing Alex. I pushed my way toward the front of the room as the guards began to lead Jerome Singer out a side door.

"Jerome," I said softly.

He turned at the sound of my voice, and I looked him full in the face. His warm, brown eyes were wide with terror.

He was a child. He didn't even look thirteen, more like eleven. He barely saw me as he gazed around the crowded room trying to find someone. His mother? No. I watched him focus on two heavily tattooed African-American men standing to one side near the back of the room. They nodded to him. I thought his eyes couldn't be more fear-filled, but the panic in them seemed to increase, and his knees buckled. The guards hoisted him between them and almost dragged him from the room.

I was willing to bet that at this moment Jerome couldn't even remember who he had shot, or even that he had carried a gun and pulled the trigger. What kind of threat had the gang held over his head to force him to kill Alex? Something to do with his family, I'd wager. And it was also a sure thing that Jerome would never speak any words in his defense. The gang was safe. This boy would say nothing to incriminate them.

I shook my head and walked out of the courtroom, looking outside for the woman I knew had to be Alex's mother. I found her soon enough. She was yelling about how "Negroes in this country could get away with murder and only get their fingers slapped." *Lovely woman*, I thought, but she had lost her son.

"Mrs. Montgomery," I said, "I was a friend of Alex's. I'm so sorry about your son."

She turned to look at me for a moment, then the anger she had been venting on others was directed at me.

"I know who you are. You're the one who broke my son's heart. And you show up here. What for? Now you feel bad, do you? Well, it's too late. He's dead, for all you cared about him."

"Edith," said the man I assumed was her husband, "Let's go back to the hotel. You need to get some rest."

He gave me a sad smile. "She's distraught. It was an early flight down here and she didn't get any sleep last night or on the plane this morning. I'm George Montgomery, her brother-in-law. My brother, Alex's dad, is deceased."

"I didn't know. I'm Eve, Eve Appel, and this is my grandmother and her husband."

"Oh, we know who you are, you bitch." Mrs. Montgomery drew back her arm and slammed her large purse into my shoulder. I staggered backward for a moment, regained my balance and moved beyond her reach.

Montgomery gently moved his sister-in-law toward the exit, murmuring, "Let's get you into bed."

"We're staying at the Hyatt," a woman whispered in my ear. I moved one step backwards and looked into eyes the same azure as Alex's.

"I'm his sister, Adelaide. You'll have to forgive Mom. She's got her own mountain of guilt over Alex's death and looking for someone to unload it on. Call me later, and we can talk then. Time to get some happy pills into her."

Whoa, I thought. That was a boatload more family issues than I needed to hear right now. If Mom was always this filled with vitriol, no wonder Alex didn't say much about her.

"She's just in shock, honey," said Grandy. "Don't take what she said to heart."

Maybe. Or perhaps not, if Adelaide's surprise confidence was accurate. I was certainly going to follow up with Adelaide before I left Miami.

"One thing is for certain," said Max, slipping his arms around Grandy and me. "That young lad needs a better lawyer, and I say that knowing he was probably responsible for the death of a man I truly admired and liked."

"Yes. He could use some help," I said.

"You just stay out of this," Grandy said.

"What do you mean?" I asked.

She shook her white curls and made a tsking sound.

Max drove us out of Miami and south toward Miami Beach, where we chose a New York style deli to grab some food. My appetite hadn't returned, so I picked at the eggs on my plate then pushed away from the table.

"I'm going to take a walk down by the beach."

Neither Grandy nor Max questioned my decision.

"Sure, honey. We'll meet you back here in an hour."

I cut over the short block east that led to the busy street lined with restaurants and night spots across from the sandy beach. It was still early in the day, but the "beautiful" people—those out to be noticed—sipped coffees at outside cafés, laughing and catching the eyes of others intent upon similar displays of shapely bodies and expensive clothing.

I crossed the street and stepped onto the concrete walkway, removing my shoes as I walked into the sand. The beach began to fill with sun worshippers, young men and women who wore only the briefest of clothes to enable them to perfect already dark tans. Others, including elderly singles and couples, strolled the sidewalk while families carrying beach umbrellas and chairs struggled to control young children eager to rush into the blue water. I gave the ocean only a glance, content to enjoy the breeze coming off the water and turning my thoughts inward to memories of Alex and me. Grandy was right, as usual. I had to guard against blaming myself for Alex's death. He was here in Miami not because I rejected him or because he needed someplace outside of Sabal Bay to hide. He was here because more and more he chose to take work in the area. I sighed deeply and stopped beneath a palm tree, where I slid to the sand and leaned against its trunk. I pulled my cellphone out of my pocket and dialed the Hyatt, asking for Adelaide Montgomery's room.

CHAPTER 6

———

I WAS BACK at the deli where Grandy, Max, and I had eaten our late breakfast. The lunch crowd had left, and the place was deserted apart from two police officers who were seated at the counter drinking coffee and eating slices of pie.

I had convinced Grandy and Max that they should take a quick run to Key Largo to check on their boat while I talked with Adelaide. They agreed, Grandy relieved that rather than trying to find Jerome Singer better legal representation I was instead meeting Alex's sister to find out about arrangements for his funeral.

Adelaide slid into the chair across the table from me. Her hair was wind-blown, fine like Alex's but not the same light brown. I assumed she'd altered the natural color by using a red rinse. It had begun raining and the raindrops in her hair sparkled golden in the deli's lights.

"I sneaked away while Mom was taking a nap. She wouldn't be happy to know I was speaking to you. I'd like to say you should forgive her what she said, that she's grieving, but she's always had a sharp tongue and a nasty way. One thing you cannot say about her is that she's been a good mother. Most of the time she seems oblivious to the existence of her children. She's too wrapped up in self-pity, blaming Dad for dying on her and not leaving her enough money. She's a bitter woman, Eve."

"Losing her son in this way can't be helping," I said.

Adelaide shook her head. "You're right, of course. Sorry for unloading family stuff on you."

"Alex never talked about his family. I didn't even know he had a sister."

"We weren't close. Alex left home soon after Dad passed. That was fifteen years ago when I was only in my teens."

I shifted around on the hard chair and said, "Would you like to go someplace else, maybe for a drink?"

"Let's. It's still early so the bars should be empty."

The rain had let up and the sun was again shining. Steam rose off the pavement as we made our way toward the beach and a restaurant I'd spotted earlier. We chose a table in the back where we wouldn't be disturbed by servers or patrons and each ordered a glass of wine. I might have preferred my usual Scotch, but it was early even for wine.

"Tell me about Alex when he was a kid," I said. "Where did you grow up?"

Adelaide talked about their early childhood in Virginia. Their father worked as an accountant for the local school system while their mother stayed at home. "Mostly she watched soaps on television and smoked cigarettes," Adelaide said. They had a cleaning woman who came in once a week. Until their father died, it seemed like a pretty typical family situation, although their mother always seemed to be angry, dissatisfied with their standard of living and short-tempered when it came to the children.

"I guess we were normal kids, getting into the kind of trouble kids get into, but our antics drove Mom crazy. As soon as Alex graduated from high school, he left, and he told me I should do the same when I graduated." Adelaide took a sip of her wine and stared across the room. "Mom guilted me into staying to take care of her. I know now what a mistake that was."

I looked across the table at her. In her late twenties, she was attractive and clearly bright and personable. I marveled at how an unhappy parent could ruin her child's life.

"Maybe it's not too late. If Alex knew his death would make you rethink that choice, I think he'd be very happy."

Tears filled her eyes. "Do you really think so?"

I reached across the table and patted her hand. "Sure."

We continued to talk over a second glass of wine, mostly about the kind of work Adelaide might obtain if she left her mother's home. She had followed in her father's footsteps, earning a degree in business and working out of the house taking in accounting jobs, mostly tax-related.

"I've managed to save a little of the money I made, but most of it went to Mom. There always seems to be something she needs done to the house or car repairs."

The bar began to fill with an after-work crowd eager to talk, laugh, and drink. It became difficult to hear each other, and we'd run out of conversation. I think Adelaide was feeling guilty about unloading all her family troubles.

"I'm talking your ear off." She looked at her watch. "Anyway, I've got to get back to the hotel."

Before we left, I asked her about funeral arrangements. She told me, then gave me some advice.

"Don't come to the funeral. Mom won't want you there. She'll use your presence as an excuse to start something that will make not only you but everyone else uncomfortable."

"I'll have to think about that. I need to say goodbye to him."

Adelaide gave me a quick hug and said, "I know you do, but I had to warn you."

"Thanks anyway."

She gave me a rueful smile. "So, see you at the funeral then?"

GRANDY, MAX, AND I drove back up the turnpike and onto the

Beeline Highway to Sabal Bay. It was dark when we pulled up in front of the house, and the answering machine was blinking when we entered.

I didn't bother checking the messages because I knew who had called. I picked up the land line and was about to dial Sammy's number when someone knocked on the door.

I opened it to Sammy.

"Grandfather said you should be coming home about now. Could you use a canoe ride?"

I threw my arms around him and stood on tiptoes to kiss his full lips.

Yes, oh my yes!

"Be back soon," I said to Grandy.

She gave me a knowing smile.

When Sammy opened the door of his truck, the smell of barbecued ribs wafted out from within.

"I thought you might be hungry," Sammy said. "You usually are."

"That is so sweet of you, but not tonight. I just want to get out on the water." I gazed up at the night sky, dense with stars. "How is it that there are so many more stars in the sky down here than in Connecticut?"

I knew there weren't more stars here. I knew it was simply air and light pollution in the Northeast that made it difficult to see the heavenly points of light, but I needed to believe that some of the stars, the shyer ones, had come out tonight specially to greet Sammy and me and light the way for us as he paddled down the canal to our special place.

We said little in the truck or on our way in the canoe or even when we settled on a blanket in our broken-down shack on an island in the swamp. Tonight I felt more at home here than I did at my own place. After Sammy had settled the blanket on the floor, I snuggled against his warm body. We lay there without speaking, simply taking in the comfort of each other's presence. It was after the moon came up that we realized we hadn't eaten the ribs, but somehow we weren't hungry for ribs. Sammy pulled me closer into his strong arms, making the pain of Alex's death seem to fade into the swamps.

"Sammy." I spoke into his shoulder. "You've been so patient with me, with my grief, but there's also your own. Did you have a funeral for Walter?"

"Yes. Frida came. I know the tribe didn't want her there, but I was glad to see her. She's not so bad for a cop. I think she truly wants to help."

"She does. I'm sorry we had to put off visiting the pawn shops."

"I visited a few of them after the funeral."

I was disappointed he hadn't waited until I could go with him, but I understood how anxious he was to track down the watch Walter said he'd found on the body.

"I found nothing, but Renfro Pawn here in Sabal Bay was closed. The old man who ran it died, and the body was sent back to Ohio, where he originally lived, to have the funeral there."

"Will it reopen?"

"The son has been running the shop and intends to reopen the beginning of next week. I wish it could be sooner."

For his sake, I did, too, but that did give me time to fly to Virginia to the funeral and get back here to my own shop. In the meantime, there was the phone call I needed to make to my mob boss friend, Nappi.

I shared all this with Sammy.

"Why do you need to call Nappi?" asked Sammy. I could see suspicion in his eyes. "Is it because of that kid who killed Alex?"

I nodded.

"Grandy won't like this," he said.

"What about you? I can't believe you think I should get involved."

Sammy gave me a slow smile tinged with sadness. "I know

there's nothing anyone can do when you decide to take on one of your 'projects.' I'd be a fool to stop you, but is Nappi the person to talk with?"

"Oh, I'm only going to ask him to recommend a good lawyer. I'm not going to get involved."

Sammy shook his head and laughed. "No, no, of course, you aren't, Eve."

To change the subject, I reached behind him for the bag of ribs. "Hungry yet?"

"I am, just not for hours-old, cold, dried-out ribs. I could use a cup of hot coffee and a nice sausage and egg scramble with home fries and rye toast."

That sounded good, so we left the ribs near the bank where we usually beached the canoe—kind of a present for the momma gator who frequented these parts. Not that she'd ever thank us and not that I recommended feeding wildlife, but perhaps she would see it as the one-time offering it was.

I FLEW TO Richmond, Virginia, two days later, taking an early morning flight and scheduling my return trip the afternoon of the same day. The taxi I'd hired at the airport dropped me in front of the funeral home an hour before the service. I hoped the funeral director would grant me a few minutes alone with Alex. I took Adelaide's advice to heart. I had no intention of making my presence here about me. This was for him and his family. I didn't want to make anyone uncomfortable. To make myself less noticeable during the service, I took up a position in the back of the room in a far corner. I wore a hat to cover my spiky blonde hair, a dark, full-length raincoat, and low-heeled shoes so I wouldn't stand heads above the rest of the mourners.

When I entered the room, I was glad for the long coat. The air was cold and smelled of the flowers draped over the end of the casket and arranged around the front. Somehow the scent of all those blooms made the temperature of the room seem more frigid. Why did arrangements for the dead seem to do that while at weddings the flowers made the room feel happy and warm? I pulled my coat around me and stood a few steps inside the entrance. Did I really want to see Alex or would it be better to remember him as he was—sometimes with a broad grin on his face. At other times his features had been pinched with irritation and aggravation as he confronted me over one of my intrusions into some case. This would be my last chance to talk to him. I squared my shoulders and walked up to the casket.

"Sweet Alex," I said, "we did have a time of it, didn't we? You were such a good man. I hope these last months have been happy for you."

Someone touched my shoulder, and I whirled around, thinking it was his mother, here to give me hell for intruding on her grief. But it was Adelaide and another woman.

"I knew you'd come, Eve, and I knew you'd be careful that Mom wouldn't see you. I have someone for you to meet."

The woman standing beside Adelaide was about my age, much shorter and much rounder, with soft brown hair in waves that hung to her shoulders. Her eyes were also a soft brown, shiny with tears.

"This is Margaret Spaden. She was one of Alex's classmates in school here. She now lives in Miami."

Adelaide didn't need to say more. I knew. Alex had found someone to love, someone from his past he reconnected with. The weight on my heart lifted. I smiled.

The woman reached for my hand. "That's a pretty good disguise, but even without the heels, your height gives you away. Alex talked about you." There was no bitterness or jealousy in her voice.

"We were good friends. I'll miss him," I said.

She nodded. We seemed to understand each other without needing words.

"Well, I think I'll find a seat somewhere back there so the family isn't upset."

Margaret smiled. "You mean so that Alex's mom doesn't go ballistic. She hasn't changed since we were in high school. I feel kind of sorry for her, but she's ill, you know." She paused. "I mean she's mentally ill, but she won't go for help."

"How do you know this?"

"I'm a psychologist. I have a small private practice in Miami. Thank you for being so sensitive about all of this."

"I just needed to—"

"I know. Say goodbye. Of course. I'm glad you came. Alex said you were loyal to your friends."

And Alex had been a good friend as well as a lover. Being here was what I needed to do, to be able to come through for him this one last time.

I nodded and walked to the back of the room, where I found an empty seat between two men—uniformed police officers who must have known Alex through his work. A tall man sat in the row in front of me, effectively hiding me from the gaze of anyone near the casket.

Several minutes later, Alex's mother entered the room on the arm of her brother-in-law, Adelaide at their side.

"Is she here? Is the bitch here?" asked her mother in a loud voice. "I won't have it, you know." She twisted her head in every direction, searching the far corners of the room. I slid down lower in my seat.

Adelaide and her uncle quieted the woman and seated her in the front row. Just when it seemed she had settled down, she jumped up and went to the casket.

"You were a shitty son, d'ya know that? You abandoned me and left me here with your useless sister."

I sighed deeply. I'd done what I came to do, said goodbye to Alex. I'd even been given a surprise gift out of this. I now knew Alex had reconnected with Margaret, and the two of them had found some measure of happiness in the last several months. *Good for you, Alex*, I thought as I slid from my seat and slipped out of the back door.

* * *

THE DAY I'D heard about Alex I promised myself that I'd get my PI license. I'd finally let the world know I was more than a snoopy gal who loved a bargain. I was a professional sleuth. The first step was to return to Crusty McNabb's office and inform him of my intentions. As much of an old curmudgeon as Crusty was, I trusted Alex's recommendation of him as a possible mentor. As was so often the case in my life, that visit would have to wait because I'd neglected my responsibilities at the shop, actually both shops. With Madeleine tied up in baby feedings and changing and all the duties that went with two new ones, I'd relied on Grandy to open the shop in the strip mall and left the motor home, our store on wheels, sitting idle in the local flea market where we usually parked it. Shelley had volunteered to take over the shop and let Grandy pilot the motor home to the coast to sell on the weekend, but it contained so little merchandise that it seemed not to be worth the gas it would take to drive the thirty miles there and same distance back. If I didn't step up and visit our ladies in West Palm to procure some clothing and household items, we would soon find ourselves with nothing to sell. I pushed my grief over Alex's death into the back of my mind and put the PI license on hold. I had to focus on the business and also accompany Sammy to the pawn shops he hadn't already visited to look for the pocket watch he was sure was his father's. Frida had entrusted this work to me, and I wanted to do it well, to prove to her and to myself that I had the stuff to work the clues, to be professional about my assignment. I was determined to lay the groundwork for my future.

The night I got back from the funeral I tossed and turned in my bed, looking for an answer to this dilemma: how to divide myself into enough parts to go around. Knowing that sleep would not come, I got up around three in the morning and went to the kitchen to make a pot of coffee. If I was going to find an answer to my problems, I might as well be wide awake and not simply in a state of anxious sleeplessness.

The coffee did the trick so well that my caffeinated brain added another item to my already overcrowded list. I wanted to call Nappi, and I should do it soon. The coffee failed in other ways. It didn't keep me awake or aware, and I was startled into consciousness when Grandy came into the kitchen at seven the next morning.

"Wouldn't you be more comfortable sleeping in a bed than face down on a table?" she asked.

"Here's my problem …" I began, deciding I should run all the issues by her to get her input.

Before I could continue, Grandy gave me a puzzled look. "You never run things by anybody, girl. Why now?"

"Now it's clear even to me that I'm trying to do too many things. I need help."

"Well, you've got help. Max and I are here, and we'll do anything you need us to do in the shops. And you might want to involve Shelley more. She's eager to become more of an asset to you and Madeleine. As for the other, that's up to you to work out, but maybe you could put Crusty on hold for a while."

For a moment I was tongue-tied. So Grandy had figured out how Crusty fit into my life. "I already decided to do that."

She gave me a wry little smile. "Good. Now get yourself into that shower and head on out to West Palm this morning for merchandise to sell while I mind the shop. You and Sammy can do your snooping this afternoon."

"Madeleine—"

"I'll call her and tell her you're back and that everything is taken care of."

I got up from the table and grabbed Grandy around her waist. "I owe you big time."

"Yes, you do. And I'm going to give you a piece of advice I know you won't follow, but since you asked for my help, you have to listen."

Oh, boy. Now I remembered why I didn't usually seek out the input of others. People who love you often tell you things "for your own good," and in my case that meant things I already knew but was too stubborn to admit I knew.

"First of all, don't you drag Sammy into your snooping. You know that man will do anything for you, even when it gets him into trouble. And second, I like Nappi Napolitani as much as you do, but leave him out of this thing. In fact, you might want to take yourself out of it too. And finally, if you need a partner in your usually not-well-thought-out detecting schemes, I'm your gal. That's all."

"I'm only going to give Nappi a call," I said in my defense.

"Then he'll be coming up here to talk with you, and we'll find ourselves doing something on the far side of legal."

"You're just jealous I might choose someone other than you as my sidekick."

"Damn right I am." She shoved me toward the bathroom.

CHAPTER 7

———

I HAD A plan. It wasn't one I had developed, but one Grandy laid out for me. Of course, she'd also given me advice I had no intention of following, but the rest of what she said made good sense. I put the top down on my convertible and sped down the Beeline Highway toward West Palm. If I located enough merchandise today, I might be able to stock the motor home store and let Grandy drive it to the coast this weekend. Madeleine and I offered a special service to our consignors: for our regulars who lived out of the area in places like West Palm or even Stuart and Wellington, we picked up from their houses, making it convenient for them to consign with us rather than with another shop. There were plenty of other places they could take their used clothing and other items. The problem today was that I might find more merchandise than I could carry in my car. Oh well, then I'd have to make another run, maybe tomorrow. If I could find the time.

Sammy and I were scheduled to meet when I got back today and visit the pawn shops. I passed through Indiantown, halfway to my destination, and decided to pull into the McDonald's there to get myself a coffee and an Egg McMuffin. My appetite had returned, and I couldn't take the risk of not keeping up my strength as I attempted to fit everything into one morning's work.

As I turned into the parking lot to proceed to the drive-thru lane, I noticed a black SUV turning behind me. On the driver's side, I spied the Gator Construction logo. The windows were tinted too dark for me to see who drove it, but after I ordered my food and was heading for the window to pick up and pay, the driver of the SUV rolled down his window and stuck his head out. It was the construction company's lawyer, Danny.

"I thought I recognized you. Eve, isn't it? We met the other day."

"I remember," I said. What did he want?

"Got time to pull in, so we can have our morning coffee together?"

Of course I don't, said the part of me that wanted to accomplish my errands and get back home. *Why not*, said the curious part. I pulled into a parking space. I was about to get out of my car and go into the restaurant when he motioned me over to his car.

"I'll leave the air conditioner running and we can talk. It's so darn noisy in there."

I liked his idea. Every time I sat in a fast food place, I ended up smelling like a burger and fries.

I wasn't aware we had anything to talk about, but what the hell? He was associated with the construction project and came to the site soon after Frida and I were called to look at the bones. Maybe he knew something I should know … I mean, maybe he knew something *Frida* should know.

"Nice car," I said, sliding into the passenger's seat and noting the soft, black-leather seats. "The company offers its employees fine rides, I guess."

"Not everyone gets a ride like this. The construction foreman drives a truck, but all the other executives have use of a car. The company owns a line of identical SUVs."

"Yes, well I noted that your back-hoe operator didn't drive one of these, not even a truck." Of course I knew the laborers wouldn't be given cars, but I loved making a point of it. He seemed so smug about his ride.

He ignored my comment. "Sad about the back-hoe operator. The foreman told me he was good at his job. A tragedy. Hit-and-run, I understand. I guess the cops haven't found who did it yet? No clues at all."

Was he trying to pump me for information? It seemed like it.

"You wanted to talk?" I said.

"Just being friendly. I thought maybe we could get together for dinner some night."

What an arrogant so-and-so. I was about to say no, when I considered that fishing for information could go both ways.

"Look, I have to get on the road—I've got client to meet— but here's my card. Call me." I handed him one of the cards from the shop and got out of his car and into mine.

I backed out of my parking space and turned onto the main road. He tooted at me, and I waved.

Something about that man bothered me. Maybe I just didn't much care for lawyers. I'd made a comment once to Sammy that most lawyers' pictures made them look like felons, and Sammy said in his opinion they were. I knew it was unfair of me to feel that way. I'd met only one lawyer I liked. He'd been recommended to the Egrets by my friend Nappi. Someday I might need the help of an attorney—probably *would* need one with my propensity for sticking my nose into things that were none of my business and engaging in behavior that skirted the wrong side of the law. Speaking of which …. I picked up my cellphone, pulled up the list of my contacts, and chose one.

The phone rang once and then Nappi's smooth voice spoke my name. "Eve, my dear. I haven't had the chance to tell you how sorry I am about Alex."

"That's why I'm calling. I could use some help."

I needed the name of a pit bull attorney. Who better to ask than Nappi?

I told Nappi I was heading down to West Palm, so he invited me for lunch at a brew pub in City Place.

"I've got just the man for you. I'll see if he can meet us there," he said when I asked him about a legal representative.

I looked at the deep-fried pastry I'd purchased at McDonald's. I loved their fry pies, but I decided to leave room for lunch, a meal I determined would be neither fried nor fatty. I considered tossing the pie—without its wrapper, of course—onto the side of the road to feed the wildlife, but decided they shouldn't eat that much cholesterol either. I wrapped it carefully and tossed it on the passenger's seat. I pressed on the accelerator and let the wind ruffle my hair and the sun warm my face. Nothing better in Florida than a convertible with the top down.

My visits to several West Palm matrons who consigned with our shop were so successful that I had to put up the top and stash the clothes and a few household items like two Tommy Bahama side tables in my backseat. I was only a few minutes late to the restaurant, but Nappi and another man were already seated at a booth in the back near the glassed-in area that held the fermenter and brewing vats. They'd worked their way halfway down the dark ale in the glasses in front of them.

I slid into the booth across from them and apologized for my tardiness. Nappi reached for my hand and planted his usual gentlemanly kiss on it.

"No problem," said Nappi. "I took the time to fill Nathan in on your situation. Nathan Hardy, this is Eve Appel. Eve, Nathan."

We nodded at each other. Nathan appeared to be younger than Nappi, if his unlined baby face was any indication, but his youthful visage was offset by silver hair. It made him look like a child playing grownup, but when he spoke, his voice was deep and authoritative with the touch of a Southern accent, perhaps Georgian. He did not look like a felon at all, although knowing Nappi must have put him in contact with many who broke the law, I wondered if he had done so himself a time or two. I wasn't being prejudiced. *Come on*. He was a mob lawyer.

I sneaked a peek at my watch and got right down to business. I needed to be back in Sabal Bay to go pawn shop hopping with Sammy.

I told him what I needed: a tough, smart lawyer with enough connections to make it possible to get a young kid off a murder charge.

"Pardon me for saying this, Ms. Appel, but you don't look like the kind of person who hangs out with gang members, even young ones. Do you really think this is something you want to get involved in?"

"I was hoping it was something *you* might get involved in," I said. "This kid was coerced somehow to kill a friend of mine. I suspect his family was threatened by the gang. I want the best deal you can make for him, preferably no time in either a youth facility or prison, and for you to make certain that being back home with his mother doesn't expose him to consequences from the men who put him up to the killing. I'd like it if you could manage to get them some jail time, preferably long sentences."

He tapped his buffed and trimmed nails on the wooden table top and looked at Nappi, who nodded.

"Can do," he said.

"I'll pay you whatever you need," I said.

He again looked at Nappi, who shook his head.

"My secretary just this morning told me I haven't done my pro bono work for the month, so it's all taken care of."

I snorted in disbelief. "You think I can't pay my bills?" I directed this to Nappi.

"I know you can, my dear, but you needn't worry."

"Nappi, I love you, you know that, but it's against my moral principles to owe too many favors to mob bosses. I am already in your debt. Let's not put me in the poor house."

He grinned.

The lawyer chuckled and took the last swallow of his beer. "I'll send you a bill."

"You'll need my address." I started to pull a card from my purse, but he put up his hand to stop me.

"I know where to find you," he said.

Spoken by someone who didn't have his pleasant manner, his words might have been considered a threat, but I took them the way he meant them, as a friendly reassurance.

The waiter, sensing we had finished transacting our business, approached the table to take our lunch orders.

"Not that your company isn't wonderful, but I've got to be in Sabal Bay shortly, so I'll take my order to go."

My luncheon partners waved away my apology.

As I left the restaurant with my turkey club, I heard Nathan Hardy ask Nappi, "Don't you think it would have been wise to talk her out of getting into a gang-related matter?"

Nappi's reply made me smile. "You don't talk Eve Appel out of anything when she has that determined look on her face."

It was good to have friends who understood you.

I PLANNED TO drop the household goods at the store for Grandy and Shelley to tag and put out on the floor and also to sort the clothing into the items we would sell here and the ones that would go into the RV for the weekend flea market at Stuart. I was surprised to find Madeleine nursing the twins in the backroom of the shop.

"Hiya, Eve," she said as she expertly handed one baby to Grandy and accepted the other from Shelley's arms. How did women learn all this stuff? Or was it hardwired into their girlie brains? Was this stuff in my head, too, just sitting there waiting to be tapped into until the right moment came along? I tried to envision myself with a baby in my arms. Nope, couldn't do it. Maybe something was missing in my genetic programming.

Madeleine gave me one of her looks, the one that expressed her worry for my wellbeing as well as her judgment that I wasn't in touch with my inner feelings. "How are things?"

"I'm fine, just fine. I attended Alex's funeral and met the

woman he was seeing in Miami. She's a great gal. I think they had something wonderful going."

Grandy settled one of the twins on her shoulder—the girl, I guessed, because of the pink trim on the little shirt. God, babies were tiny. I worried that they might break if you jostled them too much. And then that little bundle of pink flesh let out a cry. Maybe babies weren't as delicate as I thought. This one had the lungs of a bull alligator.

"Did you accomplish what you wanted in West Palm?" Grandy asked, shifting the yowling babe and rhythmically rocking her in her arms. Little Eve quieted.

"What do you mean by that?" I asked. "Did Nappi call you?"

Grandy has mastered the innocent little old lady look, blue eyes all round and wide, mouth pursed in a tiny smile. She gave me that look now, but I wasn't deceived. Nor was she.

"I know you've got your fingers in the case against that boy who shot Alex. I just don't know exactly how."

I tried the Grandy innocent look.

"Why are you doing that funny thing with your face?" asked Madeleine as she held the other baby out to me.

"I'm not too good with babies," I said. As soon as David Jr. was in my arms, he looked up at me and began to cry. "See? I told you."

"He needs burping. Put him over your shoulder and pat his back."

I did. He burped up something foul smelling on my shoulder.

Madeleine got up and took him. "Sorry about that."

I saw Sammy's truck pull up in front of the store. "Gotta go. I'll be back to close up shop."

Grandy came back from the bathroom and held out a wet cloth. "Better clean off the baby burp."

I did the best I could with the cloth, then raced out the door and jumped into Sammy's truck.

"What's that smell?" he said before I could fasten my seatbelt.

Jumping back out of the truck, I ran into the store, past the clothes' rounds and into the backroom. I pulled out a woman's shirt hanging in the small closet at the rear of the store. Balling up the shirt I was wearing, I tossed it on the closet floor to be retrieved later and pulled the other shirt on. It was missing several buttons, which I had intended replacing but hadn't found the time. It would have to do for now. Back out the door I dashed and jumped into the truck. Out of breath, I panted, "Let's go."

Sammy gave me a look. "Not until you button up your shirt. You're showing more cleavage than usual."

"No buttons." I showed him. "Don't worry. It'll work in our favor when we question people. You can scare them while I seduce them into giving us information. It's a new version of good cop, bad cop."

Sammy seemed amused at my description. He shrugged and shifted into gear. "Renfro Pawn is our first stop. The shop should have reopened after the older Mr. Renfro's funeral."

It was open for business again. The man behind the counter listened to Sammy describe the watch, but since his father had owned and operated the shop until his death, we had little hope the son could be helpful.

"The watch isn't here; I can tell you that. But it's really funny because when I was a kid I sometimes hung out here in the shop after school and on weekends. One Saturday I remember well because my dad insisted I help out if I was going to be underfoot all the time. That day he had me doing what I hated most: dusting the shelves. An Indian came in. He had this gold watch. Dad remarked it was unique. I'd never seen anything like it with that bird etched on its cover. I would have given a year's allowance to own that. The guy seemed kind of nervous, like he wanted to make the deal for the watch real quick. I think Dad gave him fifty bucks for it."

"Fifty bucks!" said Sammy. That watch was worth hundreds."

"Not in a pawn shop," the owner said.

"So what became of the watch? The guy reclaim it?" I asked.

"I don't remember if he did or if someone bought it. That was over thirty years ago. I can check back in Dad's papers to see what I can find, but I can't promise anything."

Sammy and I left the store dejected that our search had come to this dead end. I could tell from Sammy's face that he was thinking the same thing I was.

"It must have been my father who pawned the watch all those years ago, but why? As near as I can figure it was around the time he disappeared."

"Maybe he needed the money to leave here?" I said.

"For the bones in that construction site to be his, he had to go back and claim the watch, but did he? And if not, then whose bones are there? And what was the dead guy doing with my father's watch on him?" Sammy kicked a stone on the ground in frustration. "I wanted that body to be my father's. I needed that, so I could stop wondering where he was. I finally had an answer and now I only have more questions."

I put my hand on his arm. "We have to go forward. Let's find the watch and see what that gives us."

"Two murders and neither of them seem to be of any interest to the cops."

I heard the bitterness in Sammy's voice.

"You know Frida's trying, but she's handling all the cases in the department because of budget cuts and Linc being out sick."

"I know," Sammy said. "I just want to find out what happened and get the killer or killers who are responsible."

I could tell part of Sammy's disappointment and anger was directed at himself for not being able to track down the watch.

"At least we know the watch was at Renfro Pawn once, and maybe the owner will find some record of what happened to it. We have other pawn shops we can visit. No one would dare keep a watch that distinctive, not when it would lead back to Walter's murder. And as you said to Mr. Renfro, it is worth hundreds."

.Sammy perked up and nodded. "Where to now? I think there are only a few more pawn shops left around here. Should we try them?"

"Sure."

I was almost certain checking the shops in Sabal Bay was a dead end. They were too close to the crime for the person or persons responsible to pawn the watch here. Too much chance someone like Sammy and me would track it down.

One of the smaller shops had gone out of business. In the other one, the owner hadn't seen the watch. I was right. A dead end.

I looked at my watch. It was still early afternoon.

"Let's try Stuart. It's just far enough away that the thief might feel safe trying to unload it there."

We sped down the Canopy Road to the coast. I regretted we hadn't the time to slow down so we could take in the beauty of the live oaks with the Spanish moss hanging off them and their branches arching over the road to form an awning shading us from the hot sun. Still, the drive soothed us so that by the time we reached Stuart, we were both in a more hopeful mood. We first tried all the shops north on Federal Highway to the Roosevelt Bridge. Having had no success, we turned back south. Again, nothing.

"Let's go home," said Sammy.

"I guess you're right."

Sammy had whipped the truck right into a small strip mall and was about to turn around to pick up the light onto US 1 when I spied a tiny pawn shop tucked into the side of the mall.

"Wait. Pull in here." I pointed at the beaten-up sign hanging akilter over the shop door.

Sammy nosed into a parking space across from the store. At first I thought the store was closed, but when I tried to look in a window so filthy it obscured a view of anything inside the store, I saw an open sign propped on its side in the window on the other side of the door. This looked promising, the kind of place a criminal might want to pawn what he'd taken from a man he killed.

"This place sure is stuck back here where no one can find it," Sammy said.

"Yup. It's just the place a slimy character would choose to do business in."

The dirty window hid a shop filled with merchandise that would have been better taken to the dump. *Who would buy this stuff?* I asked myself as I strolled by shelves holding broken items, appliances decades old, and tools so rusty no worker would consider using them. The store smelled like aged Parmesan cheese and cooked collard greens. The man behind the counter looked as if he belonged here. His hair was long and oily and his skin was wrinkled in a crosshatch pattern as if he'd been a beach bum until he had found his calling as a shop owner. His rumpled shirt had stains down the front. Gray chest hair sprouted out the top of a yellowed tee beneath the shirt. His pants were equally stained. As I approached, I realized the smells in the shop came from him. The only neat thing about him was his well-trimmed goatee, which was blond in color. I stepped back and let Sammy take the lead.

"Hep ya?" he asked, then turned away from us and spit a wad of tobacco to one side. I hoped he'd aimed at a can or container, but given the state of his shop and himself, that might be too much to hope for. Okay. Now I got it. His facial hair wasn't really blond, but yellow from the tobacco, and the teeth he showed when he smiled were just as yellow.

Sammy didn't return the smile. My original plan was to let Sammy appear as threatening as possible, and if that didn't produce any answers, I would sidle up and be nice. I rethought the being nice part. I didn't want to get any closer to the man.

Sammy described the watch. The man didn't react, but reached under the counter. Maybe Sammy had been too scary, and the man thought we were going to rob him. Was he reaching for a gun? No, instead he held out his hand and laid something on the counter.

"You mean this watch?"

CHAPTER 8

———

THE OWNER PLACED the watch in Sammy's hand, which trembled slightly. He turned it over in his palm to inspect the etching on the cover.

"It's his, Eve. It's my dad's watch."

"Well, now," said the owner, bending over to spit, "that's not strictly true. It's mine, unless the guy comes back to claim it, and if he doesn't, I sell it."

"Tell us about the person who brought this in," I said.

The man squinted at me and rubbed his goatee as if grooming it for my benefit.

"Who wants to know?" he asked.

"Actually, the police in Sabal Bay would be interested."

"You them, are ya?"

"We work for them. Kind of," I said.

"Lemme see some identification." He held out his hand, which was surprisingly clean. His nails looked as if they had been recently trimmed and buffed. The guy was a bundle of contradictions.

"We're not cops. I'm looking for the watch that someone stole from my brother after running him down. The watch belonged to our father, and this is it. I can tell by the etching on the cover."

The man's eyes widened with Sammy's information. "Stealing and killing. That is serious. Still, I got to protect my customers, so unless you can show me something official, I ain't gonna say much."

I took my cellphone out of my pocket and contacted Frida.

"Here's what I got on the watch, Frida." I told her where we were and that we had found the watch.

"Good work, Eve, but there's not much I can do. I only have Sammy's word and the phone call from Walter to indicate the watch was taken from that body."

"But Frida, those are the only leads you have on the body."

"Not the only ones. I've got the evidence we gathered at the site." I heard her sigh and then continue, "Look, I'll try to get over to the coast later today or tomorrow. Meantime, put the guy on the phone."

"Detective Martinez from the Sabal Bay police wants to talk to you." I handed my cell over.

He listened, saying nothing, then finally, "Okay, okay, but I think this is gonna take a court order." He handed the phone back to me.

"I tried to put a scare into him. I hope I succeeded. You might find him cooperative now. I'll get more from him later. Thanks, Eve. Good work." Frida ended the call.

The owner gave me a defiant look, then stooped to spit. When he stood back up, he smiled and said, "Well, lookee here. The guy's address fell on the floor. You wanna pick that up for me? My back's actin' up."

I picked up the pawn tag. The name on it was no surprise—"John Smith," it read—but the address looked real, and it was in Stuart, only blocks back up Highway 1.

I handed it back and thanked him for his cooperation.

"Glad to help the police. I don't want no trouble with them, you know, but that's all I'm gonna say for now."

"How about a description of the guy?"

"Nope." He crossed his scrawny arms.

I said goodbye, and he gave me a yellow-toothed grin and a wink. "Stop by anytime."

I grabbed Sammy's shirt and pulled him out of the store.

"Finally," I said to Sammy as he backed the truck out of the parking space, "our time paid off. Take a left at the light onto the highway. The address should be close to the flea market we sell at on the weekends. Dumb guy. He used a fake name but put down his real address."

Dumb me. The address was as fake as the name. It wasn't a residence, but the address of the flea market itself. Yet another dead end.

"I know what you're thinking, Sammy, but there's no use going back to the pawn shop. We won't get anything more out of the guy, and he's on notice now. Frida will take care of it."

Sammy said nothing, but he was chewing over the frustrating day. I saw his jaw working as he focused on the road back to Sabal Bay.

We got back into town in time for me to close the shop as I had promised. Grandy looked up at me when I entered.

"I'm just cashing out," she said. "We had a good day. The new merchandise that Shelley and I were able to get out on the floor was popular. Those end tables netted us a good two hundred dollars." She stopped counting the money and looked up at me. "I can tell from your expression that your day wasn't quite as successful."

I told her about the watch having been pawned years ago at the Renfro shop and that we had found it today on the coast, but there was nothing we could do about it.

"The owner did let me know the name and address of the guy who pawned it, but they were fake. I think if I had been the cops I might have gotten something more out of him. This story gets more and more confusing. Sammy, like his brother Walter, was so certain the body was their father's, but if he pawned the watch years ago, how did it get on that body?" My head was spinning with possibilities, but absolutely no certainties.

I did wonder what would have happened in the pawn shop on the coast if I'd had some kind of official credentials to shove in that owner's face. *Hmm.* There were credentials, and then there were credentials. Some were licenses or badges, but others took a more human form.

"What are you scheming now, Eve?" asked Grandy as we left the shop.

"I'm thinking we should consider ribs tonight."

I know Grandy didn't believe my interest in ribs took much scheming, but she agreed we should pick up Max at the house and head for the Biscuit.

"Maybe we should see if Nappi wants to join us. I mean, if he's around."

Grandy brightened. "And there you have it. The scheming thing. When are you going to do it? Can I come along? I haven't had a good nighttime caper in oh so long." She was fairly wriggling off the seat in anticipation.

"What would Max say?" I asked.

"Oh, he doesn't mind if I go party without him on occasion."

I laughed, dropped the top, punched the accelerator, and we drove off into the fading afternoon light.

"I DIDN'T EXPECT to see you so soon after our lunch today," said Nappi after he had kissed Grandy's hand in greeting, hugged me, and shook hands with Max.

"It was a business lunch and too short," I replied.

"And this dinner will be dinner with friends?" He looked skeptical.

"We might throw in a little business," I said.

"But only if I can come along," said Grandy.

"And where would we be going?" Nappi leaned forward and waggled his brows.

"How do you feel about pawn shops?"

"What are we pawning?" he asked.

"Persuasion," I replied, and his eyes lit up.

We finished our ribs and were sipping coffee when my cell rang. I looked at the caller ID and was surprised at the name. "I'll take this outside.

"Mr. Cypress. You are a fast worker. What has it been? Less than a day since I gave you my card?"

"When I see something I want, I like to act on it."

"I have a boyfriend, Mr. Cypress."

"The grapevine tells me you have recently changed partners due to the death of Mr. Montgomery. And I believe you helped hire a lawyer to represent the boy who did the shooting. Very peculiar."

"We don't run in the same circles, Mr. Cypress, yet you know as much about me as my closest friends do."

I heard him chuckle. "I make it my business to know about people I find interesting."

"Or peculiar. Let's get on with it, Mr. Cypress"

"I like a woman who's direct, and call me Danny."

"Let's move on. What do you want, Mr. Cypress?"

"Dinner for two in the Club restaurant. It's right on the water off Salerno road. Do you know it?"

Did I? It was the most expensive, most elegant restaurant in that area. I'd jump at the chance to dine there even if it meant I'd have to put up with Danny Cypress for an evening. I knew he wanted to find out through me how much the cops knew about the body uncovered at the construction site. If anyone had a reason for moving what might be Indian remains, it certainly had to be the development company for which Mr. Cypress worked. I knew Frida would want me to seize the chance to pick his brain.

"Why, I'd love to have dinner with you. When?"

I heard someone come up to me from the back.

"Dinner with who?" asked Sammy.

"Uh, just a minute." I put my hand over the phone. "Tell you in second."

Sammy nodded and stepped into the Biscuit. "Catch you inside."

"Hi. Sorry about that. When?"

"Tomorrow night? Around eight."

"Great. I'll meet you there."

"I'll pick you up."

"Mr. Cypress, as I told you, and you already know, I have a boyfriend. I don't need to rub his face in my seeing someone else, even if it is for just one evening."

I had every intention of telling Sammy what I was doing, but I wasn't going to tell Danny Cypress the real reason I didn't want to get into a car with him: I didn't trust him. And he made my skin crawl. And did I say I didn't trust him?

I ended the call and entered the restaurant to join Sammy and the others.

"Do I detect some scheming going on?" asked Sammy.

The man knew me so well.

"I've enlisted Nappi's help to extract some information from our pawn shop owner on the coast."

"And I'm going to come along and help," Grandy said. "How about you, Sammy? Want to join us?"

"When is this happening?" asked Sammy. "I've got to work at the airboat business tomorrow afternoon. My nephews can't cover for me. Besides, I can't ask them to spend so much time doing my work."

I knew exactly how Sammy felt. I'd often asked others to jump in and do my work, and with Madeleine caring for her twins, we were already short one worker. Grandy had helped out when she could, but the time would come when she and Max would want to return to Key Largo and their fishing charter business. Shelley was doing her part, but we needed more help.

"Hey, Evie." *Oh shoot.* It was Jerry. I'd thought we might have Nappi to ourselves for the evening without his gofer, my ex-husband Jerry.

"Don't call me Evie," I said. I always said that to Jerry, but he never seemed to understand how much the name irritated me. Or did he? Maybe he liked irritating me.

"Sorry, Evie, uh, Eve. What's up?"

Nappi started to speak, but I butted in. "We've got something big we're planning, and if you're a good boy, we'll let you be a part of it."

Jerry pumped his arm in the air and yelled, "Yes!" Did I know how to manipulate this guy or what?

So that was how I got Jerry to take over the shop the following afternoon. It wasn't the role he had wanted, and it wasn't a permanent solution to our need for extra help, but it would do for just this once.

"You've done this before, so I don't have to run through what your responsibilities are, do I?" I asked Jerry the next afternoon as Nappi, Grandy, and I gathered in the shop before heading to the coast.

"Ah, Evie, honey, this isn't what I had in mind."

"Don't call me—"

"This is important, Jerry," Nappi broke in. "Eve needs you here so we can find out who pawned that watch."

"I don't understand why that's my job," Jerry whined.

"Because you have a way with the ladies, Jerry," I said. "You can sell better than any of us."

"Even you?" He sounded doubtful.

"Even me. Remember you sold me on you. I married you, didn't I?"

"Then you divorced me."

"You wanted me to." I was getting tired of trying to get his full cooperation. One more comment from him, and I'd toss him out of the shop and call Grandfather Egret to come take over the afternoon's selling. He'd done it before and very well at that. I wondered why I'd asked Jerry in the first place. *Oh right.*

I did it to get him out of the way while my reliable help did the real work.

Jerry seemed to read my mind. "Let's ask Grandfather Egret. He'll be happy to be here this afternoon, and then I can come with you to the coast."

Nappi stepped close to Jerry and scowled at him. "Look, buddy. This is the deal. You work here or you do nothing to help Eve because you're not coming along with us. Hear me?"

"Yes, sir." Jerry swallowed hard and stepped back.

"And another thing," Nappi said, "don't call her Evie. Don't you get it by now? She hates that name. It makes her feel like a child."

"Yes, sir." Jerry took another step backward. "I'll straighten the clothing rounds." He began fidgeting with the displays, moving clothing from one to another.

"Jerry," I said, "could you not redecorate and just sell?"

He nodded, and we left him standing in front of the cash register trying to look like someone who knew something about women's clothing.

We piled into Nappi's Escalade with Grandy in the passenger seat and me in the back. Once in Stuart, I directed Nappi south to the strip mall where the pawn shop was located. I walked in first, Grandy on my heels. I could practically feel her breath on my neck. Turning, I saw a big grin on her face.

"Could you try to look more businesslike and not as if you were in a toy store?" I suggested. She replaced the smile with another look, this one more like she'd swallowed something that tasted bad. It would have to do.

The owner scowled for a moment, but when he saw my sweet, chubby, and harmless-looking Grandy, he smiled. "I see you brought reinforcements. What is she going to do? Feed me cookies until I tell you about the guy?"

And then Nappi entered the shop. The smile disappeared from the owner's face. "I know you," he said.

Why was I not surprised the owner recognized him?

Everyone who had occasion to dabble in the world of crime knew Nappi—if not personally, then by reputation. And I was certain this guy had done some dabbling.

"I know you, too. What name are you using today? Edward Borden, Eddie Brookfield, or perhaps Ed Sanford?"

I figured we might as well call him Ed, last name unimportant since it wouldn't have been real anyway.

Ed spread his hands in supplication. "Name's Ed Lawton. Look. I didn't know she was friends with you," he said, reaching under the counter.

"I wouldn't pull out that shotgun, if I were you," said Nappi. "You might accidentally shoot yourself with it. You know how accidents happen with firearms." Nappi gave him one of his disarming, scary smiles.

"I could shoot you," he said.

"You could, but then my mama here," he gestured toward Grandy, "would be forced to pull out her automatic and shoot you. You know how hard it is to control those automatics. They've been known to go off by themselves. That would be a terrible accident and painful, if she misfired and you didn't die. How about it, Mama?"

A brief look of surprise crossed Grandy's face, but she quickly hid it with a nod and a silly grin like the one you would find on a lunatic's face. She reached under her jacket as if checking her weapon.

"I can hit what I shoot at, but I can't guarantee a clean kill," she said.

Ed's face turned green with terror.

"So how about it?" said Nappi. "The authorities should have made it clear to you how important this is."

"Cops haven't been here, so I thought the whole thing had kind of blown over."

Nappi let out a bark of a laugh. "Just because the cops didn't visit you doesn't mean they've forgotten about you. You know how it is. Cops get busy with other things."

Ed spat his tobacco and gave Grandy a weak smile as he brought his hands back up from under the counter.

It was my turn now that Nappi had softened up the guy. "So how about a description of Mr. Smith. He been in here before to pawn stuff? And we'd appreciate a real address."

"He's been here before, but I don't know his name or an address. I just take down what my customers give me."

"Okay. What did he look like?"

The owner hesitated, and I got the feeling he knew more about the man than he was telling us. I was also certain the next thing out of his mouth would be a yet another lie.

"He was tall, heavy-set, and bald."

"I don't think so," I said.

Grandy wandered the store, taking in the broken, dirty, and mostly useless merchandise. "I'd like to see the watch. Where is it?" she asked.

Ed-Eddie-Edward What's-His-last-Name-Lawton gulped and looked at Nappi. "You're not gonna like this. It's gone."

CHAPTER 9

NAPPI SLAMMED HIS hand on the countertop so hard I expected to see the glass shatter.

"Not my fault. He came in here this morning and bought the watch back. Said he wanted to give it as a gift."

Lies, lies, lies. Did the guy sell anything else but fabrications here?

"I don't think so. I think you called him and warned him the cops wanted to talk with him," I said.

Nappi reached out for the owner, who jumped when he grabbed his shoulder. Obviously, he expected something more violent than the pat Nappi gave him.

"Well, I guess we'll have to turn this whole thing over to the authorities then. You know what they'll do, don't you? They'll come here and arrest you, close the shop, and you'll spend time in jail for impeding a murder investigation. And you don't like jail much, do you?"

"I'd rather do jail time than mess with the guy who pawned the watch," said owner Ed.

"But you're messing with me, and you know that makes me mad," said Nappi.

The guy pointed up at the corner. "That's a camera recording everyone who comes in here. If you do anything to me, it's all there for the cops to see."

Oh, sweet Jesus. The guy had given away the store. Nappi and I looked at each other. We had the same thought.

"Let's take a look at the footage on there. It probably records for twenty-four hours and then you can erase it if you like, but I'll bet you haven't done that yet today. Right?"

"Huh?" he said. Then he got it. The guy who pawned the watch and came to pick it up earlier today would be on that tape.

We shuffled through the store and into the backroom to view the tape. All the stuffing seemed to have been pulled right out of the owner. So defeated was he that he offered us coffee—as if I'd ever consider putting my lips to anything that came out of the store. He did have some leftover donuts that looked tasty, however.

The man on the tape—the only customer in the store this morning—was not tall and heavy, but small, barely five feet five and scrawny. He could have been the younger brother of the shop owner.

"You two related?" I asked him.

"Cousins," he admitted.

"Family is important, even when it comes to murder," I said sarcastically.

His line should have been, "My cousin wouldn't kill anybody," but he didn't say it. I guess he knew his cousin was capable of murder, had probably done a couple in the past. And I was betting the cousin didn't have a soft spot in his heart for family. But try as we might with threats of having the police shut him down or having Nappi and Grandy help him into the next world, Spitting Ed's family loyalty won out. Or maybe it was simply fear for his life that made him mute. We got no name, no address, and no number.

We knew what the guy looked like, but we walked out of

the store with nothing else to go on. I thought Nappi could have been scarier, but I wasn't about to suggest ways to torture information out of the guy, not to a crime boss. That's their specialty and not mine.

When we got into the car, I called Frida to let her know what we'd uncovered.

"You took Nappi with you?" she said, irritation in her voice. "What the hell were you thinking? What did Nappi do to the guy?"

"Nothing. He just talked to him, patted him on the shoulder once, and we looked at a surveillance tape with the guy who pawned the watch on it." I thought it was best to keep Nappi's intimidating comment about my gun-toting grandmother to myself. It wasn't a real threat anyway.

"You saw the guy?" she said, both joy and disbelief in her voice. "Tell you what I'm going to do. You sit tight in front of that shop and make certain he knows you're there. I'll be over in half an hour. I want to see that tape and have a talk with the owner. Damn. If I hadn't been so tied up here with processing the evidence we found at the construction site, I would have been at that shop yesterday or this morning."

I told Nappi what she said.

"Yeah, Eddie knows we're still here. I just saw him peek through the door. I don't think she'll get much out of him, but it's the cops' show now, unless you think I should go back in there with Grandy." He bent down and pulled an automatic pistol from under his seat.

"You know how to fire this?" he asked Grandy.

Her big blue eyes got bigger.

"Hey, Nappi. Forget it. Grandy isn't going to threaten anyone with a gun."

"Well, now, honey. If it would help Sammy, I …" she said.

"No!" I said. "Frida will take it from here."

Nappi laughed. "Not necessary anyway." He shoved the weapon back under the seat. I couldn't tell if Grandy was relieved or disappointed she wouldn't get another crack at owner Eddie.

"What do you mean?" I asked him, puzzled by his attitude.

"I recognized the guy on the tape."

"You *what*?"

"I know him. Name's Connie Russo. He does contract work for various mob folks. He's the guy you hire when you think you need backup."

"Do you know how to find him?" I asked. "Can we go there now?"

"I don't know where he hangs out, but I can find out easily enough. I have friends who have friends who have contacts who, well, you know."

"Could you call them now?" I asked, trying to hide my disappointment that we wouldn't be able to find him right away.

"Patience, Eve. I'll see what I can do." He got out of the car, and I saw him put his cellphone to his ear and begin talking. He moved out of the sun and toward the rear of this side of the strip mall where a palm offered a bit of shade.

We rolled down the windows in Nappi's car, but there wasn't much breeze or shade in our parking place.

I had spotted a convenience store at the far end of the mall when we drove in, so I jumped out of the car and decided to take a walk down there to get us some cold sodas.

"Be back in a minute," I said to Grandy.

"I think I'll sit on the curb back there where there's a bit of shade," she said. "Get me a diet soda. I don't care what kind." She walked past Nappi and toward the store fronts beyond the pawn shop. One of them had an awning out front, and Grandy plunked down in its shade.

I turned the corner and walked past the stores making up the long arm of the backward L-shaped mall. The icy air inside the convenience store made me shiver for a minute when it hit my damp shirt, but it felt good to be out of the humidity and the piercing sunlight. I pulled three bottles of soda from the convenience store cooler and paid for them, then began my walk back to the corner. Before I turned it, someone grabbed my arm from behind and spun me around.

The guy with the pincer-like grip was shorter than I, and I recognized him at once. Our pawn shop owner had been busy while we stood guard in front of his business.

"I guess Eddie called you. Did he tell you the cops were on their way?" I managed to say while the cousin wrestled me down the sidewalk.

"Keep your face shut. I got some questions for you, girlie." He pulled me back down the row of store fronts toward the convenience store. An old, battered SUV, rusty orange in color, was parked there. He pushed me toward the passenger's side.

"Git in there."

"No." I tried to pull away from him as he opened the door.

"No? We ain't having an argument here. You do as I say or—"

"Or what?" said a voice from behind him. Frida had pulled up in her cruiser and seen the guy trying to put me in the car.

The guy Nappi had ID'd as Connie Russo let go of me and struggled out of Frida's grasp. One look at the police insignia on her car sent him running, bolting for the back of the strip mall and the overgrown area there. Frida and I took after him. We had the advantage on him. He was short and—although his stringy body indicated he could have been a sprinter—smelled of cigarettes. From the heavy odor, I guessed he didn't have the lungs for a long run. Frida and I, both long-legged, gained on him. He'd almost made it to the road that cut in back of the strip mall when a car pulled up and braked abruptly.

"Get in," said the driver of the vehicle.

Our runaway jumped in, and the car drove off.

"Who the hell was that?" asked Frida.

I mentally hit myself on the forehead for stupidity. "That was Ed, the owner of the pawnshop. I think he made a call to our escapee warning him that we were on his tail, so the guy came here thinking he'd use me to get information on what was going on. You foiled that plan, but how stupid of us to watch the front of the shop and not realize the owner parked his car around back."

"I don't get it. Why should the pawn shop owner care? Why get involved?" asked Frida.

"They're family."

"You mean family or 'Family'?" she asked, putting air quotes around the second family.

"They're related."

"Our suspect has bolted, but I might persuade the owner to talk. The guy won't want to lose his shop."

"You think he'll come back to his shop?"

"Sure. He might even turn himself in with a lawyer in tow claiming he was only protecting a customer being harassed by mob members. You brought Nappi into this, remember?"

Damn. And Grandy had played along with Nappi's threat. My Grandy, a mobster's hit woman.

Frida and I walked around the corner to where Grandy and Nappi stood beside his car. I hadn't confided in Frida that Nappi knew the guy who accosted me because it might not be something he wanted made public, especially to the police.

"I want all of you to clear out of here," said Frida. "This is police business."

"What are you going to do?" I asked.

"Sit on this place and hope the owner will return, maybe tonight." Frida gave a sigh of resignation. "I hate surveillance work—it's the kind of job I like to farm out to a PI—but I've got no choice but to do it myself. Next to the information I have on the stolen bones, this is the best lead I can follow."

I was curious to find out where the evidence at the construction site was leading her, so I asked, assuming she wouldn't share. I was right. She shrugged and smiled. As she walked off toward her police cruiser, she stopped and turned. "Um, could I have a minute, Eve?"

I hopped out of Nappi's car and followed her out of earshot of Nappi and Grandy.

"What's up?"

"Do you know anything about Danny Cypress—you know, the attorney for the construction company?"

What now? Was Frida the latest in a long line of friends and family who could read my mind?

"Why?"

"I thought perhaps the Egrets, being Miccosukee also, might have said something about the Cypress family."

"Funny you should ask, because Danny has an eye for the ladies, specifically this lady. I have a dinner engagement with him tonight."

Frida eyes brightened with surprise and eagerness. "So what does Sammy say about this? Or didn't you tell him?"

"I told him. He knows I'm only doing it to pump Cypress for any information he may have about the construction area and the body there."

"You know Cypress is probably doing the same with you."

"Are you saying he wasn't swept away by my charm and beauty?"

Frida snorted, and I laughed, but then she sobered. "I can't encourage you to snoop into his affairs or that of the construction company, but ...."

"But you'd be happy to hear what I find out."

"If the company and their lawyer is involved in the body's disappearance, this could be dangerous for you, Eve."

"Don't worry. I've got backup. Sammy will be following us in his truck, and although Jerry doesn't know it yet, he'll be sitting in the restaurant at a nearby table just to make certain I'm not hustled out a rear door."

"Good plan. You saw what can happen today unless you have someone close enough for a quick rescue."

"I didn't thank you for that, Frida."

She waved off my thanks. "It's my job."

* * *

"Something on your mind, Eve? You're unusually quiet." asked Nappi on our way back to Sabal Bay.

"Just thinking about what to wear tonight."

"I didn't know you and Sammy had plans," said Grandy.

"Oh, we …." *Oops*, I should keep my dinner engagement quiet, or I might have more than the two tails I'd planned on. Knowing how Grandy and Nappi worried about my schemes and capers, the trip to the restaurant might look more like a convoy of cars.

"I'm going to meet him at his place, and then we'll decide what we're going to do," I said quickly, hoping that story would satisfy any curiosity about my evening.

"Well," Grandy said, "take a wrap of some kind. The wind's coming up, and I think we're in for some weather." She turned in her seat to face Nappi. "Do you think I really could handle an automatic weapon?"

He nodded. "With training."

"I might like that," she said.

"Are you crazy?" I asked. "You're an old … uh, you're a senior …. You're just fine without one."

"Eve's right about that," Nappi said. "I don't recommend that people arm themselves, except in unusual situations." This from a mob boss.

"You mean 'unusual' like threatening a pawn shop clerk?" she asked.

"No, I mean 'unusual' like an alligator invades your house. If you interrupt their search for a snack, they're capable of doing bodily harm, but they don't shoot back." Nappi pulled into a parking place in front of the shop.

Inside I was surprised to see Shelley behind the counter, but no Jerry.

"Did Jerry cut out?" I said, thinking I'd have to get Nappi to talk to him. My threatening Jerry never accomplished much.

"No. he's back there." She pointed to the room in the back of the store.

I could hear Shelley's sewing machine whirring away, and when I stepped into the room, I saw Jerry in front of it, humming to himself and pushing fabric through the feeder.

"He's quite good at it," said Shelley, coming up behind me, "and he has a real design sense. I let him refashion a dress for one of the women this afternoon. He's working on it now."

"Where did you learn to sew?" I was so shocked I could barely get the words out of my mouth.

"My mother taught me. We were so poor when I was a kid that she had to make most of our clothes, curtains, even coats. She was a whiz, even doing work for others. I helped. Haven't done it for ages."

Nappi walked into the room after me, and I heard him groan. "He's ruined for Family work."

"Well, maybe not. He can alter your shirts and pants, even monogram your handkerchiefs. That handmade touch," I said, trying to hold back a laugh.

Nappi shook his head and left.

"All done." Jerry held up the dress he had been working on. It looked pretty good to me.

I put my arm around his shoulders and walked him out into the hallway where no one could hear us. "As a reward for doing so well today, how would you like to help me tonight?"

"I can if I finish the matching jacket to that dress."

What? This from the guy who was always so eager to be in on any adventure I cooked up.

I held back what I wanted to scream at him and cleared my throat to calm myself. "And how long will that take you?"

He scanned my face carefully, perhaps catching the note of anger in my voice. "An hour? Would that be okay? If not, I could come in early tomorrow to finish it. I don't want to miss out on anything. I love the crazy stuff you do … I mean as long as it's not too dangerous."

"That's what you'll be there for. To make certain I'm not in danger." I laid out the plan for him.

"Okay, but if I have to sit in the restaurant, I'll have to order a dinner. Who's going to pay for that?"

I ground my teeth. "You'll pay for it out of the money you earned at the store today."

He gave me a pleading look. "But it'll take all I earned today. That place is pricey."

Any scheme where I involved Jerry always meant I had to fork over money. I wanted to tighten my grip on his shoulders and squeeze hard, but I stopped myself. He was right. He was doing me a favor.

"Put it on your credit card, and I'll reimburse you."

He grinned.

I held up a warning finger before he could say anything. "But don't order the most expensive dish on the menu and limit your alcohol consumption to a drink and a glass of wine. You're supposed to be protecting me."

"Okay. It's a deal."

I sighed with relief.

"One more thing," he said before I could leave.

"We already shook on it, Jerry."

"That's a place where a guy takes a date. I need a date."

CHAPTER 10

THE JERRY AND a date scenario wasn't going to happen, and I pointed out the reason why to Jerry.

"I don't think anyone is in danger, but I'm not going to involve some innocent woman and take the chance she gets hurt."

"But it's okay with you for me to be in danger," he said.

"Yes," I replied, and that was that.

I chose to dress conservatively for the evening, a black sheath dress, sleeveless but with a boat neck. I had no intention of looking provocative and sending the wrong message to Danny Cypress. At seven thirty I pulled out of my drive with Sammy's truck on my tail and got to the restaurant about ten minutes late, conveying, I hoped, the message that I was not overly eager for this rendezvous.

My date appeared even later, at around eight thirty. I chose to wait for him in the bar area, not caring if the restaurant held the table for us or not. They did.

He didn't apologize or ask if he'd kept me waiting too long, but simply slid onto the barstool beside mine and ordered a martini.

"I hope this dinner engagement isn't interfering with something else, something more pressing for you, Mr. Cypress," I said. I couldn't help being sarcastic about his tardiness.

"What? Oh, no. I got caught in traffic, that's all."

Traffic? At this hour, on a week night? Hardly.

Out of the corner of my eye, I watched Jerry being shown to a table in the dining room. Then, to my surprise, Nappi appeared and joined Jerry at his table. What was that all about? Ah well, Jerry would have company for dinner—not the company he hoped for, but company. They were seated in a far corner of the dining room.

For someone who wanted to find out what I knew about possible evidence the police had found at the site where the bones were found, Danny Cypress seemed uninterested in pursuing the topic, or any topic for that matter. He appeared distracted, staring into space, acting as if he didn't really want to be here.

"Is there something wrong?" I finally asked, after he had gulped down his drink and suggested we be seated.

"No, of course not. I've just got a lot on my mind. Busy day, you know."

"Your company must be concerned that the police will think they are responsible for stealing those bones," I said, deciding I needed to move along the conversation.

"Why should we do that?"

"You know darn well why. If the bones are found to be Indian, then the whole construction site will be shut down. Now, however, there's no way to confirm that. The company is in the clear."

I finally had his full attention.

"It's stupid to think that area would be a burial ground."

"Not really. The land once belonged to the Seminole and Miccosukee tribes. You should know that."

His face got red. I'd insulted him.

"Of course I know that, but that's not where we Miccosukees

bury our people. We have our cemetery on our land in the Alligator Alley Reservation south of the lake, or there are private cemeteries. You're good friends with the Egrets, so you should know that."

What a lovely evening this was turning out to be, trading insults as an appetizer.

"It could have been an area used by the people hundreds of years ago and forgotten by the tribe in the last several hundred years."

"The bones weren't that old," he said.

"How do you know?"

After a moment's discomfort, he smiled. "The foreman mentioned it."

"And he's some kind of expert on dating bones?"

Danny shrugged. "He could be wrong, I guess, but he's been at this work a long time and has run into bones on other sites."

Really? I doubted that.

"So, do the cops have any clues as to who took the bones?" asked Danny. His question sounded like casual curiosity, simply part of the conversation we were engaged in.

"Tire tracks, I guess."

He stopped eating and looked at me. "Really. I would have thought it would be hard to isolate one set of tracks from all the others around there."

Now it was my turn to shrug. "I don't know how the cops do that stuff, but they do."

He looked amused, probably at my use of "stuff" to describe evidence.

The remainder of our meal was spent chatting about his work as an attorney. He liked to talk about himself, and I encouraged him to go for it. Maybe he'd spill something that would tie the company to the removal of the bones.

"I worked in Miami for a while, but decided to move closer to home. Mom and Dad like to have all of us children close by."

I'd done a little homework on his family. I knew his father

ran large numbers of cattle on his ranch west of the Kissimmee River outside Sabal Bay. Two of his brothers worked the ranch with their father. Danny was the only one of the brothers who attended college and then went on to law school, although his younger sister completed two years of college before coming home to live as well. My research had turned up something interesting about a third brother, the oldest sibling in the family.

"I understand your older brother left home years ago."

Danny squinted at me. "How do you know that?"

"Frida told me. And of course, as you mentioned earlier, I'm friends with Sammy and Grandfather Egret, so you know how closely knit the tribe is when it comes to its members."

"Albert left some years ago—I don't remember how many. I was still a kid. We heard from him once, but we haven't had any news in the last ten years or so."

"That must be distressing for your parents."

"Yup."

"From what I heard, he was a pretty wild teen."

"Could we change the subject? Albert was a problem, always getting into trouble. In some ways, it's good he left. He made life difficult for all of us." He picked up the dessert menu. "They have killer cheesecake here."

Conversation lagged through coffee. Danny glanced at his watch several times, then excused himself from the table. "I have to make a call. Business."

Nappi got up from his table and walked past me, dropping a folded note beside my plate.

It read, "Careful with this guy. He used to do legal business for a mob family. Handle him carefully." It would have been nice if Nappi has told me earlier, not that I would have turned down the invitation to dinner. I guess Nappi thought the two of us looked too cozy tonight, and he was worried I wasn't being cautious enough. I tucked the note into my purse.

When Danny returned, he acted as if a burden had been

lifted from his shoulders. "How about a nightcap at my place?"

"I have a drive home, and I already have a glass of wine in me. I'm under the limit now, but there's no sense in taking chances."

"Leave your car here. I'll drive us to my condo, and you can stay the night. I've got an extra bedroom. I promise I'll be a perfect gentleman … if that's what you want me to be." He gave me a come-hither look with hooded eyes. He was an attractive man, but not for me. Something about him made me uncomfortable. I'd have passed on his invitation even if Sammy hadn't been in my life.

"That's an interesting offer, but no."

"Some other time then." He said it as if it was a given. Such arrogance.

He walked me to my car and backed me up against the door, then leaned in as if to kiss me. I turned my head.

"You're not like other women, are you?"

"I guess not."

To my surprise he smiled. "I like that."

He left for his car, which was parked across the lot. I watched him go, thankful the night was at an end. I didn't like him. He made me jittery. I wasn't going to repeat the event; I'd pumped this well dry in any case. He wasn't about to let down his guard again the way he had when he told me the bones were not that old. Although he covered his slip-up with a story, he knew more about the bones than he let on. The only way he would know the age of the bones was if he was involved somehow. How long had he worked for the construction firm as its lawyer? Questions whirled around in my head, but I had no answers, just the conviction that he was covering for the construction company. The only other thing I'd picked up from tonight was more an impression than specific information. It concerned his older brother. It was the only subject that made him uncomfortable. I'd ask Sammy and Grandfather for the whole story. As I watched his car pull out of the lot, I sighed.

The evening was over, and I couldn't have been more relieved.

Seeing Sammy by his truck on the other side of the lot, I waved. He walked over with Nappi at his side.

Sammy put his arm around me and hugged me close. "Are you okay? I saw his attempt at a goodnight kiss."

"Yes. Fine. Get in, and we can talk for a minute."

"How about we talk in my car?" said Nappi.

That was easier than one of them having to struggle into the Mustang's small backseat.

"I hope there won't be more dates with this guy," said Sammy as I got into the back of Nappi's SUV.

I knew his comment was made not out of jealousy, but out of worry for my safety.

"So how did you know Danny Cypress was mob connected, and why isn't he anymore?" I asked Nappi.

"The lawyer I introduced you to at lunch mentioned Cypress' name. He did work for a Miami crime syndicate, but according to my lawyer friend, they found his work unsatisfactory."

"Did he say why?" Sammy asked.

"Danny Cypress seems to have bouts of severe depression," Nappi said, "and when he's in one, he tends to drink a lot. You can't trust secrets to a man who can't hold his liquor."

"He seemed distracted tonight. He was off somewhere else most of the evening. His only genuine reaction was when I asked him about his older brother. That seemed to be a topic he was adamant I not pursue. There's a story there, right?"

Sammy nodded. "Grandfather told me most of what I know about the family. There were five children. The father married out of the tribe, a woman from Guatemala. All the boys in the family were wild when they were teenagers, drinking, riding around at night terrorizing other ranching families, driving off their cattle, staying out all night …. Eventually they all settled down. Two of the boys married tribal members and worked the ranch with their dad, and Danny went off to college. But the older brother? Albert was on his way to real trouble. First he started stealing other kids' money; then when he was a teen, he started shoplifting from local stores. He robbed a convenience store and got probation, probably because of his dad's standing in the community. A few months later, he broke into a home and took money, jewelry, and other valuables. He threatened the owner with a gun. I guess it wasn't loaded, but given his thieving background, when he went to trial, his father had a difficult time convincing the judge not to throw him into a juvenile facility. It might have been a good thing if he had done some time. Next thing the tribe heard, he had left town. No one knew where he went."

"Danny said the family got a few letters soon after he disappeared, but he said they haven't heard from him in years. I got the feeling the family is just as glad to be rid of him."

Sammy nodded. "Despite working as a lawyer for the mob, I guess Danny Jr. is the success story in the family."

"What about his sister?" I asked. "She did two years of college then came home. Why, to marry?"

Sammy shook his head. "No. I understand the mother is very ill, and I think the daughter is caring for her. Danny's mother was never very sociable. I heard she came to a few tribal events, but after Albert left, she stopped attending. I don't think anyone has seen her for years. Grandfather drops by on occasion to see if there's anything he can do, but he's told the family is fine and is never invited in."

"Maybe he should pay her another visit," I said. "I could come along."

At this suggestion, Nappi's face darkened. "You should stay out of this, Eve. I've got a real bad feeling that something's not right. Danny Jr. is not a man to be trifled with. Don't you think he'd be suspicious if you suddenly turned up, feigning concern over his mother? He'd interpret that as the ultimate in snooping."

"That's what I'm known for."

"Not in this case. Leave it alone," Nappi warned. Sammy nodded in agreement.

"I know the construction company is involved in those bones disappearing. And I have proof."

Sammy's eyes widened. "What kind of proof?"

"Danny said that he knew the bones weren't very old. Now how could he know that unless he moved them?"

"That's enough for me. Those bones have to be my dad's. Maybe I should pay Danny a visit, and we can have a little talk." Sammy's face looked as I'd never seen it before: savage. It was the countenance of a warrior bent on revenge.

I reached out to touch his hand. "Let me check something first. He said he knew the bones weren't old because the foreman said so. Let me talk with him before you have your heart-to-heart with Danny."

His visage changed, softening into the kind and loving face of my Sammy.

Nappi interrupted our moment. "Well, if you have to snoop, I recommend telling Frida what the foreman allegedly told Danny. Let her talk with him to find out if what Danny said is true. Frida would appreciate the information, Eve. It is her case, you know."

"You're right, but she did ask for my help," I said.

"Help to find the watch," Sammy pointed out.

"It's all the same case," I insisted.

"Look. Eve, if I can wait until Frida talks to the foreman, then you should too. Let her do what cops do. I'm not worried about confronting Danny, but I won't risk alerting him to my suspicions and sending him off to disappear like his brother."

That sounded reasonable, the kind of thing I had little patience for. Maybe I could think of another way to talk to a member of the Cypress family without setting off alarms.

Someone tapped on the window. I jumped. Only Jerry. I'd forgotten about him.

"I thought you'd left already," I said, rolling down my window.

"I ran into a buddy as I was leaving the bar. If you don't need me anymore, I'll be on my way. And here's the receipt for my dinner." He handed it through the open window to me.

"Pay it yourself," said Nappi.

"What? I did this as a favor. The place cost me a lot of money."

"That's what friends do. Pay it. You don't see me handing a bill to her for my evening, do you?"

I could see Jerry wanted to argue, and I was ready to foot his bill, but if I paid for his dinner, I would feel guilty not paying for Nappi's too. Sure, they were friends, but they had gone out of their way for me. I owed them.

"I …" I began.

"Shut up, Eve," said Nappi. And that was that.

I'd find some way of returning the favor. Nappi especially seemed to always have my back.

"Let's go home," said Sammy. "Grandy will want to know all about the evening."

"She and Max went around the lake to Clewiston to eat dinner at that catfish place. I doubt they'll be back until late. And I'm just beat. It's been a long day."

"Are you okay to drive yourself home, Eve?" asked Sammy.

"Sure. You can follow me back."

When I pulled into my drive, Sammy pulled his truck in behind me.

"I'll walk you to the door. It appears Grandy and Max aren't home yet because their car isn't here."

I knew Sammy wanted to come in, but I also knew I was so tired I probably wouldn't be able to get to my bedroom before I fell asleep. He took me in his arms and kissed me gently on the lips. What began as a sweet kiss soon erupted into something more passionate. I broke free of his embrace.

"Every time I'm near you my hormones kind of take over," I said.

"I'm just a roll in the hay for you, is that it?"

I knew he wasn't serious from the twinkle in his eyes.

"Well, I think you'd have to do most of the rolling tonight. A passionate romp sounds good now, but by the time we reached my bedroom, I'd be asleep."

"Okay, then how about right here, on your front lawn?"

"Sammy!"

"I'm kidding. You get some sleep, and we'll paddle out to our favorite place tomorrow if you're free."

We hugged again, avoiding a kiss, which we knew would plunge us into trouble. I watched Sammy as he walked to his truck, backed out the driveway, and waved goodbye. I entered the house, leaving the porch light on for Grandy and Max.

Tossing my purse on the couch, I slipped off my shoes and walked across my living room carpet past the front window. I watched Sammy's taillights as he drove off. Yawning, I opened the door to my bedroom. That's when the smell hit me.

CHAPTER 11

———

SMOKE. HEAVY, STALE, like a burned-out campfire.

I moved out of the doorway and back into the hall. Someone was in the house. I knew it. I stopped and listened, but I heard nothing except my own heart racing in my chest until the compressor in the refrigerator kicked in. Wherever the intruder was, he or she had to have seen the lights of my car and Sammy's truck. Wouldn't the person be eager to get out of here to avoid discovery? Unless my unwanted visitor had something else in mind. I tried not to let my imagination provide unpleasant scenarios. I sniffed again. The smell seemed less pronounced. Maybe they had left. Better not to take chances.

I retreated down the hallway toward the living room. I'd turned on the ceiling light when I came in the door, but turned it back off at the switch on the wall by the hallway leading to the bedroom. I flipped the light back on and sighed with relief. No one was in the living room, and I could see across the way into the kitchen. The door to the garage was closed, but was it locked? Had my unwelcome visitor left by that exit and was now hiding in my garage? Or maybe in the bathroom or my guest room? Perhaps they'd gone out through the back door. I glanced at my purse on the couch. *Get the hell out of the house, Eve, and call the cops.* I moved toward the couch and reached for my purse to get my cellphone on my way out. The overhead light went out. Before I could retrieve my purse and retreat to the door, a hand encircled my throat in a steel grip. I tried to pull it away, but the hold tightened, and I thought I might pass out. I stumbled backward, reaching for the door knob. Another hand grabbed my arm.

"Quiet or you're dead." It was a man's voice I thought I'd heard before, but he hadn't spoken enough words for me to identify it. I tried to pull back, but he brought both his hands to my throat and tightened them. The pressure around my eyes mounted. I could no longer see the shadowy objects in the room. A red cast like blood flooded my vision.

"What do you want?" I managed to squeak out. He said nothing, but pressed his thumbs into my throat and rammed his body against mine, moving me out of the living room and into the hallway.

If I'd left my stiletto heels on, I might have been able to stomp on his instep and do some damage. They were, miraculously, still in my hand, but I was too weak to take any kind of a swing at him. My shoes had never failed me before. They'd always proven to be an effective weapon. Now they just seemed like silly shoes worn by a woman too vain to consider sturdier footwear.

He relinquished his chokehold and shoved me toward my bedroom. "Get the door," he said.

I did as ordered, and then lurched toward the wall to the right of the door, hoping I could use my hand to turn on the light. Maybe if I could identify him he'd think twice about doing anything. Or maybe he'd kill me if I saw his face. He caught my move toward the switch, pushed me away from the wall, and threw me onto the bed. I tried to roll away, but he was on me too fast. He was strong. I slapped at his face with my hands then tried to gouge out his eyes. He hit me across the mouth. I felt something warm trickle down my chin. Blood. My blood.

He grabbed my head and held it still. "I got a message for you. Stay out of that hit-and-run. It's none of your business, ya nosy bitch." He released my head and delivered another blow to the side of my face.

I tried to cover my head with my arms. I'd dropped one of my shoes when he shoved me into the bedroom, but absurdly I'd held on to the other. *Eve and her damn shoes*. What was wrong with me? I should toss it on the floor, so I could use both hands to defend myself. Or should I? I still had a move, if I could pull it off, if I had the resolve to do it. My head hurt, but I knew if he punched me again I would be too weak to fight anymore. I didn't much care for what I was thinking, but I had no choice. As his arm came back to deliver yet another blow to my head, I moved the heel of my shoe upward and shoved it into his eye.

The shoe connected with the side of his nose then slid into his eye socket, not as hard as I'd intended but enough to inflict a lot of pain.

"Bitch!" he yelled and fell off the bed. It was dark enough in the room that I couldn't tell if he was writhing around on the floor or had gotten up and was about to jump on me again. He was moaning and swearing. "I'll get you good now." I felt him throw himself onto the bed, but I rolled to one side and onto the floor. At that moment, I knew I was lost. I hadn't wounded him seriously enough. He was hurting. And he was furious. Now he was more than a messenger. Now he was going to inflict more damage. Now he was a killer.

Suddenly the room lit up with the lights of a car shining into my bedroom window. My attacker turned toward the window, and I caught a brief glimpse of a bloodied face, one hand covering the side where my heel had done its damage, but I couldn't identify him before the headlights swung away from the window. He turned and ran out of my bedroom. I heard the back door open and close, and then silence. He was gone.

"We're home." It was Grandy.

I curled up in a fetal position and let out a sob. Then everything went black.

"EVE, HONEY. CAN you hear me?" Sammy's voice came to me from a long distance as if he was on the other side of the dense fog that enveloped me. I struggled to move, to find my way out, to go to him, but my legs would not obey my brain's instructions. The fog turned black and wiped out the sense of a world beyond me, then moved inward to take away any awareness of myself. *This must be what it is like to die* was my last thought before I whirled downward into a vortex of nothingness.

There was someone standing over me, but I couldn't see them clearly. I blinked my eyes, and the image came into focus. A woman. Someone I didn't recognize.

"Who are you?" I asked. My voice came out in a raspy whisper.

"My name's Susan. I'm a nurse. You've been hurt and in a coma for several days. There are some people here who'd like to see you if you're up to speaking with them."

I blinked again and saw Grandy and Max standing at the foot of my bed.

"Oh, Grandy," I said, choking back tears. "I hurt all over. What happened to me?"

"Someone attacked you, but you're going to be fine now. You need rest. We'll be back later."

"Where's Sammy?" I asked.

"I'm right here." He stepped forward and took my hand.

"He's been here since you were admitted," said the nurse. "We couldn't get rid of him."

"Sammy," I whispered and reached up to touch his face. It was wet. "Is it raining outside?" I asked.

"No," Sammy replied in a choked voice. My Sammy was crying.

"Don't be sad. I'm going to be fine." I wanted to reassure him further, to say I'd be back to my old self in a few days, but I was too tired to get the words out, and the medication I'd been given must have taken me off to the fog, which settled on me once more. And I was wrong about being back to the usual Eve. That would take some time and a change in my life to accomplish.

I WAS STILL in the hospital. They had weaned me off the heavier pain meds, but now I had trouble sleeping. I was twitchy, jittery. *Maybe it's a drug reaction*, I thought. I jumped at the slightest noise, and I worried someone would come into my room at night and finish the job the intruder had begun at my house. I was torn between wanting to go home and not wanting to stay in the bedroom where the attacker had almost killed me. It wasn't only fear for myself. I fretted about the safety of my friends and my family, and felt anxious when they were out of my sight. I wanted them near me to protect them and for them to protect me. This was no way to live, but I couldn't seem to pull myself out of it. The old sassy up-for-an-adventure Eve was gone, and I didn't know how to get her back.

Frida came to interview me the evening of the day I woke up. While describing the details of my attack brought back much of the horror, I felt a sense of hopefulness as I tried to detail what I knew of my attacker.

"I know he was shorter than I, slight of build, but muscular. And there was a smell about him that made me think of smoke."

"Cigarette smoke?" asked Frida.

"Maybe some of that, but stronger. As if he'd lived for years in a place where people smoked and his clothes were permeated with the smell of it."

"You said his voice was familiar?"

"I think he was disguising it, and he didn't say much—only

threats and the message about the hit-and-run—but I've heard that voice before. I just can't think of where."

"That's good then," said Frida.

"How can that be good, if I can't place the voice?"

"If he disguised it, it meant he didn't intend to kill you."

"Maybe not to begin with, but once I stabbed him with heel of my shoe, he went ballistic. The guy should have a really black eye and a sour attitude toward footwear, if you run across anyone fitting that description."

Frida laughed. "I guess the old Eve is back. That's great."

No, I was not really my old self. As soon as Frida left, I got out of bed and went to the door. There was no way to lock it, but I shivered as if a cold wind was blowing down the hallway and into my room.

The nurse found me later on the floor of the bathroom, shaking and crying. No. The old Eve was gone. I wondered if she was gone for good.

THE NEXT MORNING a woman dressed in a charcoal pantsuit tapped on the door frame. "May I come in?"

"That depends. Who are you?"

"My name is Dr. Alice Halsey. I'm a psychologist on staff here. I understand you could use my services."

"Can you help me get control of my life again?" I asked.

"Well, maybe the two of us can work on that together."

I was skeptical, but when I perused her from her cap of short brown curls down to her shoes, I decided to give it a try. She was wearing stiletto heels, after all.

We talked for an hour, and she agreed that I shouldn't go back to my house just yet. She suggested I stay with Sammy and Grandfather Egret, in a house so far removed in structure and amenities from my own that I couldn't mistake it for the place where I was attacked.

"Will I ever be able to go back?" I asked.

"Of course, but these things take time, Eve. You must be patient."

"Patience is something I've never had much of."

"So I guess that's a part of you that hasn't changed." She made it sound as if that was a good thing.

"I don't seem to be able to be alone," I said to Sammy and Grandfather as I settled into the small bedroom that was Sammy's at the house by the airboat business.

"You'll have Grandfather here when I'm working at David's ranch or piloting folks on airboat rides," Sammy said. "And Grandfather is taking care of Walter's three boys several afternoons a week."

"Children? I don't know. I'm not really good with children." Well, I didn't know if I was good with them or not, did I? I'd never been around any, except for briefly holding Madeleine's twins, and I wasn't good at that.

"Let's give it a try, and if it's too much, you can accompany me to David's ranch while I work there."

Sammy had been so accommodating, giving me his single bed and sleeping on the couch, that I couldn't say no. Three little boys? Well, some days I'd be back in the shop, so perhaps an afternoon or two of them would be bearable. Grandfather carefully explained that it was part of Miccosukee and Seminole matrilineal heritage that, if children lost their father, their mother's brother would take responsibility for them. Walter's boys had no mother, and she had had no brother, so Grandfather and Sammy had stepped in to help with their care. I understood family responsibilities. Grandy has taken care of me when my parents died. I certainly would make no fuss about the boys being here.

Madeleine and David had visited me in the hospital, and Madeleine arranged to pick me up and take me out to lunch the day I moved into the Egrets' place. I'd meet the three boys later in the afternoon.

"So … any preference as to where we eat?" asked Madeleine when I got in the car.

"Any place other than the Biscuit. I don't want to run into anyone I know."

Madeleine's soft lips drooped with concern gave me a concerned look. "Your face doesn't look that bad, you know."

"That's not it. I just … I don't know. I'm not ready to explain anything to friends yet."

"They know an intruder broke into your house. Your friends won't expect any explanations. They'll just want to know how you're doing."

"Not well. Not yet."

A shot rang out behind us. I jumped and grabbed for Madeleine's arm. Sweat poured down my face. "Get down!" I yelled.

"Eve, it's okay. It was a car backfiring."

I relaxed a bit. "That's how I'm doing. Oh, Madeleine, what's happening to me?"

"What does Dr. Halsey say?"

"She says this will take time. But I feel like my life is so out of control now."

Madeleine pulled over to the side of the road. "Don't push yourself so hard. You're your own worst enemy, thinking you should be able to simply slough off this attack like it was nothing. That guy tried to kill you."

"And I couldn't do a thing to save myself."

"I heard you did some damage by plunging your heel into his eyeball. That's a lot."

I gave a bitter laugh. "It only made him madder. So stupid to think I could take care of myself …."

"You've always taken care of yourself, even when others wanted to help. Could you just let us help you now? A little? Please?" Madeleine leaned across the seat and put her arms around me. "Please forgive yourself for not being able to kill someone."

She was right. I knew I was being too hard on myself, but I wanted the old in-your-face Eve back again. Maybe Alex was wrong about my becoming a PI. I might have the curiosity and the intelligence necessary for the job, but did I have the right attitude? It wasn't only that I felt I couldn't fight well enough. I also worried that from now on my first impulse would be to flee any encounter with personal violence. Who would hire a PI who bolted in the face of danger?

We ate at a new little café in town, a place too upscale for all my cowboy buddies, but I did see some of our clients there. As Madeleine predicted, they asked after my welfare and told me to get well soon.

I looked at my watch.

"Got an appointment?" asked Madeleine.

"Not until later. Dr. Halsey and I set up appointments three times a week. I feel like some kind of emotional cripple. I never thought I'd need a therapist. But I like her, and I trust her. I was wondering if we could drop by the shop. I haven't been there since—"

"Great idea. I told Grandy and Shelley I'd be there after lunch anyway."

"You're working afternoons, according to Grandy. Are you certain you want to take that on right now?"

Madeleine waved at the waitress for our bill. "It's good for me. Gets me away from talking only baby talk and gives David the chance to do daddy stuff. He likes it. His ex-wife didn't let him get too involved in raising his daughter, so he's excited to be a hands-on parent. And I bring the babies in some afternoons."

"You got yourself a good man there," I said.

Madeleine smiled. "And two wonderful babies, even if they do keep me up most of the night. That's the issue with twins. They take turns crying."

I enjoyed the feeling of sitting and riding while someone else did the driving. Sabal Bay is a sprawling town, neighborhoods interspersed with commercial establishments. There's a town center, a four-block strip of pharmacies, gift shops, several coffee places, my favorite diner, and two furniture stores. Our business was located south of town center. The back roads Madeleine took to the shop were sheltered by stands of live oaks, their shade interrupted by fields dotted here and there with palm trees. Large herds of cattle grazed on the grass, sometimes lifting their heads to stare back at us as we sped by.

"Do you ever miss Connecticut?" I asked.

"Never. I love this place, and I'm happy I'll be raising my kids here." Madeleine smiled at me, then her happiness turned to a look of concern. "Don't you like it here? You're not thinking of going back to the Northeast, are you?"

"I don't know. Sometimes I miss the order there. The malls and cities with their businesses are separate from the neighborhood where people live. Here everything is jumbled together. No zoning of any kind."

"That's what makes it charming," Madeleine said.

"I guess so."

Out of the corner of my eye, I caught Madeleine's uneasy look.

"Sorry I brought it up. Don't worry. I'm not about to book an airline ticket to Hartford."

At the shop, Grandy and Shelley greeted me with hugs. Clearly they interpreted my visit as evidence I was healing from the attack. I assured them I was feeling better and would be coming into the store to work several days during the week.

"Don't rush on our account," said Grandy. "Shelley, Madeleine, and I are taking care of everything just fine."

"What about the RV shop?" I asked. "And who's picking up merchandise from the coast?" I looked around the store and saw the racks were half empty. The three of them couldn't do everything here. It was time I dedicated time to our business.

"I know the shop looks bare," Grandy said, "but Max and I are going down to West Palm this evening. I've scheduled appointments with several of our best customers. After hearing about your, uh, mishap, they've been gathering merchandise from their friends for pick-up. The store and the RV should be packed by tomorrow."

Grandy to the rescue, as always, and I loved her for it, but I had to get back up to one hundred percent and soon.

"Maybe I can talk Grandfather Egret into accompanying me this weekend, and I can drive the RV over to the flea market in Stuart," I said.

"Are you certain you're up for that?" asked Shelley.

"Yup. I'm good." I hoped the bravado in my voice hid the uncertainty I felt inside.

As Madeleine and I left the shop, Crusty McNabb stuck his head out the door of his office.

"I hear you got yourself in a bit of a scramble," McNabb said.

I walked over to him. "Yep."

"I also heard you gave the guy what-for."

"Well, if you call plunging my high heel into his eye what-for, then I guess I came out the winner."

"You might have done better if you'd simply shot him in the eye. That would get his attention."

"Mr. McNabb, I didn't want to kill him."

"Didn't you know? He wanted to kill you, from what I heard."

On the way back to the airboat business, I thought about what McNabb had said, rolling the thought of using a gun on someone who was attacking me around in my mind. I wasn't Crusty McNabb, and I didn't have his casual attitude toward using a weapon, but the idea of apprenticing myself to McNabb as a PI in training made me again consider learning more about guns. I knew private detectives usually had gun permits. Alex had sometimes carried one, but I'd never heard him talk about using it.

I felt a spark of the old Eve reasserting herself.

CHAPTER 12

———

"Frida stopped by this afternoon while you were gone. She told us her boss wanted her to put Walter's hit-and-run on the back burner," Grandfather Egret told me when Madeleine dropped me off at my new home.

"It's a hit-and-run. Isn't that murder?" I asked.

"Yes," said Sammy, "but Frida's captain believes it was an accident, and whoever was responsible is too scared to turn himself in. Given what Walter found at that construction site, I can't believe that. There's also the threat your attacker made, Eve."

"I know Frida informed her boss about the threat. What did he say? If the hit-and-run wasn't intentional, why send someone to warn me away from investigating it?" I asked.

"She's not happy with her orders, but she's overwhelmed with the cases assigned to her. Although the threat seems to confirm Walter's death was no accident, your head injuries from the attack at the house make it possible you were only imagining the threat. Or so says Frida's boss. It doesn't look as if Linc will be back on the job anytime soon. He's in the hospital now with pneumonia. Frida feels really awful about that, especially since your assault has been pushed aside also." Sammy paced the room as he spoke.

"What about the bones?" I asked.

"That case is also on hold," said Grandfather.

"Well, what's so important then?" I asked.

"An old hunter's cabin on the edge of the swamp was burned to the ground last night," said Sammy, "and the fire marshals have declared it arson. A guy's body was found inside with a gunshot wound in the back of the head. Frida says it looks like a professional hit."

Uh-oh. I felt icy fingers on my spine. Frida and the local authorities knew Nappi Napolitani spent time in this area visiting me. Frida knew he and I were close, close enough that he helped me in some tricky situations. I worried they would see this as a situation where Nappi used his influence. What I couldn't see was why he would bother with some guy in an old cabin.

"We need someone to help us with Walter's case," said Grandfather.

"Yes, I can understand that," I said. "I hear that Crusty McNabb is a good detective. And his rates are reasonable. How about hiring him?"

"No, we were thinking of hiring you," Grandfather Egret said with calm determination.

"You can't hire me," I said. "I'm not a detective. I've got no license. And I wouldn't say this to anyone else, but I'm having a difficult time adjusting to life after my assault. I'm really not myself, not the Eve who takes on impossible missions. I can hardly get out of bed in the morning. I'm not the person you want to do your detecting."

I heard a ruckus out back. Three children slammed through the door, then stopped in their tracks when they caught sight of me. Three sets of black eyes regarded me with curiosity. They were all boys, neatly dressed in clean jeans and crisply ironed, colorful shirts. The oldest came forward and shook my hand.

"I'm Jason Egret, and these are my brothers, Jeremy and Jerome." He pointed to the other two boys, lined up by their older brother, each a head shorter than the one next to him. The smallest boy had his thumb in his mouth and held onto his older brother's hand. Jason's manner was grave and polite. "I understand you'll be finding the man who killed our dad."

I what? I gulped.

I looked at Grandfather and Sammy for help in explaining my position, but they simply smiled at the boys and me.

"Well, I don't know about that," I said. "I'm not a detective, you know."

"But Grandfather says you're as smart as one, and you're like a coon hound once you've got the scent," said Jason.

I'd never thought of myself as a hound. Sure, I was one determined gal, or had been, but now?

The middle boy dropped his brother's hand and stepped forward, then looked up at me with a serious expression. "Sammy says everyone loves and admires you, and I know Sammy wouldn't love someone who wasn't as strong and brave as him."

Oh gulp. How could I refute that argument?

"Look," I said, "here's the thing. I'm not a real detective. Real private detectives have licenses, carry guns, and have training in detective work. I don't, so Grandfather and Sammy can't hire me to find the man who ran into your father."

"Is that the law?" asked Jason.

I looked at Sammy. He was still no help. "Uh, I'm pretty sure it is."

"That's white man's law, but we're Indians," Jason said. "We know you don't need a license and a gun and stuff like that. Sammy says you're real good at snooping into things, so we say we can hire you." He gathered his brothers in a huddle, and they whispered among themselves. Jerome, the middle boy, ran off toward Grandfather's bedroom and came back with a glass jar.

"We've been saving to go to Disney, but this is more important." He handed the jar to me. "There's more than thirty dollars in there. We want you to be our detective."

I took the jar and examined its contents, mostly coins, but a few dollar bills and one five.

"We did work around the house and Dad paid us. He'd want us to use it to help him. It's yours," Jason said.

"I can't take this money. What about Disney?"

"We'll go some other time," said Jerome. "When we're older," he added in a mature tone of voice.

"I-I-I ..." I stuttered, so shaken by their request and their confidence in me that I wanted to cry.

The youngest boy tugged on my shirt to get my attention. "I miss my daddy," he said, a single tear spilling from his chocolate brown eyes and streaming down a chubby, round cheek.

"I can't bring him back to you, you know," I said, kneeling and putting my hands on his shoulders.

He brushed away the tear and nodded.

So that's how I became the Egret family's private PI for the sum of thirty dollars and fifty-three cents. The children insisted upon paying me and calling the arrangement an "Indian contract."

SAMMY DROVE THE three boys back to their own house, where an adult cousin was caring for them in the evenings and at night.

"It's not a good arrangement. They need a permanent home," said Grandfather. We were sipping tea on his porch, waiting for Sammy's return. The phone in the house rang.

"I'll get it." I ran in and picked up.

"I'm trying to get in touch with Sammy Egret," said the male voice.

"This is his home, but he's not here. Can I take a message?"

"This is Cal at Renfro Pawn Shop. Are you the gal he came in with the other day?"

I assured him I was.

"I found out something interesting about that watch you were asking about. Can you come down here tomorrow so we can talk?"

I said yes and arranged to meet him at his shop at noon. I didn't want to take any more time than necessary away from my own business, and I knew Sammy was working David's ranch tomorrow afternoon, but this was important to squeeze in somehow.

I told Grandfather about the call.

"There's something about that watch," he said. "I think it's the key to everything—the bones, the hit-and-run."

"And the disappearance of Sammy's father, don't forget that."

Grandfather poked around in the bowl of his pipe and said nothing for a minute. "Maybe, maybe not."

What did this old man know that the rest of us did not? Or was it simply his ability to read a world beyond this one, like his kinship with the swamp and all its creatures, human and others.

The headlights from a truck lit up the porch.

"Sammy's back," said Grandfather. A good guess because he expected Sammy or that second sight again?

Sammy bounded up the porch steps and took me in his arms. "Thank you, Eve, for taking this case on for the boys and for us."

"I may find out nothing. And if I don't, they will have wasted their hard-earned money."

"You'll find out plenty," said Grandfather. He got up and went into the house, calling back to us, "It's leftover stew for dinner." I heard him bang around several pans. After ten minutes or so, the smells of meat and onion began to drift out way.

I told Sammy about the call from the owner of the pawn shop.

"Hurry up, Grandfather. I want to eat fast and get over to the Renfro place as soon as possible," Sammy said.

"I told him we'd meet him tomorrow."

"Not soon enough, Eve. Something wrong with your snooping sense?"

Sammy was right. I'd simply have tossed and turned all night thinking about what the pawn shop owner had to say to us.

Less than twenty minutes later we were in Sammy's truck and on our way to see Cal Renfro.

"I've never eaten so fast. I think I burned the roof of my mouth." I snuggled close to Sammy. We'd had little time to ourselves, and I missed the feel of his strong body next to mine. "Maybe, if we get back early enough, we could take your canoe out."

"Let's see what Renfro has to say, and we'll go from there."

I looked at Sammy's face. His mouth was set in a tight line. Was he keener to get to the bottom of this case than I was? I mentally shook my head. No one was snoopier when it came to crime than Eve Appel. Or that used to be the case. I slapped my hand down hard. It still was the case. I was just a little slow in getting back up to speed.

"Ouch!" yelled Sammy. "You slugged me with your fist."

Did I? "Sorry!"

Sammy gave me a questioning look.

"Just thinking what I'd like to do to that guy who attacked me."

"Good girl." He turned into the house at the address Mr. Renfro had given us.

When we rang the bell, the outside light came on. Renfro opened the door and invited us into his living room. I noticed papers spread over the coffee table.

"Have a seat. Can I get you anything? Coffee?"

I ran my tongue around my burned mouth. Coffee was the last thing I wanted. "Cold water?"

He gestured toward the couch, and then walked into the kitchen. I heard the water run in the sink, and he returned with three glasses. Sammy ignored his, but I downed mine in several gulps and murmured my thanks.

"Something about that watch kept nagging at me," said Renfro. "Then I remembered. The week after the watch was pawned, the shop was broken into and a lot of items were taken."

"Was the watch one of them?" I asked.

"Now that's the problem. I can't find my father's papers on what was stolen. I know he made a list, but it's gone. I looked everywhere."

"So it's a dead end." I could hear the dejection in Sammy's voice.

"Perhaps not. I'm sure the police have a record of what was taken. You could check with them."

"So if it was on the list, then that's it, unless the items were recovered. Were they?"

Renfro shrugged. "I can't remember if anything was recovered. I was just a kid back then. But again, the police would know."

"Wait a minute. Even if the items weren't recovered, maybe the police had some suspects in mind. This might be a good thing." I was excited. The trail might have gone cold, but it was heating up once more.

Renfro gestured at the papers on the coffee table. "The only papers I found from back then were newspaper clippings recounting the robbery. I thought you might want to take a look at the story."

Sammy and I looked over the newspaper account. There was little detail, only several lines about the location of the shop, its owner, and a final sentence indicating the police were following some leads. That sentence got me more excited.

"We need to talk with the police," I said.

Sammy didn't look as eager to pursue this lead as I.

"They won't tell us anything." He got up from the couch and shook Mr. Renfro's hand, thanking him for the information.

Sammy didn't start up the truck. Instead he stared down the deserted street and sighed.

"It's late to go to the police station now, but I'm going to call Frida and tell her what we found," I said, rubbing Sammy's arm to comfort him.

"Her boss said Walter's case wasn't important enough to pursue now."

"I know, but she might help smooth the way for us to find out what the police had on the pawn shop robbery, and she could find out the names of the detectives who handled it."

"I'm sure they're long gone, dead or retired. That was decades ago."

"We'll see. Don't lose hope, Sammy. I have a feeling this is only the beginning." I gave him an encouraging smile and got a tiny one in return.

On the drive back to his place, Sammy pulled over to the side of the road. "I owe you an apology, Eve. I'm being too negative about this while you are so upbeat."

"No need to apologize, Sammy. And don't think I'm being positive just to make you feel better. A few hours ago, before I met your nephews and even after I told them I'd find their father's killer, I wasn't sure I could do the job, but now I'm raring to go. This is the Eve you fell in love with, the old in-your-face, damn-the-consequences Eve." I sat back in the seat and crossed my arms over my chest. I wasn't lying. I felt as if I'd drunk a whole pot of coffee. My body was quivering with anticipation.

ONCE I LAY down in Sammy's bed, the adrenaline rush I'd experienced in the truck drained away, and I felt limp with fatigue. Sleep came quickly, but I awoke toward morning with the feeling that someone had their hands around my throat, squeezing. I gasped for breath and awoke bathed in sweat. I must have cried out because the door to the bedroom slammed open and Sammy rushed to the bed.

"Are you all right?" he asked, folding me into his arms.

"It was just a bad dream."

"About the attack?" He smoothed the damp hair off my forehead and kissed my cheek.

"Yes."

"Maybe helping us find Walter's killer is too much for you now. Maybe you should let it go. We could hire Crusty as you suggested."

I sat up and drew back from Sammy. "No! This is my case. I'm fine."

"Well, at least visit Dr. Halsey tomorrow. Tell her about the dream and see what she thinks."

I promised him I'd see the doctor first thing in the morning. Sammy crawled into the narrow bed with me, and we cuddled until I fell asleep. The next thing I knew, sunlight was bright in the window and moving across the bed. A limpkin called from the canal behind the house. All remnants of the dream had passed, and I jumped out of bed.

"Bathroom's free!" Sammy called.

I turned on the shower to warm water then jacked the faucet to cold. By the time I poured my coffee from Grandfather's old metal pot, I was ready for the day.

I CALLED FRIDA and told her what Sammy and I had learned from Renfro.

"I'll find out who handled the robbery and get back to you," she promised.

A few minutes later, my cell rang.

"Bad luck, Eve," Frida said. "The guy on the case is not only retired, but he died a few years back. The other guy working the case has relocated to San Diego. I've got his name, but no address."

"Oh, damn."

"But there is some good news. If I sit with you, the captain says he'll let you look at the notes on the case. That's kind of unorthodox, but he says he knows the tribe is anxious for a solution to the hit-and-run, and if this will do it, he's willing to stretch the rules. I also told him I thought the hit-and-run was connected to the robbery of the bones, not that either one is top priority right now. I convinced him solving one might solve the other."

"Do you believe that?"

She paused. "Maybe. I don't really know."

Frida was coming around to seeing things the way I did. Great minds and all that. "I'll be at the station in a few minutes."

"Cannot do, Eve. I've got to interview a witness to that shack fire this morning. I should be back at noon or so. I'll let you know."

I hated waiting, but it gave me the morning to go to the shop. I hadn't forgotten my promise to see Dr. Halsey, but the dream seemed so unimportant now that I told myself the good doctor could wait. I called Grandy and told her I would open this morning.

"Madeleine will be in around noon with the babies. If neither of you mind, I'll take the day to go fishing with Max," said Grandy.

I thought I caught a note of relief in her voice. I couldn't blame her. She'd dedicated far too much of herself to the business. By the time this whole thing was over, I'd owe so many debts to so many people, I'd have to give Grandy, Shelley, and even Grandfather—who had agreed to accompany me to the coast with the RV this weekend—a percentage of my share of the business. And then there was Nappi. Madeleine and I had not been able to pay him for the RV, not that he'd accept any money for it, but I felt indebted to him for that and so many other things he'd done for me over the years. I *should* work as an apprentice to Crusty McNabb. I needed the income.

FRIDA CALLED ME at one in the afternoon, but we put off looking at the robbery of the pawn shop case. Instead Frida had news that shook me to my toes.

"The guy we found in that burned-out shack with the bullet

in his head?" said Frida. "We identified him as the cousin of
the pawn shop owner on the coast."

"And the watch?" I asked.

"No watch anywhere. But there's more bad news."

I held my breath.

"The pawnshop owner has split. His shop is closed, and
when I visited his residence, it looks as if he's taken a runner.
No car, the front door was open, and all his clothes were gone.
And before you ask, Eve, there was no watch on the premises
or in his shop, which we just searched."

The cases—the hit-and-run, the uncovered bones and their
subsequent disappearance, and the missing pawnshop owner
and his dead cousin—had just come together in one confusing
puzzle. Was there some other horror that went along with
these cases, some piece we were overlooking?

CHAPTER 13

——

"I GUESS LOOKING at that old pawn shop robbery case is as good a place as any to begin unraveling this mess," said Frida.

My head was still spinning from the confluence of all these cases, but I agreed to meet Frida at the station in fifteen minutes.

The file on the pawnshop robbery was slim and not very revealing. I expressed my disappointment to Frida.

"It wasn't a big deal. A small heist of some jewelry from a local pawn shop," she replied.

The theft had occurred during the night. There was no surveillance camera. The thief came in through a back window. Two of the bars protecting the window had been pried loose using some kind of tool—perhaps a chisel, perhaps a hand drill of some kind. The thief obviously was worried about the noise made in entering and had rushed through the store, grabbing merchandise in a few cases and drawers. The safe was unopened.

The list of items taken was in among the papers. "One pocket watch, cover etched with a wading bird," it read. Although the detectives had tried other pawn shops in the area, suspecting the thief might have tried to pawn what he had stolen, the watch never showed up at another shop. Several of the rings and other jewelry stolen did.

"I think maybe the guy wanted the watch for himself," I said.

The file indicated the detectives followed up by interviewing several suspects who had been involved in other thefts in the area. One of the neighbors had spotted someone running down the alley that night. The witness thought the person they saw was an Indian.

"Oh, boy," I said to Frida. "It's beginning to look as if Sammy's father broke into the pawn shop, took a bunch of stuff, then kept the watch for himself. I guess he didn't have the money to buy it back after he pawned it."

"That makes sense," said Frida.

"And then someone killed him and buried his body with the watch on it. Walter recognized the watch, took it, and was killed for it." The pieces began to fit. Except I wondered why Sammy's father was killed.

"Are you going to tell Sammy and Grandfather what you think happened?" asked Frida.

"Not just yet." I kept thinking about how the thief got into the pawn shop.

"I'd like to see the pawn shop window where the bars were ripped out," I said.

Frida gave me an odd look, then shrugged. "Sure. Why not? I'm going to follow your lead until I come up with a better approach."

When we got into Frida's cruiser, my nose caught a smell that tickled a vague memory.

"What's that funny smell?" I asked. I thought I'd caught a whiff of something in the police station when we were looking at the files, but in the enclosure of the car, the odor was stronger.

"Can you smell it too? It's from my trampling around that

burned shack this morning. I guess I should have popped home and changed my clothes. Sorry about that."

"No need to apologize. It reminds me of something."

"What?"

"I can't put my finger on it. Something just out of reach."

We pulled into the alley behind the pawn shop. Frida went around the front to tell Mr. Renfro what we were up to while I examined the window. The bars were old, clearly the ones that were here when the robbery occurred, and it looked as if they had been cemented back into place after someone—the thief from all those years ago, I assumed—had ripped them out.

"Satisfied?" asked Frida. "What did you hope to find after all this time?"

"I'm not sure." I stood back and looked at the space the thief must have opened to get into the shop, then walked back to the window and placed my hands on the bars to get a sense of how wide the space was.

"Tight squeeze," I said.

Frida nodded. "Ready?"

We walked back to her cruiser.

On our way to the station to pick up my car, Frida slid down in the seat and heaved a deep sigh. "I really didn't need this case or cases to get so complicated. And now I have no time to look into who broke into your house and tried to …" she stopped short, but I finished for her.

"Kill me?" I remembered my promise to Sammy to get in touch with my shrink this morning and realized I hadn't called her. I had something more important on my mind.

"Can you give me the name of that detective who worked the pawn shop burglary case, the one who moved to San Diego?"

"Sure, but it'll be a bitch to get in touch with him."

"For me, maybe, but I have resources."

Frida gave me a warning look, which I ignored. She knew I was about to call on my pal Nappi for some help on the West Coast.

"Tell him I said hi. And I hope he had nothing to do with the disappearance of the pawn shop owner and the hit on his cousin."

"You think the murder looked like a mob hit—the bullet in the back of the head. But the shack was burned. That doesn't sound like what the mob usually does. They like to leave the body to make a statement, not cover it up with a fire."

"Maybe not, but still it looked like a professional hit to me. The shack was probably burned to destroy evidence."

Like a watch?

"I thought the mob simply tortured people until they found out what they needed to know," I said.

"The guy wasn't tortured, but he's just as dead. You sure seem to know a lot about mob hits. You must have learned it from someone, maybe a friend?"

"I read a lot."

"Sure you do."

"Nappi had nothing to do with those murders," I said, but then remembered he knew the pawnshop owner's cousin. What else did he know about the guy? Anything my cop friend Frida should also know?

"You'd tell me if there was anything I should know. Right?" Frida asked.

I searched her face for any sign of suspicion on her part, but she shot back her most innocent look, the one I always thought highly suspicious.

SPEAKING OF NAPPI, I hadn't talked with him for a long time, so I invited him to share dinner with Grandy, Max, and me. I also invited Sammy, but he had promised to take Walter's two oldest boys to the early movie while Grandfather took care of the youngest. He then confided that the boys were eager to see me again so I could report on my progress in their father's case. Jason had been reading about private detective work. Sammy said Jason expected both a written and a verbal report of my progress. Kids are just too smart for their own good. Next thing I knew they'd want an itemized list of my expenses and a time sheet. How far could I stretch that thirty-plus dollar retainer without the boys having to do extra yard work or quit school and take part-time jobs? The case had just gotten more complicated, but I told him I'd be at the house tomorrow when they got out of school. If he could get away from the hunting ranch, I'd make a picnic, and we'd take the canoe out into the swamps.

Not only did I want Nappi to help me find the detective who moved to San Diego, but I also wanted an update on how the lawyer was proceeding with the case of the young boy who shot Alex. As it turned out, Nappi was willing to offer me even more services, most of them legal.

I NEVER UNDERSTOOD how anyone could eat ribs at the Biscuit and not wear the sauce on the front of their clothing. In Nappi's case, he was the king of keeping his cuffs white and his cufflinks shining gold in the restaurant's lights while I was up to my elbows in the stuff. The soiled napkins were piled up next to my plate, and I grabbed for another one, noting that he had barely used his. I didn't feel too bad. Grandy and Max ate like I did, with gusto and utter disregard for how saucy our fingers were. I had been in a restaurant up North where they offered plastic gloves with rib dinners. Where was the fun in that?

"I am so sorry for what happened to you, Eve, but I'm happy to see your encounter with the intruder didn't ruin your appetite." Nappi dabbed gently at his lips, and I could swear he left no trace of sauce on the napkin.

"Thanks, but it took me some time to recover. Being hired by Sammy's nephews to take on their father's hit-and-run was just what I needed." I dipped my fork into my coleslaw and stuffed a forkful into my mouth.

"Hired?" Nappi said.

"Miccosukee contract. The nephews are only kids," I managed through a mouth filled with coleslaw.

Nappi pushed his plate away and tented his arms on the table in front of him. "I hope I can be of help."

"Sure can. Let me bring you up to speed on what we know so far." I told him about the murder of the pawn shop owner's cousin and what I'd found out about the robbery at Renfro Shop here in Sabal Bay.

"And of course the police here are wondering if I had anything to do with the hit," he said.

"I assured Frida you did not. And no one here knows that you were familiar with the guy murdered in that burned shack."

"We should keep it that way. Just between us." Nappi looked to Max and Grandy for confirmation.

"There's just one thing," said Max.

We all looked at him in surprise. Max was usually so quiet, we never expected him to say much.

"Go ahead," said Nappi.

"If there's going to be any stuff like surveillance or a bit of breaking and entering, you know, work that's just this side of illegal …. What I mean to say is, I want to be in on the fun. Eve and Grandy are always in the thick of it while I'm fishing or captaining a boat. Fun for me, sure, but I like a walk on the wild side sometimes, too."

"We don't purposely leave you out, honey," said Grandy.

"Well, if you're worried about my health, I'm just fine." He shifted back in his chair and gave us all a stern look.

"I'm sure Eve can find some way to use you," said Nappi. "There's always room for another member on this team."

He made it sound as if we were about to take the field for a game of football.

I watched as someone familiar walked up behind Nappi. Danny Cypress, a man I wasn't keen on seeing again.

"Enjoying your dinner?" Cypress gave me a smile filled with sexual promise.

Nappi turned in his seat and stood up. "Mr. Cypress, I believe." He put out his hand in greeting.

The smile disappeared from Cypress' face, replaced by a wary look. "Have we met?"

"Once, perhaps, and only in passing. Back when you worked for some folks I know in Miami."

Cypress took the proffered hand and shook it. "I don't remember the occasion."

I introduced him to Grandy and Max.

"Would you like to join us?" asked Grandy.

No, no, no, Grandy. I kicked her under the table.

"I'm sure Mr. Cypress is too busy to bother with us," I said.

"I'm never too busy for two beautiful women," Cypress oozed.

Max rolled his eyes, and Grandy shot me a sheepish little grimace of apology. Cypress moved a chair from a nearby table to ours and inserted it between Grandy and me.

I looked across the table at Nappi, whose eyes never left Cypress' face.

"Ms. Appel and I had a lovely dinner the other night, and I was hoping we could repeat it." Cypress snapped his fingers together to get the attention of the waitress.

I hate that. I wanted to snap mine at him and yell, "Hey, fella! Get some manners."

Nappi continued to stare at Cypress with a pleasant expression on his face. "Perhaps I can get some service for you, Mr. Cypress." Nappi took his gaze away from Cypress and smiled across the room at the waitress, who rushed over.

"This *gentleman*," he said, pronouncing the word with a sneer in his voice, "would like to order a drink."

"I'll have what Ms. Appel is having," said Cypress.

The waitress nodded and hurried away. She returned with a glass of water, which she set in front of Cypress.

"What the hell is this?" he yelled at her.

"It's what I'm drinking. Water. I'm still on pain meds and

can't have alcohol." I brought my glass to my mouth as if to drink, but I was hiding a smile.

Cypress recovered his smooth quickly. "Yes, I think I heard something about someone breaking into your house and assaulting you." His face grew red and his voice got louder. "Whoever would do a thing like that should be shot. Or worse."

"The police are looking for him. I'm sure they'll find him soon."

Cypress raised his glass and sipped. "Did you get a good look at the guy?"

"Not really," I said. "I was too busy stabbing him with my shoe."

This brought a smile to his lips. "That's my girl."

"Actually, Danny, I believe that's *my* girl." Sammy leaned down and kissed my cheek.

"Hi, honey. How was the movie?" I returned his kiss and pulled him down into the chair next to mine. "Mr. Cypress stopped by to say hello and was just leaving."

Danny Cypress' face was red, not with embarrassment—he didn't have the social sensitivity for that, I was sure. Anger might be closer to what he was experiencing.

"I was merely commenting on how glad I was to see our Eve was back on her feet so quickly, given her recent experience. She certainly is resilient." Danny pushed back his chair.

Sammy gave Danny his best smile, the one he reserved for those he didn't like, the one that didn't light up his eyes. They remained black, like those of an eagle on the hunt.

"So good of you to stop by." The words were hardly out of Sammy's mouth before he turned his attention back to me, slipping his arm around my shoulders.

"I guess I'll say goodnight." Danny nodded to all of us and donned his hat as he left.

No one paid him any mind except for Nappi, whose gaze followed him until the exit door closed behind him.

I watched him go with relief. "Mr. Cypress doesn't seem to

like being around you, Nappi. Why is that, do you think?"

Nappi leaned back in his chair and finished his Scotch. "He thinks I know about his past work in Miami."

"With a 'family' there," I added.

Nappi nodded. "He thinks I know more than I do, but I believe he's hiding something, and I intend to find out what it is."

THE NEXT MORNING my cell rang as I was drinking a cup of Grandfather's strong coffee. One cup was all it took to get my brain working and put my body in motion.

"About Mr. Cypress, Eve …. As a lawyer for the mob in Miami, he used our pawn shop owner's cousin, Connie Russo, for a number of jobs."

"Nappi?"

"And I think it might profit us to find the hidey hole of the pawn shop owner and have a talk with him."

The way Nappi said the word *talk* sent shivers down my spine. I knew he meant something quite different from friendly chat.

"But no one knows where he is."

"I'll find him and get back to you. Oh, and there's something else, Eve. I didn't have time to tell you last night, but the kid who killed Alex? He'll probably end up in a youth facility."

"That's good, right?"

"Not really. It leaves his mother and sister in the same neighborhood where the gang members can get at them. So far the kid isn't implicating the gang, and he's not naming names, but if he decides to talk, they'll come after his family. He needs to be moved beyond their reach. He should be sent out of state, but it will be difficult to talk any judge into doing that or providing protection for his family members."

"I want the gang held responsible for what was done to Alex."

"So do I," Nappi said. "It may be that the only way to do that is to put the mother and sister into a witness protection program."

"I thought that was only for witnesses who were going to testify or who had testified and whose lives were in danger."

"I said *a* witness protection program, not *the* witness protection program. I have connections."

Of course he did. Before he could continue, I said, "Your 'connections' will move the family someplace else, and the kid will be placed in some facility where your 'connections' can ensure his safety. What then?"

"Then that gang and its members might be out of business for a long time."

"I don't want to know any more."

Nappi was my friend, but he had ways of dealing with situations. He got results. I just didn't want to know how he did it.

"I'll keep you posted."

"Please don't."

"I mean on the pawnshop owner, our Mr. Ed, Edward, Eddie Lawton."

I had asked for his help, but now I worried what form that might take, and whether I would share responsibility for whatever happened.

CHAPTER 14

———

I FINALLY SCHEDULED a much-needed session with my friendly shrink, Dr. Halsey, and we decided I was ready to move back to my own house. Sammy and Grandfather would be sad to see me go, but there were a few advantages to my being back in my own bed. First, it was mine, and more importantly, it was big enough to fit Sammy and me in it together. I couldn't fault my treatment at Grandfather Egret's place. They fed me well, treated me like royalty, and did not expect me to lift a finger when it was time to clean or cook or wash dishes, but having Sammy in the next room so close and yet so out of reach was difficult for both of us. We sneaked away in the canoe whenever we could.

Oddly enough, when I thought of leaving, my mind kept straying to Walter's three boys. They were often at the Egrets' when I was there, and I enjoyed their company. They were fascinated by my punked hairdo and asked endless questions about it, so many that I finally had to confess the color came out of a bottle and the spikes were the result of globs of gel. I found the youngest boy, Jeremy, using the stuff on his hair one day. The result was hilarious, but the hopeful look on his face prevented me from laughing. It was clear he wanted approval for his little experiment, which I awarded him, but I also said I liked his natural look better. When Jason gave a snort of scorn at his brother's hairdressing attempt, I shook my head, warning him not to make fun of his brother. He shrugged and said he guessed it was an okay look "if you liked that sort of thing." The middle boy was quiet, but I thought I caught a look of jealousy that his younger brother had the courage to experiment, even if the outcome wasn't so great.

ONE EVENING SAMMY and I took the boys to the local carnival in nearby Indiantown. I think they were glad to have me along because Sammy said the rides made him sick to his stomach. Since I loved any kind of ride, I took the boys on all of them, although Jeremy was too short for the more thrilling ones. Instead he and I did the twirling teacups, which seemed to make me queasier than the tilt-a-whirl or the Ferris wheel. Jeremy, Sammy, and I did the merry-go-round while the two older boys played some of the carnival games like pick-up-ducks. They each won a goldfish, which made Jeremy cry with envy, so I spent about ten dollars to get him one too. I think the guy running the game saw what was happening and scammed me. I didn't mind. The boys were all happy, filled with carnival food, and sleepy on the way home later that evening.

As they slept in the back of my car, I snuggled close to Sammy, who was driving.

"So my big guy is afraid of a few fair rides, is that true?"

I could tell by the way Sammy kept his eyes on the road that he knew I was on to him.

"Sammy, I'm more than happy to share our time with the boys. It's no burden for me. I like them. You don't have to make up stories about not going on the rides so the boys and I can bond. The kids are great."

"You figured that out, did you? I was worried you found the

boys a bother, so I thought, if you got to know them better, you'd like them more."

I punched him playfully in the arm. "I like them. I like them a lot. And I'm going to miss them when I move back home."

I hadn't talked with Sammy about my move, but now was a good time with the boys snoozing in the back.

"I have to go back to my life, Sammy. You know that. I can't sleep in your bed and have you on the couch forever, you know."

He nodded. "But isn't it a little too soon?"

"I talked with Dr. Halsey, and we agreed. It's time for me to take my old life back, to work in the shop, to tempt you into my big bed at night, and—"

"To find out who killed Walter and who attacked you," he finished for me.

"Yes, all of that. To get back my fearless, Eve-on-the-scent persona. I have a job to do for those boys and for you and Grandfather. I hope I can count on you to help."

"We'll help," said a chorus of voices from the back.

I turned around in my seat. "How long have you guys been awake?"

"Long enough to hear how you're going to have a sleepover at your place with Sammy," said Jeremy.

"She's not having a sleepover," said Jason.

"Or a slumber party then. Are we invited?" Jeremy asked.

Sammy and I looked at each other.

"Why not? How about this weekend?" I said. "Now go back to sleep. Tomorrow is a school day."

"You want the truth?" Sammy asked after the boys had quieted down.

"The truth? You mean you don't want to share me with the boys this weekend?" I kept my voice low so the boys wouldn't hear.

"Well, there's that. No. I meant the truth about carnival rides."

"Huh?"

"I really do get sick on them."

I heard giggles from the backseat.

The next morning, I packed my bag with the clothes I'd brought to the Egrets' and kissed Grandfather goodbye, thanking him for having me as a guest. Sammy and I were planning a canoe ride this evening, so his goodbye could wait for a more private place where I'd deliver kisses plus something more.

I drove to the shop and opened by myself. Today would be the first day in weeks where I was responsible for taking care of the business on my own. It suited me fine that my first day back to the old Eve—as I'd put it to Sammy last night—would be tending to the business Madeleine and I had started here in Sabal Bay. Although the place seemed familiar, I almost felt as if I was beginning anew, and that made me optimistic about the future. I roamed the store touching the merchandise, as if the items for sale were old friends I'd not seen for some time. When I felt satisfied that the shop was still mine, I took out my cell and dialed the number Nappi had provided earlier this morning.

There was something about the robbery over thirty years ago at Renfro Pawn that bothered me. I needed to talk to the detective who worked the case. I hoped Nappi had given me the right number, but I also worried that once I made contact with the detective, he wouldn't talk to me. I had called Frida right after Nappi's call and asked her to call the detective first. I liked snooping around in criminal matters, but I had found that saying you were the curious sort didn't get you far as a credential. I needed the force of law in my corner.

The phone rang about ten times, and I was about to hang up when a machine kicked in. As I started to leave a message, the recording was interrupted.

"Yup. What can I do for you?"

"Is this Detective Burt Wayman?"

"Retired. Just plain Burt Wayman now. You that gal the detective from Sabal Bay said would call today?"

"Yes."

"She said you had some questions about an old case, the one where Renfro's Pawn was robbed. That right?"

Frida had given him the details, making it easier for me to get right to the point.

"The neighbor who thought he saw the thief running away ... did he give you a description of the guy?"

"Yup. Said he thought he was an Indian."

That I already knew.

"Any other details? Height, build, age, what he was wearing?"

There was silence on the other end. Darn. I was out of luck. Just as I feared. Most people who saw Indians, saw Indians, and that was all they saw. The details were lost.

"Let's see. I remember he thought the guy was young."

"Young? That's kind of vague." I was getting nowhere.

"Young like a teenager. He was short and lean—small guy, he said. Had to be, I figured. Otherwise how could he have gotten through that rear window? He only removed two of the bars."

Right. I'd noticed that too. Sammy's father was a big man like Sammy, according to Grandfather, and he would have been in his twenties back then.

"I wondered about that," I said.

Since things were going so well, I tried another question, a way-out one.

"Any idea who it could have been?"

"If I knew that, I'd have made an arrest back then, now, wouldn't I?"

Oops. I'd unintentionally insulted the man.

He continued after a brief pause. "But there were a rash of robberies back then. What we knew was that there were some kids up to no good. We figured they might have been stealing stuff, but we had no proof."

"Names?"

"Uhm, sorry. I can't remember. You know how those Indian names are—like animal names, some of 'em."

"I know. Listen, you've been very helpful. If you think of anything else, could you call me?" I gave him my cell number.

Putting down the phone, I leaned back into the counter with a sigh of satisfaction. I'd learned something important. Whoever stole those items, including the watch in that robbery at Renfro's years ago, was a kid, not Sammy's father.

The bell signaling a client tinkled as the front door opened. I looked up and saw the last person I wanted in my store. Danny Cypress.

"You look like the cat that swallowed the canary. Did you find out something about who attacked you?"

"Now, why would you think that?" I asked.

"Because of your reputation as an inveterate snoop—always on the case, never defeated." He walked up to me and got close enough that I could smell he'd been sucking on a peppermint. Trying to impress me with his fresh breath?

"I don't spend much time thinking about the guy who broke into my house. It's up to the cops to get him, not me. And my doctor says it's not good for my mental health to dwell too much on that night."

"I'll bet that's hard for you, being the nosy gal you are."

He was annoying me with his insistence that I was some kind of super sleuth.

"Let's just drop the subject, can we? What can I do for you? Looking for a gift for someone?"

He laughed. "As a matter of fact, I am. My mother's birthday is next week, so I'm looking for a dress for her."

"I would think you'd be more interested in buying new."

"Maybe I would, but my sister was in here last week several times, and she had someone here hold a dress she said would be just the thing for Mom."

"I'll check on it. It'll take just a minute."

I went into the backroom and looked through the clothes hanging on our "hold" rack. I found a blue chiffon dress with the name "Cypress" on it and pulled it off the rack. When I turned around, Danny was right behind me. I collided with him, and he reached out his arms to steady me.

"Sorry," he said.

"I didn't know you had followed me back here."

"Was I not supposed to? Oh, sorry again."

He had to know he shouldn't be back here. He was the most annoying man.

"Well, let's go up front where the light is better."

He followed me to the front windows.

"It's a beautiful color. I assume your mother has dark eyes and hair. This should be perfect for her."

"It is," he said, fingering the material, "but my sister was worried it was too long. Mother is pretty short and kind of small through the shoulders."

"If she comes in, my tailor Shelley will fit her."

A moment ago Danny's face was lit up with a kind of joy at how perfect the dress would be for his mother. Now a cloud seemed to settle over him.

"Mom is in a wheelchair. She almost never leaves the house. Would it be possible for your tailor to come out to the ranch and fit her there?"

"Sure."

"And I'd like you to come along too, if you'd be so kind." He flashed his white teeth in a friendly smile. Sometimes the guy could be okay. If he'd just lay off that smarmy romantic stuff.

"Would next Tuesday work for you and your mother?"

He nodded, and we agreed on ten in the morning. This was working out better than I could have expected. I wanted to know more about the Cypress family, especially the older brother who had left years ago. A visit to the ranch with the family there would present the perfect opportunity to ply them with questions. I'd be subtle, if I could manage it.

* * *

THAT EVENING SAMMY and I took his canoe out to our swamp hideaway, and we almost got reacquainted. It wasn't that the mating roar of a bull alligator disturbed us. We were used to that and considered it "our song." Nor were we put off by the mossy, moldy smell of the swamps. That was like perfume to us. Even the rain that began to pelt us and force us farther back under the sloping roof was like tiny caresses of teardrops against our skin. It was my fault when Sammy cried out "Damn" and I followed with, "I'm sorry." I had brought my cellphone with me, and it rang in the middle of one of the most sensual and loving moments Sammy and I had experienced in weeks.

Sammy leaped up and yelled something in Miccosukee to the clouds overhead. Then he stomped off into the dense vegetation, leaving me behind holding only that damn cell.

I shrugged. Might as well answer it. "Hello?"

"Am I disturbing anything?" asked Nappi.

"Not anymore."

He hesitated. Perhaps he caught something in my tone of voice. If so, he dismissed it and continued talking. "I've been using some of my contacts to find our pawn shop owner. You know, Eddie of the numerous last names."

I quickly forgot my mortification at having my cell ring in the middle of Sammy and my romantic interlude. "Where is he? Have you told the authorities yet?"

"I'm telling you first. I thought if you weren't busy tonight we might pay him a visit and have a little chat before I turn him in to the police. He'll just lawyer up then, and we won't get anything out of him."

"Uh, okay. But what kind of a chat are you thinking of? 'Chat' as in baseball bat or tire iron, or the other kind?"

"What other kind?"

"That's what I thought. I don't want to be a party to that kind of rough stuff."

"Aren't you interested in getting to the bottom of the stolen watch mystery?"

"Of course, I want to find out about the watch, but …."

Sammy, who had reappeared out of the dark, took the phone out of my hand and held it so both of us could hear.

"I'm interested in the watch," he said. "What's up?"

"How about we meet in an hour at your airboat business?"

"Good. I'll leave Eve at home if she's queasy."

I heard Nappi laugh. "By now the two of you should know me better than that. I can get information from a stone by just giving it a bad look."

Sammy disconnected and handed me the cellphone.

"It was a good thing you brought it. Otherwise we might have missed out on all the fun."

"You have no idea what Nappi is capable of," I said.

"I think I do. He's capable of scaring the bejesus out of someone and getting the information he needs with nothing more than sustained silence. Don't be so worried about his methods, Eve. He'd never compromise his friends."

Sammy was right. I wasn't giving Nappi enough credit.

"WHERE ARE WE headed?" I asked as I jumped into the backseat of Nappi's SUV.

"We're going north of town on 441. Once we get past the golf course, we'll take a dirt road west and into some swampy area past the Martin ranch." Nappi hit the accelerator and the big car surged forward. "It seems that Eddie, like his dead cousin, likes to go to ground in cabins out here in the boonies. Thinks no one will find them."

Yeah, well, that didn't work out so well for Connie, now lying on the medical examiner's table in Sabal Bay. I wondered what we'd find tonight and hoped it wasn't another burned-out cabin with a body inside.

For the next few minutes, he concentrated on the road. I was curious about how Nappi found the pawnshop owner, but knew better than to ask. What I didn't know I couldn't tell anyone. That included Frida or a jury, should I be asked to testify in court if Nappi was brought to trial for kidnapping or miscalculating the impact of his hard look on a terrified man's heart.

"There's the turnoff to the golf course," I said.

He slowed as we searched for the unmarked dirt road.

Sammy spotted it. "Right there."

As we passed the drive leading to the ranch, the road got smaller and ruttier. Soon it appeared to be nothing more than two tracks, water on either side. A weak light shone up ahead. Nappi turned off his headlamps and stopped the car.

"We go the rest of the way on foot. I hope you wore sensible shoes, Eve."

Everyone laughed at that comment, including me. When did I ever wear anything but the most outrageous designer footwear, always with at least a three-inch heel? Tonight was no exception.

"I'll just have to clean them when I get home."

"More like, you'll have to throw them out when you get home." Sammy looked at my boots and shook his head.

We couldn't see much in front of us and would have lost our way if the light up ahead were extinguished. I stepped into knee-high water.

"Oh, crap." *There go my patent leather ankle-high boots.*

"Hah," said Sammy. He grabbed me up in his arms, and we continued to wade through the water. Several hundred feet from the cabin, we hit dry land and Sammy put me down. My boots made squishing sounds as we continued.

"Can't you be any quieter?" Nappi asked. "We want to sneak up on the guy, not announce he's getting visitors."

Suddenly the light went off.

Nappi whispered to Sammy, something I could not hear, and Sammy disappeared into the darkness.

"It's Nappi Napolitani. I need to talk with you," Nappi called out. He extracted a flashlight from his pocket and shone it on the building in front of us.

No sound came from within, so Nappi stepped onto a small rickety porch and knocked on the door. No one answered.

"Well, hell," said Nappi. He turned the knob and shoved the door inward, shining his light around the one room inside. No one was there, and there was no place to hide—we saw only a tiny table, three mismatched chairs, a wood stove, and a bedroll on the floor in the corner.

"He was here," I said. I pointed to the pot of soup on the stove, the flame beneath it still lit. "We missed him. I ruined my boots for nothing."

CHAPTER 15

—

I SANK DOWN into onto one of the chairs and examined my footwear. My shoes had suffered too many times before and always when I was in hot pursuit of a criminal or was being pursued by one. Maybe I should rethink how I dressed for these missions.

Nappi lit the kerosene lantern on the table, looked around the shabby room, and laughed. I heard a ruckus outside, yelling followed by a thud, as if someone had been thrown against the building. The floor shook from the impact, and the back door was flung open. Sammy stood in the doorway, holding Eddie by his collar. He looked like a large dog with his chew toy.

"Back Door Eddie," said Nappi. "I figured you'd try that again, so I sent my friend here to help you reconsider your flight plans."

Eddie looked up at Sammy, terror emanating from his bugged-out eyes. "Don't let him hurt me!" he said.

Sammy shoved him to the table and into the chair across from mine.

"We need to have a talk." Nappi spun the other chair around and straddled it.

Eddie's gaze traveled from Nappi to Sammy and back again. Then he looked at me, but apparently found no sympathy in my face as I snarled at him, brandishing my boot.

"You owe me a new pair of boots, you little rat."

"Anything, anything. Just don't let them hurt me." He reached across the table, but Sammy slapped his hand away.

"Don't touch her." Sammy's voice was menacing. I knew he was putting on more threat than he felt, but I decided it couldn't hurt to follow through with a bit more of the same.

"You'd better cooperate with Nappi or I'll have my Indian friend here give you a haircut."

Eddie looked puzzled at first, then got what I really meant by *haircut* when I added, "He likes to cut it real short." Sammy grabbed Eddie by the hair. I saw his eyes roll back, and I was certain he was going to faint. Or just die of fear.

I sneaked a peek at Nappi. His face registered only cold threat, but I caught a twinkle in his eye and knew he was enjoying the way Sammy and I were handling Eddie, kind of softening him up for Nappi's go at him.

"I knew you'd find me and do to me what you did to Connie." Eddie struggled in Sammy's hold then went limp, as if resigned to whatever horrible fate awaited him.

"What are you talking about?" asked Nappi.

"I heard what happened to Connie. You put a bullet in the back of his head like you mob bosses always do. I don't get why. Connie was always a good soldier for the mob. He's always kept his mouth shut. You know that."

Sammy, Nappi, and I exchanged looks. What was Eddie talking about?

"I didn't do in your cousin, believe me," said Nappi.

"Well, I don't. Why do you think I'm holed up in this godforsaken dump, trying to lie low until I can get out of here and move someplace where you won't find me?"

"But we did find you, Eddie. So you'd better level with us. Nappi is my friend, and if he says he had nothing to do with

Connie's murder, then he didn't. Some other mobster must have taken him out. Maybe someone he recently did work for until he took what wasn't his to take," I hinted.

"You mean that watch? That damn thing has been more trouble than it's worth. I mean it was a great watch, but not if it meant Connie's death."

Eddie sat in his chair for a minute, staring into the flames in the wood stove. We let the silence fall, giving him the opportunity to rethink his situation.

"If you weren't responsible for hitting him, then who was?" he finally asked.

"You tell us," Nappi insisted.

"I don't know." Tears filled Eddie's eyes. "I really don't."

"Why don't you tell us what Connie was up to in the days before he brought the watch in to you? Maybe we can figure out who killed him. He must have been working for some mob boss. Maybe one out of Miami?"

Eddie shook his head. "Nope. Connie said he didn't want to do any more mob stuff. It made him nervous. But when he died the way he did I assumed you had something to do with it. You came into my shop and all, looking for that watch. I just assumed it was yours and you were pissed he had taken it."

"If you believed he wasn't doing mob work, why did you think Nappi was after him?" I asked.

"I knew he didn't want to have anything to do with the mob, any mob, but I figured someone coerced him. Like you." He nodded at Nappi. After a pause, he added, "It's funny though, now that I think about it. He told me when he brought the watch to me that he was working for some construction company, and that he'd made so much on that job he wouldn't need to work for a while."

My heart did a backward flip in my chest. "What construction company? What was the name of it?"

"Don't know that. He didn't say."

It was clear we weren't going to get anything else out of Eddie, no matter how we threatened him. He'd told us all he knew. I called Frida on my cell and told her we'd found the pawn shop owner. After determining our location, Frida dispatched a police SUV to pick up Eddie for more questioning.

"I don't think he'll have anything to say to you, but he did tell us something interesting about Connie Russo's most recent job."

Frida gave an interested "Hmmm?" on the phone.

"Some construction company, no name available."

"That could be any company, Eve." She paused, then said, "But it can't hurt to look into Gator Way's work on that sportsmen's resort where Walter indicated to Sammy he found the watch. Maybe the foreman saw Walter take the watch and alerted his bosses."

"Alerted them about what? The foremen called in the bones, and they were the only real threat to the project going forward that we know about, so no one was trying to hide the fact they had been uncovered."

"You forget that the issue with the bones is if they are Indian, indicating a burial ground," Frida said. "That would put the entire project on hold, but since we can't find them to determine if they are, a judge could give the go-ahead for continued construction."

"There's something we're both forgetting," I said. "The bones could be from a body someone didn't want to be found. If found, they might tell us foul play was involved."

Frida was silent.

"Are you still there?" I asked. "Are you grinding your teeth? I think I hear frustrated grinding noises." I wouldn't have blamed her if she was. I'd have joined her if I thought it would do any good.

"I wish I could find those damn bones. Or find out who took them. I know it doesn't make sense, but they're the answer to this whole thing: Walter's hit-and-run, the watch, Connie Russo's murder. Why won't the pieces come together? I must be looking at them wrong."

"Listen, sweetie, if you can't see the picture, neither can we."

"Yep. I'll get back to you." Frida disconnected.

Oh damn. I'd forgotten to tell Frida what I found out from the detective in San Diego. *Oh well.* I could tell her tomorrow, but I needed to fill Sammy in on my thoughts about his father not being responsible for the theft of the watch. Then there was another lead I needed to follow up on. Maybe Sammy's father wasn't the person who pawned the watch at Renfro's shop. I was about to talk with him when we heard a car approaching from the rear of the house.

"Your ride's here, Eddie," said Nappi.

Eddie looked relieved to see the two officers who cuffed him and led him to the car. I guess he was worried Nappi and Sammy might decide his lack of information merited some kind of punishment.

"Let's get out of here," said Nappi. "You two up for a drink or a quick bite to eat? Interrogating is hard work."

We both shook our heads. "I think we'll just go back to Eve's place and sack out for the night."

Nappi gave him a knowing smile.

LATER, IN MY king-sized bed—after a session of getting reacquainted—I had turned off my cellphone and taken the land line off the hook.

Sammy turned on the bedside lamp. "I've got a bone to pick with you, my love." The look on his face was serious. His mouth quivered at the corners, as if he was trying to prevent himself from yelling at me. "Miccosukees do not scalp people."

"But they did once from what I've read."

"White folks' history. Who knows if it's true? Anyway, we don't do it now."

"But Eddie didn't know that."

The quivering of Sammy's mouth finally gave way to laughter. "True that."

I punched him in the arm. "I thought you were really mad at me. You scared me."

"I'm sorry. Let me make it up to you." He moved toward me and kissed my hair, face, mouth, neck … then abruptly stopped.

"Don't stop there," I said.

"Are you sure?"

I grabbed a handful of his thick black hair and pulled him on top of me. "I'm sure."

He reached for the lamp.

"Leave it on," I said.

As his muscular arms encircled my body, the part of my brain that was still functioning rationally sent a message that there was something important I was going to tell Sammy. Something about the watch and Sammy's father. The message was ignored.

THE NEXT DAY was Saturday, and I had promised the boys I would host a sleepover. I had a feeling only Sammy and I would be sleeping. Maybe I should include Grandfather so someone could keep an eye on the children.

Madeleine was in the shop for the day—David having baby duty at home—and Grandy and I headed to the coast with the RV. The flea market there closed around three in the afternoon. Assuming traffic cooperated, we should be back in Sabal Bay in time for supper. Grandy and Max planned to leave for Key Largo and spend the night on their boat after we ate. The man captaining it for them had booked Sunday morning and afternoon fishing charters. Max was feeling fit enough to take a day of charter work. I know he was raring to get back on his boat, and both Grandy and I were thrilled he appeared to be recovering from his heart attack several months ago.

"You look a little exhausted," Grandy observed on our way down the road to Stuart. "But you also look happy, and I'm happy for you."

"Oh, gosh." I could feel a flush working its way up my neck. I looked at Grandy in embarrassment. "Were Sammy and I too loud last night?"

"Eyes on the road, Eve. We don't want to drive this thing into the ditch. Max sleeps without his hearing aids, and when the noise from your room got too much, I simply turned on the little fan by my bedside. It drowns out most noises."

I yanked the wheel to the left, barely avoiding the feral pig someone else had hit on the side of the road. The vultures that had been enjoying the carrion for a late breakfast flew off and circled for a minute. When I glanced in my rearview mirror, I saw them settle back on the carcass.

"Nature's sanitation engineers," I remarked.

"That's enough to put me off barbecued ribs at the Biscuit for a month," Grandy said.

"Well, I assume you'll be dining on freshly caught Florida pink shrimp tomorrow," I said. "I wish Sammy and I could get away for a weekend in the Keys. He's lived all these years in Florida and never been there."

"We'll set a date for the two of you to spend with us on the boat."

I chewed on my lower lip. I knew Max wanted to move back onto the boat soon, but I would miss having Grandy and Max with me full time. "When do you think the two of you will return to the charter business?"

"Maybe never, if I had my way," she said. "It's hard work, and the pay isn't great because our boat doesn't have the amenities other newer vessels have, like gourmet meals and fancy linens, a mixologist. We just give 'em burgers and beer. That used to be enough for someone wanting to fish the waters off Key Largo. Now they want someone to bait their hooks, reel in the fish, and serve them cocktails in crystal glasses."

"I assume you've not shared your feelings about resuming the charters with Max."

Grandy spit out a laugh. "Are you kidding? I know better than that. I'll let him find out for himself. And he will."

"Before or after his next heart attack?" I asked.

"That's what I worry about too. The old goat." Grandy folded her arms across her chest. "But some things can't be rushed."

I knew she was right. I'd been rushing things since I lost my parents. Pushy, snoopy, impatient Eve. I had no time to just let things be. I had to make them happen. Control. I had to be in control of my world.

As if reading my mind, Grandy said, putting on a Southern accent, "I'm not like you, darlin'. You might could learn something about taking your time."

Now where did my Connecticut born and raised grandmother start talking like the locals? "Might could learn?" What was that about? Maybe I should get her back to the Keys or she'd be saying things like "Get 'er done."

Me? I did not like taking my time, or letting things happen. Not ever. I liked to run things. I liked to do it at my own hurried pace. The world would just have to adjust. I was "get 'er done in a hurry Eve Appel."

As we pulled into the flea market, I saw a black SUV behind us and recognized the driver. Parking our rig in the designated spot, I got out to set up our sign. The SUV pulled in alongside us.

"Hi, Nappi. Are you here looking for bargains?"

"I'm meeting Jerry to pick up some fresh fish at the market. How would you like it if I brought some by tonight? I could cook them up the Italian way."

I didn't know what the "Italian way" was, but if Nappi was the chef, it had to be good.

"Sure. You and Jerry can stay for the slumber party."

Nappi looked puzzled, then I explained about Walter's boys staying at my place for an overnight. I also told him Grandy and Max were leaving after dinner for Key Largo.

"Will the boys like fish?" Nappi asked. "All the kids in my family did, but what about them?"

"They'll love it, and you'll love them. They are the sweetest boys."

"Hi, Evie," said a voice from behind me.

It was my ex-husband Jerry calling me by the name I hated. As usual. I turned and gave him a stern look.

"Sorry," he said. "So we're dining at your place. Will Sammy be there? Grandfather Egret, too?

I wished I could find some way to exclude Jerry from our gathering, but my heart softened when I looked into his sad brown eyes. I reminded myself that Jerry wasn't so bad if you weren't married to him. I wasn't, and he was good with kids.

As Nappi and Jerry left for the fish market, I yelled after them, "Is it okay if I call Madeleine and David to come also or will that be too many?"

Nappi stopped and looked at me. "My dear girl. Of course. I'm used to cooking for a big family."

I waved at him and turned my attention to business as several women entered the rig and began to look around.

EVERYONE LOVED NAPPI'S Italian fish with basil, tomato sauce, and fennel, baked in the oven until the smells coming from my kitchen almost made me sob with culinary joy. Nappi encouraged the three boys to help him prepare the dinner, and he quickly became "Uncle Nappi." He shooed the rest of us into my living room to drink the fine Chianti he'd bought in Stuart. Grandfather and Sammy rarely drank anything other than an occasional beer, but they each had a glass of wine. They laughingly pronounced it really fine "firewater" and drank a second glass with dinner. Everyone helped clean up. Grandy and Max were on their way south by nine and the others left shortly thereafter—except for Grandfather, who retreated to my front porch to smoke his pipe and think whatever deep thoughts he liked to think. It was just Sammy and me and the three boys. We played a few board games, but after our activities of the night before and working all afternoon at the flea market, I knew I'd find it difficult to keep my eyes open much longer. Sammy looked like he was asleep on his feet. Grandfather shooed Sammy and me off to bed, whispering in my ear, "They'll be asleep in less than an hour." We had agreed the boys could watch television as late as they wanted. The three of them each curled up in their sleeping bags with Grandfather in the lounger nearby. He was right. He looked wide awake, but the boys' eyes were drooping, especially Jeremy's.

Sammy and I hugged them and said goodnight after saying no to their request for another helping of Nappi's tiramisu, which would only give them tummy troubles and probably wake them up to boot.

Sammy and I undressed and embraced quickly, lest we become too wrapped up in each other and face another fun but sleepless night. I didn't remember falling asleep or how long I had been sleeping when I felt warm breath on my face. I opened my eyes to Jeremy standing beside my side of the bed, holding his favorite stuffed toy, a Florida panther. His thumb was jammed in his mouth.

"Can I sleep here?" he asked.

"Sure, honey." I pulled back the covers. "Crawl in."

He snuggled into the crook of my arm.

"Couldn't you sleep in your sleeping bag?"

"I could, but I like it here with you better."

I hugged him to me.

"Would you be my mommy?"

CHAPTER 16

———

MY HEART STOPPED, and I took a deep breath before I answered. How does one respond to that question? I knew I had to give the right reply, but I had no idea what that was.

"How about you ask her that again when she's not so sleepy?" Sammy, bless him, had overheard Jeremy.

"Are you too sleepy?" insisted Jeremy. "Maybe you already have a boy like me and don't want another one."

I could hear the fear and sorrow in his voice.

"There is no other boy in the world like you, and anyone would be thrilled to be your mother. I'm so glad you asked me."

He smiled and wriggled closer. Soon I caught the rhythm of his breathing and knew he had fallen asleep.

"Thank you, Sammy, for jumping in. He just took my breath away, and I needed time to gather myself together before I said anything."

"You said the right thing."

I sighed with relief. "Did I? I'm so glad."

"But it's something you need to think about. He is a

wonderful boy. All of them are, but they need a mother. And a father."

"You and me?" I was surprised. "Is that a proposal?"

"I'm too sleepy to answer that right now. We'll talk."

"Sammy Egret, you talk to me. Now." I gave him my usual punch in the shoulder followed by a kiss on the neck, but he responded with snores. The only sound I thought I heard in the house came from Grandfather Egret in my living room, and he seemed to be smiling out loud.

SAMMY AND I got up before the boys, but not before Grandfather, who was in my kitchen making pancakes. Jeremy was still asleep in my bed.

"There's coffee." Grandfather pointed to the pot. "I couldn't find any maple syrup."

"I'm out." I grabbed two cups from the cupboard and poured coffee for Sammy and me.

"Then it will be strawberry preserves," Grandfather said.

"Oh, yum. I like that better anyway," Jerome called out.

After breakfast, the boys gathered up their clothes and sleeping bags, and Grandfather and Sammy took them back to Cousin Selena, who was looking after them for the remainder of the weekend. Sammy gave me a quick kiss goodbye and said we'd talk later. *Damn right we'll talk later*, I thought. We had a lot to discuss. Was his comment last night a marriage proposal? It sounded like it.

"Don't worry, Eve," he whispered in my ear as he got into his truck, "This is going to be a lot simpler than you think."

Really? Nothing was ever simple in Eve Appel's life. Didn't he know that by now?

I went back into the house, grabbed my keys, and went to get the rig to drive it again to the coast for the Sunday flea market. Although it took some juggling to cover both the shop and the rig, on Sundays we only opened the rig. I was on duty today to give Madeleine time with her husband and the babies. She had invited me to stop by after I got back to say hello. I welcomed the visit. I needed to talk to either her or Grandy about what had happened last night with the boys and Sammy. I parked my car behind the rig and jumped in. As I pulled onto the road to the coast, I noticed my hands were not as steady on the wheel as they usually were. This Sammy-and-three-boys thing had me in a state, one I wasn't used to. I was terrified. Or was I thrilled? I couldn't tell one from the other.

Early in the afternoon, a coastal storm swept in, making it a poor day for shopping outside in the market. Folks would be dry and warm in my rig, but I knew few would want to dash between showers and wind from the parking lot to the motor home shop. I closed up and was home by two in the afternoon. I called Madeleine to see if it was convenient for me to stop by early. She invited me for a late lunch. As usual, I could eat.

I held the babies for several minutes, and they seemed to like my attention. I didn't drop them, and they didn't upchuck on me. Maybe I was better at this child thing than I thought. Madeleine took them from me and put them down for a nap. While she looked madly happy, she also looked tired, as did David.

"Maybe I should scoot out of here and let the two of you take a nap yourselves."

"David, you go on and get forty winks. I want to talk with Eve." Even when she was dead on her feet, Madeleine knew when I needed her ear.

"No, go on. You could use the sleep too."

"I can grab a nap when David gets up. You've got something on your mind."

"I can wait until Grandy gets back later tonight and run it by her."

"And leave me out? I've been left out of too much in your life these past several months with my pregnancy and now the babies. I'm not saying I resent motherhood at all, but I do miss hearing about what trouble you've gotten yourself into."

I told her about Jeremy and what Sammy had said.

"He's right, you know," I said. "Those boys need parents. They're being shuffled between relatives, including Grandfather and Sammy. They need stability in their lives right now more than ever. But Sammy seemed to be suggesting something more permanent for them and for us. What do I do?"

"Do what Sammy suggested, Eve. Talk about it. Be honest and explore your feelings. What do you want? What does your heart tell you to do?"

"But Sammy and I have only been together for a short while. Jerry and I knew each other three years before we got married."

"How did that turn out?" Madeleine asked.

She was right. Taking time didn't mean you got the results you wanted. My impulsive nature might not always be a bad thing.

I heard a noise from the bedroom. It began with a tiny squeak, then erupted into a cry, followed by a squalling that could not be ignored.

"That's Eve, wanting attention."

"How can you tell it's her and not him?" I asked.

"They have totally different cries, different personalities. She's just like her namesake. Likes to get things going. And now."

"Oh."

Madeleine hugged me before she went to get Eve out of the bedroom. "Don't make this more difficult than it is, Eve. You know what you want. What you need. So do it."

I tried to give her a smile of confidence. "Tell David I said goodbye."

I felt better after talking with Madeleine, yet I still had no idea what I wanted or needed. She was so wrong about that. Things were not easy. They had never been for me, and I had no reason to believe they would or could change. But then I could be wrong. I'd been so off about marrying Jerry. Did people just plunge into marriage and parenthood because it felt right? Madeleine did. *I'm not Madeleine*, I told myself.

I wasn't looking forward to getting back to my house. Grandy and Max wouldn't be home until late, and Sammy and Grandfather were busy with tribal matters. I'd be alone for the first time since the intruder had attacked me. The solitary life hadn't bothered me before, but after the assault I felt more vulnerable. This would be a test to see if the old Eve was truly back. Could I once again find comfort in my home or would I dash out of the house and go … where? I had nowhere to run.

I pulled into the drive and sat for a moment, scanning the house. It was still light, and the place looked friendly enough, but how would I feel once the sun went down? Fine. I was fine. I'd have a lovely evening to myself, doing things like shaving my legs and redoing my spiky blonde hair. I looked in my rearview mirror. The dark roots were getting too long. It needed a touchup sure enough. And I could take a tweezers to my eyebrows too. Good. I had a plan.

Jumping out of the car, I ran toward the house, unlocked the door, and bounded into the kitchen. I poured myself a glass of white wine and headed for the bathroom, the place where all important girlie things were accomplished. I slathered hair dye on my re-growth, and while it did its work, I shaved my legs. I hopped in the shower to rinse the dye out of my hair and lathered the shave cream off my legs. It was still early and the evening stretched ahead, so I decided to run a bath for a long soak. I started the water, tied my robe around me, and got another glass of wine from the fridge. I poured several capsules of bubble bath into the water and stepped into the hot tub. Sliding down into the water, I let the warmth and bubbles soothe me. I sighed deeply. Tonight was my night, a night when Eve made herself into the old fashion-forward gal she used to be.

I was awakened much later by the bath water having gone cold. I had slid far enough in that the next slip would have put my nose under. No sense in drowning myself. I got out, toweled dry, and put my robe back on. I hadn't touched my second glass of wine, but it was room temperature now. I tossed it out in the kitchen sink and poured a couple of shots of Scotch over some ice cubes. It was too early for anything good on television, so I carried my drink to the bedroom and sank into my chair to watch twilight descend over my backyard. The sliding glass door was open, allowing the chill of the evening to invade the room.

I opened my closet, looking for my heavier robe, and realized no amount of clothing would take away the shiver that ran through me. Suddenly my evening took a dark turn. I realized I was scared. *Don't panic*, I told myself. *Think this through rationally*. Maybe the fear came from being in the bedroom where I had been attacked. Stupid me. This was no place to sit alone. I closed the slider and went into the living room, where a sense of déjà-vu settled over me. Bad déjà-vu, *really* bad déjà-vu. This night was too much like the one when I was attacked. I was alone then too. Grandy and Max were to return later, just as I knew they would tonight, but then ….

I turned on all the lights—the outdoor porch light, the light in the kitchen, and the backyard light. There. That was better. I'd watch television to take my mind off things. I grabbed the remote and heard the distant rumbling of thunder. Rain began to fall, first a soft shower, then more rain coming down in sheets, followed by wind, which gathered in force and blew sideways against my windows. The wind kicked up more, and it sounded as if the windows would be blasted inward by its fury. I lifted the blinds and looked out my front window to see palm fronds flying across the yard. One hit the front door, making it shake and rattle. The noise startled me for a minute, then I laughed. No one would brave this weather to come back and attack me again. The wind and rain were my friends, a kind of barrier between me and the world out there. I was safe and snug in my house.

Then the lights went out.

* * *

"Eve?" a voice called from the other side of the front door.

The storm had passed, but I didn't want to open the door to anyone.

"Eve?" the voice called again.

Ah. It was Sammy. I rushed to the door and flung it open.

"Are you all right?"

I threw myself into his arms and drew him into the room.

"What is all this?" He gestured around the room, which I had filled with candles. I had lit all of them, and their flames flickered a greeting, bathing the house in a warm, golden glow.

"The lights went out."

"I know. That's why I'm here—to see if you're safe."

"And I suppose you expected to see me cowering under my bed?"

"Maybe."

"Well, when I lost my electricity, I panicked, but just for a minute, then I thought about it. What's cozier than candlelight? I got out every candle I could find and created a warm nest for myself. Kind of romantic, isn't it?"

He crushed me to him and squeezed me for a very long time.

"Hey, buddy. You're about to break a rib."

When I looked up into his face, the candlelight made his eyes shine like obsidian.

"I worried you'd have a hard time being here alone and especially when this storm came up. But you're …."

"I'm good. I talked myself through it." I stepped back, holding both his hands in mine. "Like I said before. Romantic, isn't it?"

It took very little pressure for me to lead him into my bedroom.

"Grandy and Max are coming in soon," he said.

"Oh, that's the best part. Grandy called just before you got here to say the storm had flooded roads, and they weren't traveling until early tomorrow morning. We have this entire candlelit house to ourselves. All night."

"I think we should talk before we take advantage of the mood you've set."

I didn't reply to his comment, but walked over to the bedroom slider and pulled it open. "Smell how clean the air is. The storm did that, cleaned away all the musty, moldy mildew smells and replaced them with the fresh smell of nature, of the swamps. I think the storm did that for me too. I'm pretty clear on what I want now. I want you, Sammy, and I want the boys to be ours."

When I turned to look at him, the moonlight shone on his face so that I could see his black eyes and the single tear that glistened on one cheek.

And later we created another storm—wild, passionate, loving.

I SHOULD HAVE been tired when Grandy and Max rolled in around six in the morning, but I was awake and energized, eager to take on the day, to take on all the days that were to come.

"What time did the two of you leave to get here so early? It had to have been before four this morning. You didn't need to get back so soon."

"I told you I'd open the store this morning, and I will. I've got a few hours to get in a quick nap," Grandy said.

I wrapped my arms around my short, chubby grandmother. "I know you'll balk at this, but I'm going to open the store today, and you can come in around one in the afternoon. I wouldn't even have you do that, but I'm going down to West Palm to pick up some merchandise from one of our consignors, the one who's always redecorating. She has some more Tommy Bahama furniture for us. I'm borrowing Sammy's truck to pick it up."

Grandy seemed about to argue with me, but I held up a finger to silence her. "And I've got some news. I'm getting married, and I'm about to become the mother of three."

From her still, pale face, I thought Grandy was next in line for a heart attack, but she recovered her composure quickly. "Oh, that's good news."

"I'm surprised at you. All you can say is 'That's good news.' I thought you'd be thrilled."

Max enveloped me in his arms. "She's thrilled, all right. She's just too shocked to say much."

I reached out to include Grandy in the hug, and we three soon were sobbing and laughing, which is how Sammy found us when he came into the room. He joined the group hug.

"So, how about a cup of coffee and something to eat before you take your naps?" I wiped the tears from my cheeks.

"We need to talk wedding, Eve," said Grandy.

"We can do that some other time," I said.

"I think we're more tired than hungry," said Max. He pushed Grandy down the hallway to their bedroom.

"I could use a cup and some food," said Sammy. "Or do you want to go out and eat?"

"Let's have coffee here and then go tell Grandfather the news. Do you think he'll approve?"

"He'll act as if it was his idea."

After a quick coffee, Sammy drove off in his truck, and I followed in my car. He would take the car to his job at the game ranch while I used the truck this afternoon to pick up the furniture my client had promised me.

When we walked into Grandfather's house, he was awake and cooking something on the wood stove. It smelled divine.

He turned from his work and beamed at us. "Congratulations. When will you tell the boys?"

Wow, you couldn't pull anything over on Grandfather. He knew what you wanted before you knew you wanted it. I had ceased asking him how he knew anything about me. I assumed he either read my mind or my thoughts traveled across the swamps on the wind to his house. Either was possible. And likely.

He showed his approval of our plans in a more subdued way than my family did. He took my hands in his and pressed his forehead against mine and did the same with Sammy. Then he smiled and gestured toward the table, which was set—you guessed it—for three diners.

"This smells wonderful. Is it some Miccosukee dish?" I asked.

"Scrambled eggs," he replied and his smile got bigger.

I CALLED MADELEINE on my way to open the shop. We did a lot of joyful squealing over the phone until she said we had awakened the twins and she had to go. Before I could make my next call, which was to Nappi, my cell rang and he was on the line.

"Now you're reading my mind too?" I said.

"What do you mean?"

"I was just about to call you."

"Yes, well I thought I'd save you the trouble. Congratulations."

"Who told you?"

"Well, I think everyone in Sabal Bay knows by now."

"How can they?"

"Max went fishing this morning."

"He was supposed to be napping."

"And your grandmother has a lot of friends in the community."

"She was supposed to be napping also."

Why did I think Grandy would do as I'd suggested and get some sleep before she took over the store for me? Because she was my grandmother and we shared DNA, especially the stubborn strands of it, and she and I did as we pleased. We could have been identical twins except for our ages and outward appearances.

"Big party this coming weekend to celebrate, I guess," said Nappi.

"What party?"

"Oh, I guess I goofed. I didn't know it was to be a surprise. I was calling to see if you had decided on a place to hold it. Or even a place to hold the wedding. When is the wedding?"

"I just said yes last night around ten or so. Let a gal catch her breath, will you?"

"Sure, no problem. I'm just offering my yacht for the party or the wedding or the honeymoon, whatever you'd like. Let me know. Chow."

Just as Madeleine predicted. Once I knew my heart, things between Sammy and me were easy. Working out the details might be more difficult.

We could always elope.

CHAPTER 17

——

I DIDN'T SELL much in the morning, but I sure had a lot of visitors who all had heard about my impending nuptials and wanted to congratulate me. Jay Cassidy and his foreman Antoine stopped by. As was the cowboy way, they each removed their hats when they entered. Cowboys can be hard men, but they are gentlemen in the old-fashioned sense. I wasn't sure if our tiny store catering mostly to women could hold all the testosterone the two of them generated. They were cowboys—lean, handsome, ride-the-range cowboys—whose spurs jingled as they entered. I was honored they stopped by. It couldn't have been easy for them to enter this den of femininity.

"I'm saying congratulations, Eve, but I'm not really happy about this." Jay wrapped his arms around me and squeezed. Oh durn, was he going to say something about his barely hidden prejudice against Miccosukees, an attitude I tolerated but didn't condone?

"He means," said Antoine, speaking up quickly before I could jump to any conclusions, "that there'll be one less eligible gal in this town. Actually, *the* most eligible gal." Antoine blushed. He was another cowboy who liked to flirt with me.

"When's the wedding?" Jay let go, leaving my ribs intact. "I'm just asking because I intend to pursue you until that, uh, man puts a ring on your finger saying hands off."

I ignored his comment and changed the subject. "Nice of you boys to stop by. Can I offer you a discount on something while you're here? Maybe a nice pair of earrings for that special woman in your life?"

Jay clapped his hat back on his head, and without saying goodbye, left, Antoine at his heels. As Antoine strode past me, he winked. "Don't mind him. He likes to growl when he doesn't get what he wants, and he wants you."

Jay made a sound very much like growl. I laughed, and they were gone.

Grandy arrived exactly at noon, perky as if she had slept eight hours instead of the two or three she and Max had gotten. I could tell she'd washed her hair, because it shone brilliant white in the sunlight, and her usual curls were frizzy in the Florida humidity.

"Bad hair day," she said, fluffing her locks. "I can't tame this stuff."

"Cut it shorter, gel the hell out of it, and maybe you'll look like me. Easy." As if a new hairdo would make her grow inches taller, years younger, and pounds lighter. I liked my Grandy the way she was, frizz and all.

"Well, you're off to restock the store, so get busy." She almost pushed me out the door.

"But I haven't had lunch yet. You were supposed to bring me something."

She handed me a paper bag with a logo on it from one of the fast food places in town. "Here you go. You can eat on the road."

Grandy seemed eager to get me out of the store. *Oh well.* I shrugged and headed to the truck. It had no air conditioning, so I rolled down the windows to keep cool.

I turned left out of the parking lot to get on the Beeline to

West Palm. As I passed by a local campground, I caught the smell of brush being burned to clear an area for expansion of their facilities. The smell reminded me of the whiff I'd gotten of Frida's clothing after she returned from investigating Connie Russo's burned cabin. It was not unlike the odor in Eddie's tiny cabin with its wood-burning stove, and it jarred that memory just out of reach in my mind—the smell my intruder carried on him when he invaded my house and attacked me. It was the smell Connie Russo had picked up from his cabin. *Aha.* Now I knew. Connie Russo was my attacker, the man who had warned me to stay out of the hit-and-run, the man someone had hired to warn me off. Russo had taken a job with a construction company, according to his cousin Ed of the many last names. Could that company be Gator Way? It made sense to me.

I did a U-turn and headed back toward the Kissimmee River and the construction site. I wanted to nose around Danny Cypress' business digs. The construction company had to be the one Connie—our toasted and dead creep and my attacker—had been working for. Did he steal the watch for them? I couldn't figure out why they would have him do that, but I was certain the company was involved in stealing those bones. Did Connie kill Walter on their orders? Again, I couldn't make sense of why. Danny Cypress had been a mob lawyer at one time. There was every chance he ran into Connie and knew he was the kind of guy you could send after a loose end. And remove it. Was Walter a loose end? I had no idea why the company would consider Walter such a threat, but I'd work that out somehow.

The company had their headquarters somewhere beyond the river bridge on a road to the north. It wasn't hard to find. The buildings were a mere several hundred yards beyond the turn, and they could be seen from the highway. The sign at the entrance read: "Coastal Development Company, Gator Way Site." It sounded as if the development company had other locations around Florida. I pulled through the gate and into the parking area. Part of it was dedicated to the company cars with spaces allocated by number for their black SUVS and trucks all bearing the company logo. The assigned slots wrapped around the front of the building and partway down the right side. I selected a space labeled "visitors" and noticed a police car in the next slot. Frida stood at the entrance to the building, watching me pull in.

"Hey!" I called out.

"Hey, yourself. What are you doing here?"

"I guess I'm doing what you're doing. Snooping. Except I'm unofficial, so I'm paying a social visit to Danny Cypress." I laughed to let her know I wasn't really serious about the social part of my call.

She wrinkled her nose in distaste.

"Not a fan of his, I gather?"

"I was here after the bones were stolen to talk with his boss and other executives as well as the foreman from the construction site. They claim to know nothing about the theft. Now I'm here to see if they might know something about Walter Egret's death. Eddie the pawnbroker said his cousin was working for some construction firm. Like you, I'm betting it was this one."

"Speaking of Connie Russo, I think he was the one who attacked me." I told her about connecting the smell when I came into my house with the odor on her clothes from when she investigated the fire at Russo's cabin. "It's a reach, I know, but the guy's voice was familiar, too. I'm certain it was Russo's. He also had the watch Walter found at the site. It had to come from Walter's body."

Frida agreed. "The warning he delivered to you sounds like it came from this company, but I've got nothing else to connect the company with that hit-and-run, the bone theft, or the homicide in that burned-out cabin. I'd love to get a search warrant and tear this place apart. But for now, I'll play nice and ask to talk again to the foreman and Danny Cypress because they were in that area when Walter was killed. Maybe they saw something."

"Or maybe they did something."

"Maybe they need someone to jog their memory."

"Right. And that someone would be you."

Frida nodded. "You might nose around while I talk with Danny and pals."

I looked puzzled.

"Danny has a secretary who dresses well. She might like to talk bargain designer clothes on her salary."

I gave Frida a jaunty salute, and we entered the building. The offices we wanted were on the second floor. On the stairs, we ran into Danny coming down. He looked surprised at our visit and none too pleased. His lips were set in a tight line.

"Cops. Again," he said.

"Just tying up some loose ends. Got a minute?" Frida said.

"Come on up. We'll get this over with, and then Eve and I can chat." Danny took us past a desk where a young woman with curly dark hair and a cute little kewpie-doll mouth was seated at a desk. She wore a teal blue silk dress. It had to be Ralph Lauren. I saw what Frida had said about her. If new, that dress cost her.

"Love your dress," I said.

"My secretary, Liz Coyle. This is Eve Appel. And you already know the detective," said Danny.

She nodded politely at Frida and then her face brightened. "Oh, I know you. You run that consignment shop with that little redheaded woman. I love that place. I wish I had more time to drop in, but I work long ...." She let the remainder of her sentence go and looked embarrassed.

"Do our hours interfere with your shopping, Liz?" asked Danny.

What a mean-spirited thing that was to say. As if realizing how unpleasant his comment was, Danny quickly smiled and added, "I'll leave you two gals to talk haute couture while I answer the detective's questions—questions I'm sure you've already asked and I've already answered." He showed Frida into his office.

Liz and I chatted about her favorite designers and her addiction to shoes, a compulsion I shared. As we talked, I looked out the window, behind her desk. From the second story, you could see the river and a part of the lake. Today was sunny, and the lake, usually a brown color, shone blue with sparkles like diamonds bouncing off its surface.

"Beautiful," I said.

I noted that the parking spot directly below us was painted with the name "Cypress."

"So, does everyone have an assigned place to park?" I asked.

"Oh, no, only the executives and some of the managers like the construction foremen. The rest of us don't drive company cars, so we park out there." She pointed to the back of the building and lowered her voice. "That's where the pavement ends. It's all pea rock and dirt back there."

"It must be hell on your shoes trudging through dusty gravel."

"You have no idea. I carry my shoes with me and wear my sneakers to work. And when it rains? That place is all mud. You need boots, hip waders almost." She laughed.

"You can see if Mr. Cypress is here at work even if he's not in his office."

"Yep. If his car is down there, then he's around someplace."

"And the day the bones were found at the construction site?"

The laugher drained out of her eyes. She lowered her voice. "He left here after he got the call from the boss telling him about those bones."

"And when did he come back?" I asked.

"Oh, I think it was soon after that. When I returned from lunch, his car was back in its parking slot. His car was there the entire afternoon. He was either in his office or with the boss. Those bones scared the hell out of everybody here."

"We had nothing to do with that," said Danny. Neither of us had noticed that he and Frida had emerged from his office because we faced the window and had our heads together, whispering.

"Get back to work, Liz. And now, Eve, what can I do for you? Or are you here to snoop along with your cop friend?" His tone of voice was pleasant, but his expression registered something else. Fear? No. it was anger. I'd have to be very careful how I handled this man.

As I followed Danny into his office, Frida managed to pantomime a "call me" message. I nodded.

"So what did you want to see me about?" asked Danny, and added, "Not that a visit from you isn't always a delight."

"It's about your mother's dress. I got several others in that I thought she might also like, so I was wondering … would you mind if I brought them also? She can choose, or she might like them all."

Danny roared with laughter. "Ever the little business woman, aren't you? Sure. Bring them over. You could have called me to ask that. Was there something else?"

"Not really. I was in the area, and I thought I'd drop by to see the operation. I assumed you wouldn't mind. I can call next time before I show up if you'd like."

Putting him on the defensive had the desired outcome. He hurriedly assured me that he welcomed the visit. "Not much to see here."

"I wasn't expecting it to be as entertaining as Disney, but it certainly is a big operation."

"From your tone of voice, I gather you're not impressed."

He was enjoying our war of words. He was good at it, but so was I.

"Oh, the size is impressive. It's what you do that concerns me."

"You're assuming we dig up Indian bones and hide them from the authorities so we can proceed with the project. I think we've proved we do not do that. It took only minutes after I was called before I arrived at the bones."

"And then, they went missing."

"Vandalism?" he offered.

"Or perhaps something even more sinister. Murder, perhaps."

We were rehashing the entire discovery of the bones and murder of Walter Egret in a few sharp sentences.

"What do you think about Walter's murder?" I asked.

"It was an accident. A drunk driver."

"In the middle of the day? Really?" As much as I was enjoying matching wits with him, this conversation was getting me nowhere.

He shrugged. "I suppose we'll never know unless the person who did it comes forward. That probably won't happen."

How could he be so sure?

"Frida has a lead. She located the owner of a pawn shop where we found the watch Walter mentioned in his telephone call to Sammy right before he was hit. It was their father's watch, you know."

"I didn't know anything about a watch, and I don't see how it figures into his death."

"We're working on the connection."

Danny turned his back on me as if he was interested in what was happening outside the window behind him. Or perhaps he was trying to hide the expression on his face. Had I said too much about the pawn shop owner? Or just enough? When he turned back to me, he had assumed a blandly pleasant expression, the kind of social face that put me off with its emptiness.

"Well, then," I said. "I'll see you tomorrow at your ranch."

"Dad's ranch."

"Yes. I'm looking forward to meeting your family."

He took a few steps forward. "Let me get the door for you." He reached around me and pulled open the door. As I began to walk through, he turned his body so that I was wedged between him and the door. We were so close that I could smell the garlic and mint on his breath and the smell of his deodorant as he sweated through it. Something I said had gotten to him. This was a man who didn't sweat easily.

I waved goodbye to Liz, hopped in my car, and sped out the gate. About a hundred yards beyond the entrance, I saw Frida's car at the side of the main road. I pulled over behind her, and she walked back to my car.

"Find out anything?"

"Nothing that you probably don't already know. Liz said his car was parked in his space from shortly after he returned from the construction site until he left around five."

"So he told me, too."

"From Liz's window, you can see only the line of company cars parked on that side of the building, but the ones around the corner aren't visible."

Frida shrugged. "So?"

"So. There are a lot of company cars parked in those slots, and they all look exactly alike."

"Good point, and I know what you're thinking, but like I said before, none of this will get me a search warrant to take a look at all those cars to see if one of them might have been involved in a hit-and-run."

"Maybe I can sneak a peek at Danny's tomorrow if he drives it to the ranch for Shelley and my meeting with his mother."

"I can't see how that could be the car, but take a look if you can."

I nodded, happy to help Frida with her investigation.

"But, Eve," Frida said, as I put the truck in gear, "be careful. Danny Cypress is a suspicious man, and he's dangerous."

"Roger that," I said and took off. As much as I loved this sleuthing work, I was late for my appointment with my consignor in West Palm. My paycheck still came from selling used items, not from tracking down killers.

* * *

I LOADED TWO accent chairs upholstered in a zebra print, a table with a glass top, and four matching bamboo chairs into the back of Sammy's truck. Someone in Sabal Bay would gobble these up fast.

"I've decided I don't like the island look, so I'm going with lighter colors, more South Seas tropical. I mean, everyone is doing Tommy Bahama now. It's become common." Mrs. Graymore flipped her hand in the air, her nails flashing silver in the sunlight. "They're all yours. Oh, I almost forgot … I've got some clothes too." She ran back into the house and came out with an armload of dresses, tops, and capris, some with the tags still on them.

"Great," I said, taking them from her and laying them on the passenger's seat on top of the other clothing I'd picked up this afternoon.

As I drove off, my cell rang. It was Grandy, and she wasn't happy.

"Where have you been? I closed the store at five, and it's going on five thirty."

"I got delayed. I'll tell you all about it later." I heard voices in the background. "Is someone there? Did I forget we were having company tonight?"

"No. We're absolutely not having anything tonight. I just wondered where you were. You said you'd be home by now."

"I'll be home in another hour. Do you want me to pick up some take-out for dinner? Or are you cooking? Or am I supposed to cook tonight?"

"No one's cooking. We'll eat leftovers." With a heavy sigh, she disconnected.

I must have done something to get her mad, because she sure sounded angry.

I stepped on the accelerator and coaxed the old truck to several miles over the speed limit, hoping I wouldn't attract the attention of a cop and the truck wouldn't rattle to pieces. She wasn't used to speeds over thirty or forty.

The scenery sped by on the Beeline, now a four-lane road from West Palm to Sabal Bay. Maybe that was an improvement for those traveling this route, but I missed seeing all the wild, untamed vegetation on the side of the road as well as the wading birds seeking their dinners by probing the wetlands that were now replaced by wide shoulders and recent plantings of cultivated bushes and trees. I wasn't even certain most of it was indigenous to this area. That was progress, or someone's take on it.

I pulled into my drive expecting to see Max and Grandy's car, but it was empty. Where were they? Odd. Especially after the earlier conversation with Grandy.

The sky looked clear, but I couldn't chance a passing shower ruining the furniture in the bed of the truck. After all, we sold items "gently used," not "a bit rained on."

My garage door opener was in my car, so I had to go into the house and open the door by going through the kitchen and into the garage. I'd pull Sammy's truck in and unload it tomorrow. He wouldn't mind if I kept it overnight.

I unlocked my front door and reached around to turn on the ceiling light in the living room, but before I could hit the switch, the lights came on and a crowd of people all yelled, "Surprise!"

"What is going on?" I asked. I was certainly surprised, but why was my house filled with all my friends and relatives?

"This is your engagement party. We knew we couldn't surprise both you and Sammy, so we thought we'd spring this on you," Grandy said.

Sammy stepped forward and kissed my cheek, then presented me with a small box.

"A ring?" I asked.

Sammy beamed with pride. "Yup."

I opened the box. Inside was a lovely pearl ring, its opalescent color a milky blue-green under the light. It was nestled in a heavy gold setting. The ring appeared to be very old. It was simple and elegant and spoke of love.

"It was the ring my father gave my mother. It belonged to his mother. My mother sent it to me the other day. Somehow she knew I'd be needing it."

"So if I marry into this family, will I have the gift of second sight also?" I asked.

CHAPTER 18

———

I T WAS A lovely engagement party. The three boys seemed to be more excited than anyone, except perhaps me. I felt as if I'd been granted every wish I ever wanted from my childhood until now. The only darkness in the evening was that Sammy's father and my parents weren't here to share our happiness, but we had our family and all our friends, including those about to become my family—Sammy, the three boys, Grandfather, and Sammy's cousins. Sammy's mother called from Las Vegas to add her congratulations. My house was crammed with people and joy.

It was late when we closed the door to our guests. We bedded the three boys down in their sleeping bags in the living room, and I sent Grandy and Max off to bed while Sammy and I cleaned up. It wasn't until after midnight that he and I snuggled under my comforter. It was a night so brimming with love and happiness that we immediately fell asleep in each other's arms, exhausted with the wishes of love received from everyone. I believed we shared the same dreams as we slept.

I awoke to the smell of coffee brewing and an empty bed. I expected to find Sammy in the kitchen, but he wasn't there.

"Where is everyone?" I asked Max, who handed me a steaming cup of coffee.

"Sammy took the boys off to school, and Grandy is opening the shop. I'm about to go fishing." Max drained his cup and grabbed his tackle box.

"What time is it?" I asked.

Max pointed to the wall clock. "After eight. You were dead asleep, and Sammy said not to wake you."

I yawned and stretched. Max planted a kiss on my cheek and was out the door. The feeling of happiness from last night colored my morning as I mentally prepared for my appointment with Shelley at the Cypress ranch.

At the store Shelley and I pulled several dresses off the rack as well as the one chosen for Mrs. Cypress by her daughter and approved by Danny.

"I understand you went to school with the Cypress daughter," I said to Shelley as we put the dresses in the car and left for the ranch.

"I knew her, but not well. Amanda is her name. She was quite a bit older than me, but I remember her because she rescued me from some bullies on the playground. She was always kind to the younger kids. She went off to college for a while, but came back here when her mother's physical condition got worse. She's now her mother's caretaker. She's devoted to her family, but it's not much of a life for a young woman."

"Danny said his mother doesn't get out of the house much, that she's in a wheelchair."

Shelley nodded. "I guess not, but I did hear that she liked to go to the lake and sit by the water. Amanda stopped in the store one day last week when you were out and said her mother doesn't ask to be taken to the lake anymore because the construction there is noisy and has torn up the area."

I remembered the construction site and thought it was a shame to have destroyed the serene beauty of it. "Maybe they can find her another place that will give her some peace and happiness."

"I know she still mourns for her lost son. They've heard nothing from him in recent years. It must be hard for a mother not to know what happened to her child."

"It sounds like there's a lot of sadness in that family," I said, wondering if that figured into Danny Cypress' character. Was it grief that made him so unpredictable, odd, and perhaps dangerous?

"Here's the turnoff to the ranch." Shelley pointed to a road leading off to our right. I could see buildings in the distance. As we got closer, the house appeared in a grove of palms and live oaks, the latter shading both sides of the building. I don't know what I expected, but given that the Cypress family was Miccosukee, I'd envisioned a structure much like Grandfather's, a simple house on stilts built of hand-hewn timbers. This was anything but. The exterior was stucco the shade of a blush on a woman's cheek, just pink enough to be inviting but not so much that it looked trite and girlish.

One section of the large house had two stories, unusual in these parts, while the other arm of the building was a single story. The roof was high, peaked, and made of red tiles. The tall windows were rounded at the top, giving the structure a Mediterranean feel. A semicircular drive fronted the house with a large, tiered fountain bubbling water into a pool at its base. Two vehicles were parked in the drive. One was an SUV with the Gator Way Construction insignia on its door. The other—a white, four-door pickup—also sported an insignia. It was the picture of a cypress tree with Spanish Moss hanging from its limbs. "Cypress Ranch" was lettered below the tree. Danny Cypress stood on the porch in front of massive carved-wood double entrance doors.

Danny wore his usual outfit—blue suit, white shirt, and a tie in a subdued light blue and grey print. The very picture of a successful lawyer. For some reason, I thought he'd be more casually dressed at home, but then, he probably was only taking a few hours out of his work day to meet us here at the ranch. He greeted us, took the clothing items out of Shelley's hands, and invited us into the house. We entered a cool entry with a vaulted ceiling, a tile floor, and amber walls adorned with colorful tapestries depicting rural scenes of natives in their daily lives. The hangings included wading birds—some with white plumage, others smaller and greenish-blue in color—alligators, Florida panthers, and other small mammals. Scenes of Florida as it once was.

"My mother, father, and sisters are outside. Let me introduce you." He gestured to glass doors at the rear of the room. The view overlooked a swimming pool with several chairs, lounges, and tables on its deck. A woman sat in a wheelchair, her size so diminutive that she looked like a doll in an adult seat. A young woman was seated to her right. When we approached, she looked up from the book she was reading. She and Shelley exchanged greetings.

Danny introduced us to his mother and me to his sister, Amanda. The surface of the pool water was broken by the body of a swimmer, who pulled himself out of the pool and grabbed a towel.

"My father," said Danny.

The man was not much taller than me, but his chest was broad, his arm muscles large, and his grip strong as he took my hand.

"Danny has told me a lot about you," he said.

"All good, I hope," I said.

He didn't smile, nor did he deny or agree with my comment.

"I was taking my daily swim, fifty laps."

"Every morning," said Danny. His voice held a note of respect, the kind that often comes from a child firmly disciplined and sometimes harshly punished by an authoritarian parent. Danny Cypress clearly admired his father and feared him too.

I shifted my gaze from the father and son back to the

mother. It was clear she was not in good health. Her dark skin must have once had the healthy glow of her daughter's, but now it was deathly gray as if washed with ashes. Her face was filled with sadness and lined with grief, but it registered little movement now, as if she felt too defeated to care about what was going on around her. Her black eyes told a different story. There was the shadow of mournfulness there, but they examined me carefully as if looking for something in me. A judgment of some kind or a secret I was keeping from her? Her full lips were pulled across her teeth in a grim line. As pretty and young as the daughter was—dark-skinned with blue-black hair and her mother's full mouth—Amanda carried some of her mother's sense of defeat. No one smiled here, not even to greet their guests.

As if there was a need to explain her tiny stature, Danny said, "My mother is Guatemalan."

"Ah," I replied, not really knowing what to say. "Well, I have some lovely dresses for you to look at, Mrs. Cypress. I hope you'll find them to your liking. Ms. McCleary will be happy to fit them for you."

Mrs. Cypress looked up at her husband, still standing at her side. Her eyes seemed to plead for something. I wasn't certain what.

"You can use my library to try them on and fit them." He gestured toward another set of entryway doors to the left of those we had just exited. Without another word, he strode into the house.

"We rarely have company. It's too tiring for my mother." Danny watched as Amanda pushed the wheelchair into the library, Shelley trailing behind. Was Danny trying to excuse the abruptness of his father's greeting and exit?

I smiled and turned to follow the threesome into the library, but Danny placed his hand on my arm to stop me. "Have a seat. I can get our housekeeper to bring some iced tea, if you like." His grip tightened, and he moved me toward one of the chairs around the table. I hated it when men decided what I should or could do, but Danny seemed to be eager to keep me here. I wanted to know why.

"Tea would be nice." I took the chair he held for me.

The housekeeper, short, round, and with a face filled with happiness—appeared at the door. Danny nodded to her. Her joy contrasted strangely with the overwhelming sadness of the rest of this family.

"I have some news for you," Danny said. "I was about to call your detective friend, but thought I'd wait and tell you first. I assume the two of you are working together."

I knew what he meant, but I decided to act dumb. "Working together? On what?"

"The case of the missing bones."

"We're both interested in it. You know that the backhoe operator was killed in a hit-and-run or something that looked like a hit-and-run and that his father's watch, which we assume he took off the body, was stolen from him. We're guessing the person who hit him stole it."

"So you say."

"It's true."

"I believe you, and that's why you'll be interested in what I have to say."

I said nothing, simply assumed my interested face.

"Our garage man responsible for the upkeep of the company vehicles called me this morning. He was performing an oil change on one of our cars and noticed damage to the front of the vehicle. That particular vehicle is one used by one of our associate vice presidents, so at first I assumed he had failed to report a minor accident, but our repairman reminded me of something the day the bones were found."

I was too excited to keep quiet. Damage? On one of the construction company vehicles? It was just the lead Frida needed. "What? Tell me."

Danny leaned closer to me. "I thought you'd be interested."

There he was again, invading my personal space, but I did not move back. I would not be put off by this man. "Go ahead."

"The day the bones were uncovered, I was in my office—it's on the corner of the building as you know—and I noticed the slot usually housing that car was empty. Then, later in the afternoon, the car was there."

"So your associate VP was off on business or playing hooky."

"No, and that's what's so odd. He was off, but he was off on a month-long combined vacation and business trip."

"Someone else in your company took the car out. Who?" I felt we were getting close to the truth.

"If someone in the company wanted to drive that car, they would go to the garage man for the keys. Our man there said he never gave the keys out."

"There was a duplicate key then. Who had it?" I seemed to know the answers to this dilemma. Why didn't he?

"There's another explanation, one that makes more sense. Someone must have left the keys under the driver's side floor mat. The garage man and I thought the car had been taken for a joy ride and then returned. An outsider could have wandered in and saw an opportunity for fun.""

"If you thought one of your cars had been stolen, if only for a few hours that day, why didn't you notify the police?' I had begun listening to this tale with hope, but now I doubted he was telling the truth. The story of a missing car with front-end damage left unreported to the authorities was just too convenient.

"It was my fault. Our man told me that day that the car was missing and then had been returned. I assured him I would take care of it, but with finding the bones on the company site that day and then hearing of their disappearance the next, a joyride with a car that was returned slipped my mind. It didn't seem important until today when the repairman spotted the damage."

"And why was it spotted today? Why not sooner?"

"Obviously no one was driving the car, and it was taken into our shop today in preparation for our VP returning this week from his month's absence."

I peered closely at his face. Was the entire story a tall tale? Was he telling the truth or covering for someone? "Call Frida and do it now. I hope for your sake that your garage man hasn't started to repair the vehicle."

Danny smiled. "I told him not to touch it. I knew the authorities would want to see the damage. I'm not a fool, Eve."

"I know that. I just wish I could believe you're not a liar."

The smile on his face never wavered. He leaned farther in, and I suspected he was about to try and kiss me, but his father's voice interrupted his next move.

"Your mother chose the dress your sister and you picked for her. The other two are lovely, Ms. Appel, but my wife assured me she has no use for more than one. I thank you for your consideration. Send me the bill." He gave his son a warning look, then turned on his heel and left.

"He's probably on his way to the barns to see to one of our horses who has gone lame." Danny avoided my eyes, as if embarrassed by the coldness in his father's voice and abruptness of his departure.

Shelley came back onto the pool deck with the dresses. "Mrs. Cypress seemed pleased with Amanda's selection. I'll get it to her in a few days."

"Where are Amanda and her mother?" I asked Danny.

"This is the time of day they usually go to the lake, but with the site under construction, my mother prefers to spend her time at our small graveyard." Danny pointed beyond the pool toward a field. At the far edge was a rise surrounded by fencing. Within, I could just make out the tops of headstones. Amanda was pushing her mother across the field toward the graveyard. A large mixed-breed dog with brown and black markings followed them. Like the daughter and the mother, the dog seemed to have sadness written in the slowness of his gait and the droop of his head.

"Our last old hound. His brother died a few weeks ago, so we buried him out there." Danny pointed to the cemetery. "After all, he was a part of the family, Mother's favorite of the litter of four that we adopted years ago. Now there's only one left. With the lake no longer available to her, Mother likes to sit in the cemetery. There she can find peace, think, and pray for her dog." Danny's voice threatened to break with emotion. It was the first time since we'd met that I believed he was speaking the truth.

"And I'm sure she prays for her lost son also." I placed my hand on Danny's shoulder and patted it.

His gaze shifted from the cemetery to me. He paled and his eyes widened briefly as if I'd startled him, but before I could wonder what I'd said, he gave me his usual smarmy smile. He was once again the clever lawyer. The sympathetic son I saw for a brief moment was gone.

Danny showed us to our car, slammed the door, and waved goodbye. Would he call Frida and tell her what he had told me about the company vehicle? Or would he simply assume I'd talk to her?

On the road back to the shop I tried to contact her by cellphone, but her number went to voicemail. That might be a good sign. Maybe Danny was talking with her right now. I left a message for her to get back to me.

Shelley was uncharacteristically quiet on the way back to the shop.

"Something bothering you? I asked.

"I know it was necessary for me to come out here and fit Mrs. Cypress, but I got the feeling we were here for more than that."

"Oh, you're right. We were. Danny Cypress took the opportunity to lay on me a story about one of the construction company cars. I don't know if it's true." I told Shelley what he had said.

"I think Danny has a crush on you." Shelley laughed. "Does he know about Sammy?"

"Yes, he does. And his crush gives me the creeps." I paused for a minute before adding, "I think his father was sizing me up, and not in a friendly way either. Danny gets his creep from Daddy, I'm afraid."

"Such a sad family. So much loss. Mrs. Cypress was eager to get to the cemetery. Danny told you about her dog, right?"

"Yes. I guess when you've lost a son, you hold on to what you can. He said the dog was her favorite. Now the cemetery has become the spot where she grieves, but finds solace of a kind. You'd think Danny would feel some guilt at being a part of a company that destroys the natural habitat the way Gator Way does."

"There's nothing he could do about that."

"I guess not." I wondered how torn Danny's loyalties were. On one side his mother's love for the lake. On the other his duty to protect the company he worked for. The latter duty might encourage him to go outside the law to ensure construction proceeded on schedule. I couldn't yet put it all together, but I was certain Danny Cypress' loyalties didn't extend to the truth.

THE MORNING VISIT to the Cypress family was still on my mind when I met Sammy and Grandfather that night by the airboat business. We had built a small fire in a fire pit between the house and the business only feet from the canal. The boys were with us, and like all kids, they had fun roasting hot dogs over the fire. I'd brought the makings for s'mores, and soon everyone was eating the gooey marshmallow and chocolate concoctions. Sammy dripped hot marshmallow down his chin, making it look as if he had grown a white goatee.

I reached out and wiped away the sticky mess. "You're worse than the boys. Didn't I say to let it cool first?"

Sammy pointed to my blouse, which held a glop of marshmallow and melted chocolate. "I hope that's not some designer brand."

"Of course it is, but it only cost me fifty cents at a yard sale. And it's washable."

Grandfather had been silent until now. "You have something on your mind, Eve."

"You tell me." I leaned over and gave Grandfather a kiss on his cheek.

"I can only read so much. With you, there are always too many things going on in your head. It's like a swarm of mosquitoes."

I told them about my visit to the Cypress ranch today.

"Successful Miccosukees." Grandfather spat into the fire.

"You don't like them?"

He said nothing for a minute. "I don't know them anymore. I liked her. She's a good woman and doesn't deserve losing her son."

"And now her dog."

"I heard about that. That dog was from a litter we gave them years ago. I knew she loved animals and thought it might be a comfort to her to have the puppies to raise. Her husband allowed it, which surprised me, but as severe a man as he is, I think he'd do anything for her." Grandfather stirred the coals in the fire pit. Flames leaped up, and the boys grabbed their sticks for a second round of s'mores.

"I didn't meet the other two sons. I gather they were out working in the fields."

"They're hard workers, doing what their father wanted for them. As for Danny, I guess his destiny was elsewhere." Grandfather grimaced.

"You think Danny is a bad seed?" I asked.

"I think they all do their father's bidding, the daughter included. The boy who disappeared got himself into a lot of trouble stealing, but the old man bailed him out time after time. I don't think any of the children have a very close relationship with their father, but they respect him. His word is law. The family now keeps to themselves. They have nothing to do with the tribe, never come to our celebrations or funerals. They've left their old friends behind. They tell everyone it's because of the mother's illness, but there's more to it."

I held my hand out to the fire and watched my pearl ring take on the orange glow of the flames. "Maybe pulling the family close and keeping others out is the only way he knows to prevent another child from taking off." That made some sense from the father's point of view, but it was unhealthy for the children.

"Love is what keeps family safe and close even if they are far away," said Sammy. I knew he was thinking of his missing father and of his mother out in Las Vegas. Sammy gently shifted his arms around Jeremy, asleep now but still holding his sticky treat.

Grandfather took a puff on his pipe, then looked at the bowl. "Fire's out."

Sammy and I looked across the fire pit, smiled and read each other's thoughts. Embers can always be relit with a little fuel.

CHAPTER 19

———

THE NEXT MORNING Frida slammed through the door of our shop, making the bell attached to the door bang back and forth and jangle so furiously I thought it might crack the glass. She was more excited than I'd seen her for a long time.

"You're going to love this one, Eve. The front-end damage on that car from the construction company? Well, it matches with what you'd expect with a hit-and-run. Now we're looking for transfer from Walter's body to the vehicle and vice versa. We got 'em."

"Who have we got? We don't know who was driving that car." I hated to bring her down, but if Danny's story was true, it could have been anyone behind the wheel.

"Fingerprints might give us a lead. I'm thinking it has to be someone associated with the company, so I'll compare prints in the car with those of company employees. I should find the garage man's, the VP's, and whoever drove it into Walter that day." On that happy note, she slammed back out the door.

She was being overly optimistic if she thought those were the only prints she'd find, but she knew that and would handle it when the prints were identified.

"Call Sammy and tell him," said Grandy.

I did, but didn't find him in the office at the hunting ranch, so I called the airboat business. Grandfather answered, so I told him the news

"Uhm," he said.

"Is that some kind of Indian chant for good luck or for good for you, Frida?" I asked.

"No. it means 'uhm' like you white folk do when you have no idea what to say. But here's a thought …."

I waited expectantly.

"I can understand why the company wanted to steal the bones, although in the end it might not do them any good. It's shortsighted and odd, but why would they kill Walter? And why would they have that fellow who's the cousin of the pawn shop owner on the coast steal the watch? And why is he dead?"

Those were the very questions that had been buzzing around in my mind for days. Grandfather was right. It was as if I had a swarm of mosquitoes in there.

Maybe I was wrong to see this crime as motivated by business concerns—a company wanting to prevent a possible shutdown. Maybe it was something else. I needed to swat those mosquitoes away and try another approach.

No one knew how to think criminal like my friend Nappi. It had been days since I'd talked with him about this case. He was someone whose head was mosquito-free.

"Hey, Nappi. I've got an hour for lunch." I tucked my cellphone under my neck and looked to Grandy for confirmation of my lunch hour. She nodded. "How about we grab a sandwich and meet at the construction site where those bones were found?"

I heard a chuckle from the other end of the line. "You want to talk bones over lunch? Great. I'm on my way from West Palm to your area. I'll see you there at noon. Don't worry. I'll bring lunch."

"Don't make it a salad. I'm so hungry I could eat a side of cow."

"Salads accompany a meal. They are not a meal." With an additional chuckle, he disconnected.

"Only an hour, Eve," Grandy said. "Madeleine will be here around one with the twins. We're supposed to talk wedding plans. Remember?"

I did. It was something I dreaded. I didn't want a big wedding. What was there to plan? I was certain they'd want to know if we'd set a date and gotten a venue, sent out invites …. I sighed at the thought of how complicated all this might become. Elopement, anybody?

IT WAS A kind of salad, but not like any I'd eaten before. It was filled with vegetables, yes, but it also contained several kinds of cooked seafood, including shrimp, scallops, lobster and calamari, all doing a tango with penne pasta and brought together with Italian dressing. We sat at a picnic table, one of the few remaining in the area. The construction equipment was silent, awaiting some official determination of whether the project could continue.

Nappi handed me a piece of crunchy bread. "Dip it in the dressing at the bottom of your salad."

I did, and after I'd finished that piece of bread I took another. He'd also brought along an Italian white, Soave, chilled enough to make my teeth hurt, but still flavorful.

"Someday I'd like to visit Italy," I said between mouthfuls.

"Maybe your honeymoon?"

"Not you too. I'm supposed to talk wedding stuff this afternoon with Grandy and Madeleine. I can hardly wait."

"So elope." He poured me another glass of wine.

"Where did you get that idea?"

"Isn't that what you were thinking?"

Well, yes it was, but I was tired of everyone reading my mind, being able to hear through all that buzzing noise that I couldn't seem to get beyond.

"The state has been delayed but soon it will send out an

archaeological team to dig the area. The lost bones may remain lost, but it won't matter. Either that place is an old burial ground or it's not. If it is, then that will mean construction will be delayed or permanently halted. It's as if the bones don't matter, yet they belonged to someone alive at one time and that person, whether or not it was Sammy's father, might hold the key to his whereabouts. It makes me mad on two levels. First, the bones are missing so we can't find out about Sammy's father. Second, the beauty of the area is being destroyed. Once that sporting complex is finished, no one but the very wealthy will be able to enjoy this. Why should beauty be accessible only if you have money?" I gestured to the lakeside and the expanse of lake beyond. "But my anger is doing nothing to answer any of these questions. Talk to me about what you see, Nappi."

He took the linen napkin he'd provided and wiped his mouth.

"This is what I see. Look beyond this physical setting. What does it mean to people? To people you love, Eve." He waited while I considered what he said.

"This was a place of comfort, once a place where some found peace and serenity, a place where ..." I stopped, then completed what I was going to say, "a place where bones should lie undisturbed. That's what the Egret family would have wanted for Sammy and Walter's father, wherever his bones were buried."

"Sadly, no one knows if it was Sammy's father lying here."

I shook my head. "Why would the construction company have Walter killed? What did he see that they didn't want him to see?"

"The only other person to see those bones was the construction foreman."

"That's a dead end. Frida has talked with him and asked him over and over what he saw there. He still claims he saw only buried bones."

"I'd go back to him and try again. You do it, Eve. You talk

to him. This is your family now. It's personal for you." Nappi reached out and patted my knee.

We bussed our table and loaded the empty wine bottle, plates, utensils, and other items back into Nappi's picnic basket.

"I wonder if I was any help." Nappi stepped forward and put his arms around me.

"You're always a help." I relaxed in his embrace for a moment, then looked up at him. An idea came to me. "How well do you think Danny Cypress knew Connie Russo when Danny was a lawyer for the mob in Miami? Didn't you tell me they used Connie for some work there?'

"I'll get right on it," Nappi said.

I knew he would.

I COULDN'T SNIFF around the construction company site. Someone might spot me, and I didn't want Danny to know I was so interested in the place. I knew I was a coward for avoiding the afternoon discussion of wedding plans with Grandy and Madeleine, but I couldn't think of an excuse for not showing up, so I didn't get in touch with them. I was always of a mind that you never got permission to do something you knew you shouldn't do; it was better to just do it and take the consequences later. Meantime I stopped off at some consigners in Sabal Bay to see if they had items for us. If we could provide the service of pick-up for our West Palm customers, I reasoned, why not for the ones in Sabal Bay? I killed the afternoon and collected some lovely dresses and a few pairs of shoes. Grandy and Madeleine couldn't be mad at me if I was working, could they?

My cell rang several times. I didn't need to look at the caller ID to know Grandy was trying to track me down. I'd ignored the calls until now, but I couldn't dodge them forever. I tossed my phone onto the passenger's seat and let the call go to voicemail.

The construction company site continued to call to me.

Late in the afternoon I parked my car down the road from the company and waited until I spotted the construction foreman leaving the building. I assumed that he, like all men who put in a rigorous day's work out the Florida sun, would stop by some watering hole for an icy cold one. I was right. I followed his truck to the Rusty Nail Bar, a place Madeleine and I had danced on Saturday nights before she was married.

The inside of the place was as I remembered it, dark and smelling of smoke and stale beer. It didn't have a kitchen, so all they sold for food was chips, pretzels, and some odd-looking flat concoction that passed for pizza the bartender slid into a small oven.

The foreman took a seat at the bar. I pushed my way beyond several men entering the door and sidled up to the empty stool next to my quarry.

I extended my hand to him. "Eve Appel. I thought you might be willing to talk with me about the day you uncovered those bones at the construction site out by the river. I'm Frida's associate."

He groaned and looked as if he might want to put his head down on the bar and leave it there until I went away, but I wasn't going anywhere.

He gave a tired sigh. "I've told the detective everything I saw, which wasn't much. Why can't you leave me alone?"

"Look, I'll let you in on a little secret. We found one of the company cars had front end damage. We think it's the one used to run down your backhoe operator."

"You think I did that?"

"No, of course not. Well, *I* don't think you did that, but the detective might. I need something I can give her so she'll look at someone else, not you."

"What?"

"Just walk me through that morning. Tell me everything, not just what you did and saw, but what you were thinking, what the backhoe operator said to you."

He pulled his cap off his head for a minute and scratched his sweaty head. "Okay. I'll try. I didn't know the guy real well, but he was a good worker, real competent. He almost made me change my mind about working with Indians. And he was smart, maybe too smart. When he uncovered those bones, he was the one who pointed out that we had to stop because of that damn law. He knew the name of it and everything."

"Most Indians do. It's important to them that their burial places not be disturbed."

"Yeah, well, he jumped off the machine and into the hole to take a close look at what was there. I yelled at him to get out, but he hesitated and bent over the bones. I thought maybe he touched something, and I was worried I'd get in trouble if he moved anything in the hole."

Maybe I was getting somewhere. I was pretty certain he hadn't told Frida he suspected Walter found something interesting enough in the hole to touch … or remove it.

"Anything else? How was he after that? Any change in him. Fear or excitement?"

"I think he was as eager as I was to get out of the hot sun and stop work. I immediately sent him home, and I think he was glad to leave, to go home to his family."

"Think, will you? There had to be something."

"Don't push me." He took a swig of his beer and stared across the bar into the smoky mirror.

I wanted to shake him, but knew better than to move. I'd wait him out.

"Okay, well, he kept saying to me the whole week, 'Lenny,'— that's my name—'Lenny, I got the feeling someone is watching me. I figured he was complaining because I was hanging around too close to his work. Maybe he thought I should just go back to my truck and sit and watch him from there."

" 'Someone is watching me' is what he said?"

He looked down at his beer, picked up the bottle and stared across the bar. "Yup."

"Did you see anyone?"

"Nah." He slammed his empty beer bottle on the bar and motioned to the bartender for another.

"Put it on my tab," I said to the bartender when he delivered the bottle.

The bartender gave me a weary look. "I didn't know you had a tab. You have to drink something to have a tab, lady."

"Okay. I'll have a coke."

The foreman took another long draw on his bottle. "Lotta trees around that area."

What was he trying to tell me?

"So someone could have been watching from the cover of the trees?"

He shrugged and took a long guzzle of his beer.

"You'd tell me if you saw anything, wouldn't you?"

"Sure, if it would get you off my back. Don't look good having a cop following me in here. Especially a girl cop." He looked around the bar at the tables, now beginning to fill with other workers.

I'd gotten all I could from him. At least for today. I laid my business card on the bar next to him. "Thanks a lot, Lenny. You've been very helpful." I tossed a ten-dollar bill on the bar and started to leave.

He glanced at the card. "Hey, you ain't no cop. Says here you run some kind of a store."

"I'm kind of undercover. You know."

He looked at me for a moment, then turned his attention back to his beer.

I waved at him and exited the bar to the sound of some whistles and a few comments of a sexual nature. I took it all lightly, a bunch of tired working men letting off some steam over cold beers. I smiled, and they hooted, offering to buy me drinks if I'd join them.

Not tonight, boys. I was in hot pursuit of a killer.

* * *

I DROVE UP to the shop just as Grandy and Madeleine were closing up.

"What trouble were you getting into today?" asked Grandy.

I hauled dresses, other clothes, and shoes out of my trunk and held them aloft. "I was working. See?"

"We were supposed to be planning a wedding," said Madeleine. She handed one of the twins to Grandy while she opened her car door to put the other twin into the baby seat. "I've got to get home. I'll let Grandy hand out your punishment for not being here."

I knew she wasn't really mad because she grabbed my arm and planted as kiss on my cheek. The twin in her arms began to cry.

"I think he's jealous of you giving me attention."

"That's Eve, and she, like her namesake, wants to be the center of attention. Someone said boys are easier. I thought that meant when they got older. With Eve, she's been a pip since birth."

I smiled. "Better my personality than your clumsiness."

Madeleine always took teasing about her lack of coordination well. "We don't know that yet. She's not crawling or walking. She might be like a pigeon-toed moose."

"God, let's hope not," said Grandy.

We waved Madeleine and the twins off and went into the shop.

"Okay, Eve, if you think I don't see through this," she indicated the load of clothes, "you're mistaken. I may be old, but I'm still as smart as you, maybe smarter, and I know this is just a cover for what you were really doing. How long did it take you to get this stash? Ten minutes? You were gone the entire afternoon."

"Several hours. It required an abundance of schmoozing to obtain these treasures."

"Well, before you start to beef up the lie about what you were up to, let me tell you Frida called and would like you to call her back."

"Why didn't you say so earlier? And why didn't she call me directly?"

"I think you'll find the answer on your phone. Look at it." Grandy headed for the backroom.

Oh, yeah, I had put the phone on vibrate after listening to it ring all afternoon. There were twenty-three messages. I scrolled through to find the ones from Frida. They began with, "Call me," then "Call me, dammit," followed by "Call me when they arrest you for whatever laws you are breaking," and finally "Call me or I'll never tell you another thing about this case."

Apologizing to Grandy or Madeleine for doing something I shouldn't have is one thing, but with Frida, there was no apologizing, only retribution.

"It's Eve," I said after connecting with Frida.

"Eve who?"

I decided to go on the offensive. "I'm sorry, but I've got some important information for you. You're gonna love this."

"Eve Appel?"

Now she was making me mad.

"No, Eve from the planet Mars."

"Is that where you've been? So what have you got for me?"

"You first." I thought she'd want to play the you go first, no you go first game, but clearly she was too excited about her information to hold back.

"We've got prints."

"How unusual. Prints in a police department."

"Eve, I'm warning you."

"Prints from where and from whom?"

"Prints from that construction company car. I mean, there were a load of them, including those of our favorite lawyer, Danny Cypress."

I interrupted her. "That's to be expected. He's one of the employees."

"Oh, I know. It's not *his* prints I'm interested in. Well, maybe I am, but it's a set of unexpected prints."

"Whose?"

"Connie Russo's"

I was silent. I hadn't expected that.

"Here's the interesting part. The prints are only on the passenger's side of the car."

"Someone else was driving."

"Oh, yeah. I'm pretty certain those prints had to come from the day that car hit Walter Egret. Russo's not on the construction payroll, never has been. I guess someone could have picked him up as a hitchhiker, but I think he was in that car for nefarious reasons."

"Nappi said he worked for the mob in Miami. And so did someone else we know."

"Danny Cypress."

"I asked Nappi to find out more about the relationship between Danny and Connie when they were mob-connected in Miami." I knew Frida wouldn't be happy about using Nappi for information, but it seemed the fastest way to find out about Danny and Connie.

"You know your friendship with Nappi bothers me," said Frida.

"Yes?"

"But he is useful at times. So where does this take us?"

"Without too much speculation, it takes us to Danny Cypress and Connie Russo in a car running down Walter Egret. Do you still think the hit-and-run was an accident?"

CHAPTER 20

——

FRIDA LET OUT a groan. "Mob stuff. God, I hate mob stuff when it impacts events around here. It looks to me as if the construction company is up to its ears in something it wants hidden out at that construction site. Why would it bring in a mob operative like Connie Russo to silence Walter Egret? That's heavy stuff to hit some Indian backhoe operator."

"Walter saw something at the site. Maybe more important is that he *felt* something." I told Frida what the foreman had said about Walter's proximity to the bones. "And he also said Walter was uneasy that entire week, believing that someone was watching out at the site."

"I wish Connie Russo was still alive. He was such a nervous little twit …. I know I could sweat the truth out of him."

"But he's dead. His death bothers me," I said.

"A mob killing, that's for certain."

We ended the call after more puzzlement over how and why the mob was involved in all of this. Frida was right. The company was eager to hide something about that site and those bones.

I was standing with the phone still in my hand when Grandy came out from the backroom.

"You look troubled, my dear." She placed her hand on my arm and looked up at me with her sympathetic blue eyes.

I was wound up from the conversation with Frida and had to will my body to let go of the tension. Rubbing my neck, I said, "Walter's death is all about those bones. If we could find them it would clear up a lot of things—his death, Sammy's father's disappearance, why the bones are important, the pocket watch, and how it traveled from Sammy's father to a pawn dealer, to a body and then to another pawn dealer through Connie Russo, a man killed in a mob hit."

THE THREE BOYS were with their cousin tonight. We had begun the paperwork for their adoptions, but it would not be complete until after Sammy and I were married. For now, the boys were temporarily our foster children.

"It's good for them to be with their cousin so they can have contact with their Seminole relatives." Grandfather had started a fire in the fire pit outside his cabin. The night was cool, the wind had all but died away, and the flames kept the mosquitoes from chawing us to pieces.

"Seminole? But you're Miccosukee," I said.

"Walter's wife was from the Brighton Seminoles," Sammy explained. "The boys are fortunate to have both Seminole and Miccosukee blood in them. They will grow up speaking three languages, English, Mikasuki—which is our language and that of most of the Seminoles—and Muskogee, spoken by the Brighton Seminoles."

"I guess I always wondered about the difference between the Miccosukees and the Seminoles," I admitted. "I should learn more so that I understand the boys' heritage. I don't want them to lose their roots." I knew I could never replace their mother, but I wanted to be the best adopted mother I could be.

"I'll teach you," said Grandfather, stirring the fire.

Sammy smiled his approval, and we sat warming ourselves in a comfortable silence.

Finally I broke the silence to share my confusion about what was happening with the events surrounding Walter's death.

Grandfather cleared his throat and tossed another chunk of wood onto the fire. The dancing flames lit up his face, deeply lined from years of living, the color of old leather, with kindness in every pore. "I believe the connection is Danny Cypress."

"I do too, but unless Frida can break him somehow, there is absolutely nothing to connect him to Walter's death or those bones."

"Our father's bones," said Sammy.

Grandfather stirred the fire again. "Maybe not."

"You believe your son Lionel is still alive, don't you?" I asked. I had my suspicions about those bones, but Grandfather knew something I did not.

Grandfather nodded. "You will think this is just the silly delusion of an old man, but sometimes I feel him near me. Once I thought I saw him on the other side of the canal." He pointed beyond the airboat business to the stand of palms. "There. Hidden among the sabals. Watching me, watching Sammy."

"That sounds like what Walter told the foreman just before he died." I repeated what the foreman said about Walter thinking someone was watching him.

We let the silence encompass us as the fire burned down. The night was surprisingly quiet, no birds calling or frogs chorusing. Even the cows in the far field had stopped their bellowing. Then, in the distance, a train blew its whistle as it crossed the county road. The coyotes began yipping to one another to warn of the coming of the iron beast, its whistle and ground-shaking roar disturbing the pack's evening hunting. The whistle faded away and the yipping ceased, replaced by a loud splash at the edge of the water near our fire.

"Gator," said Grandfather.

"Why did Lionel leave?" I asked Grandfather. Everyone was so puzzled by his disappearance. Sammy had carried the guilt of it with him since he was little, believing that his father had abandoned his family and rejected his sons. Yet, knowing Grandfather Egret, I couldn't believe he had raised a son who would leave his family, at least not without a compelling reason. If Grandfather knew more than he had said these years, now was the time for him to speak the truth—not simply to take away Sammy's pain, but to put to rest the idea that those bones belonged to Sammy and Walter's father. If Sammy continued to believe the bones were his father's and they were never rediscovered, the family could have no closure. Was Lionel Egret still alive? If so, why didn't he reveal himself?

Grandfather spoke with hesitation, reaching his hand out to his grandson, who watched him without moving. "Lionel left us to find himself in the swamp. He is always with us, but cannot be here. He's a man damned by what he did."

Sammy's eyes in the light from the dying fire reflected the red of its coals. His unwavering gaze held hope, disbelief, and anger.

"What did he do?" I asked.

"He killed his best friend." Grandfather's words were spoken in a whisper, as if he could hardly bear to say them out loud.

"You're saying he's wanted for murder and is hiding out?" asked Sammy. "What is he afraid of? Getting arrested? Serving time? Cowardly." Sammy got up and grabbed one of the logs meant for the fire. He threw it into the flames with such force that sparks jumped out of the pit and caught the dry grass on fire near our feet.

"I don't believe it," I said. "There has to be more to this story."

Grandfather nodded. "Sit down, Sammy. I promised your father I wouldn't talk about this to anyone, but I see now how foolish that promise was."

Sammy sat, though he clearly didn't want to hear what Grandfather had to say. He turned his face away and looked toward the canal.

"Your father and his best friend Howard Coolie grew up together. They spent much of their youth in these swamps, knew them as well as they knew the rhythm of their own heartbeats. They loved taking each other out into the swamps, blindfolded, dropping off the blindfolded one to see if he could find his way out. They timed each other to see who could do it the fastest. It was a game. I warned them the swamp was not to be disrespected by their sport, but they continued the competition even into adulthood."

Grandfather threw another log on the fire before continuing. "The night you were born, Sammy, a big storm rolled in. Howard said this was a great test of his skills, that he could find his way out of the swamp, even in a storm. Lionel thought he was crazy, but Howard insisted he was the better man in the swamps. That got Lionel's competitive spirit up, and he agreed. The storm blew in with furious winds. Howard never found his way out. Lionel felt responsible. He set out in his canoe and told me he wouldn't return until he found his friend. He was ashamed that he encouraged Howard to pit himself against the swamp."

"But it was Howard's choice," I said.

"It was Lionel's choice not to stop him when he knew better," said Grandfather. "I taught him to respect the swamp."

Sammy stood up and looked up the dark canal that led into the heart of the swamp. "He's out there, is that what you're saying?"

Grandfather nodded. "He might be, or it might be his spirit that wanders there. I do not know. Your father never approached me in all these years."

"He needs to be found. I need to find him." Sammy's gaze met mine across the fire.

I knew what he intended to do, and I also knew I would not stop him. He left the fire without another word. After spending a short time in the house, he joined us again, the big knife he sometimes wore in the scabbard at his waist, his rifle in his hand and a leather bag slung over his shoulder. He reached out and drew me into his arms.

"Tell the boys I'll be back."

I could only nod through my tears.

"Here, take this." I removed the talisman Grandfather had given me as protection a few years ago. I believed it had warded off death and severe harm for me, and I trusted in Grandfather's power to make it work for Sammy also. I placed it around his neck.

Sammy kissed me and put his hand on Grandfather's shoulder. The two men seemed to communicate something through their touching. Then he was gone into the night. All I heard was the sound of his canoe paddle as it dipped into the dark waters.

"Do you think he'll find his father?"

"I think he hopes to find more than his father. This is a journey to shed his guilt and find himself," Grandfather replied. "I should have spoken of Lionel's leaving years ago, but I was afraid to tell Sammy. This is what I feared." Grandfather stared into the dark swamp, then dropped his head to gaze once more into the flames.

The two of us remained at the fire far into the night until the ashes were cold and the sun began to rise over the canal.

THE NEXT MORNING, I told the boys Sammy had gone into the swamps to do something important. I assured them he would return soon, although I struggled with my anxiety over when this would be. Or *if* he would return at all—a possibility I could not share with the boys. It was because I was responsible for the boys and because I loved them that I held myself together. It was what Sammy would have expected me to do, but terror threatened to overtake me each moment of the day. If I gave into my fears, I wouldn't find my way back to sanity. I held steady, turning my concerns to the boys' welfare. They had lost one father. I wanted them to know they had family to turn to.

Sammy had vacation time due him as the foreman at David's hunting ranch, so I arranged for one of Sammy's cousins to take over for him there. David asked no questions when I told him Sammy had business to attend to. "Business" is what I told everyone else. My tone of voice must have indicated the business was of a personal nature, so they didn't ask questions.

Being alone with my worries for Sammy and my yearning for his return left me time to contemplate the missing bones and Walter's death.

Something told me I needed to go back to the beginning. After Grandy and I closed the shop the next day, I dropped her off at the house and headed out toward the construction site. As I passed the Rusty Nail, I spotted a familiar truck in the parking lot and thought it might be the foreman's. I stomped on the brakes and pulled in.

Lenny sat at the bar, as he had when I'd talked to him before. This time he appeared to have spent considerable time romancing his beer. He looked up and greeted me with slurred speech and a surly manner.

"Well, well, if it ain't that undercover cop. Come to harass me again? Well, surprise, surprise. Go pick on someone else." He saluted me with his beer bottle. I took the seat next to him and ordered a coke.

"You seem a little down today," I remarked.

"And ish your fault, ya know."

"Really. How can that be?"

"Cuz some of the guys that work for the company saw me in here talking to you that day, and they blabbed around the company that I was spilling stuff to the cops, so the company fired me. Said I was drunk on the job. Weren't drunk, at least not always. They thought I was telling tales to the authorities."

"So are there tales to tell?" I asked.

He drained his beer bottle and looked at me expectantly. I signaled the bartender to give him another. "On my tab."

"I might know some stuff. What's it worth to ya?"

"It might be worth your staying out of jail."

"What? I didn't do nothin'."

"I'll bet the cops are wise to the company already." Wise to what? Oh well, I'd just make up stuff as I went along. "And the company will want to blame everything on you, you know."

"Listen, I told them not to try to bribe the county when they pulled those construction permits, but they ignored me. I'm innocent. Talk to that fancy-schmancy lawyer of theirs and the big wigs. They're the ones who shoved money at the county officials." He stared into the mirror behind the bar and shook his head.

Trying to bribe county officials. Were they successful? I'd keep that information in my pocket for use at some later date. The foreman seemed to know some things that put the company in jeopardy. No wonder they'd fired him. Maybe he was lucky they chose this way to get rid of him and not something more permanent.

"I'm still interested in that spot where they dug up the bones. There's something fishy about that, don't you think? I mean, the bones were stolen the next day and haven't turned up."

His attention turned back to me. "I'd sure like to tell you somethin' about that you could use against them, but I can't."

"Can't or won't?"

"Well, I did see a truck parked in that grove of trees every day from the time we began digging that place."

"Did you recognize the driver?"

"Maybe." He tilted his beer bottle to one side to show me it was empty. I signaled the bartender again.

The foreman's tongue seemed well lubricated now, and he began to tell me a story I almost couldn't believe.

I SLEPT POORLY the night I talked to the foreman. I suspected I was in for many sleepless night as I waited for Sammy's return. But this night my restlessness might be due to all the caffeine from the cokes I drank while listening to the foreman.

I awoke often with the image of Danny Cypress' mother's face suffused with pain in my mind. I saw her sad eyes gazing across the lake, a picture quickly replaced by another of her being wheeled toward the family cemetery to grieve for her dog buried there. As the night wore on, my brain was seized up with worry and bombarded by thoughts circulating with the speed of a hummingbird's wings. And with about as much impact on my powers of rational thought. A son who left, who disappeared about the same time Sammy's father did. What was the connection? Sammy had left for the swamp. Lionel had left for the swamp. And the oldest Cypress boy had left for the swamp. No. that wasn't right. He was just gone. Or was he? His mother's face crept into my mind again.

And then the wildest thought. I leaped out of bed. Maybe I knew whose bones were in that grave. Maybe I even knew where they were now.

I dressed quickly, tiptoed through the living room, and quietly left by the front door, trying not to wake Grandy. As I started my car and backed out of the drive, I saw the living room light come on and knew my stealth had been unsuccessful. Grandy was up. I hoped she simply believed I needed to go for a late-night drive because I missed Sammy.

I drove west toward the Kissimmee River, passed the state park, and crossed the bridge over the river. Finally I took the turn toward the Cypress Ranch. As luck would have it, the night was well illuminated, thanks to the full moon shining over the swamps and fields. Maybe it would be light enough for me to see what I needed to see. At the turn to the ranch, I slowed the car and stopped along the road.

This was silly. What did I expect to find? And was my foolish errand worth trespassing and getting caught? Would I be adding to the grief of a woman already weighed down by loss? And was I putting myself in danger? The bones found in the construction area didn't just find their way there. Someone had killed whoever was buried in that grave by the lake. I could be taking on a murderer, one who had been clever enough to keep a victim hidden for over three decades.

I pulled my car ahead until I found a small turnoff that had once led to a gate. The path appeared to be unused until recently because the tire tracks were almost invisible. I nosed my car up to the gate and turned off the ignition. This felt like another caper I had tried years before, one that almost got me killed. My hand automatically went to the amulet I wore around my neck; then I remembered I had given it to Sammy. Was I foolish to be so superstitious about its power to protect me? I felt naked without it. Silly me, but I wanted to back out of what I had planned tonight. Was I losing my love of danger and adventure, or had I finally connected with the wiser, more reasonable side of Eve Appel? If I didn't find out what I needed to know I'd never be able to sleep. Still, this wasn't something I should do on my own.

I took out my cellphone.

"Hi, Nappi. Got a shovel?"

CHAPTER 21

━━

I WAITED IN the car for over half an hour and was about to give up on Nappi's joining me in my recklessness when a tap on my car window made me jump.

"Sorry if I woke you." Nappi grinned at me through the glass, his teeth showing almost an iridescent bluish white in the moonlight.

"I'm not asleep."

"Maybe you should be."

"You think this is crazy, don't you?" I asked.

"I think it's important we don't get caught. If we get caught, then it's crazy."

I got out of the car, and Nappi and I climbed the gate into the field fronting the Cypress property.

"Where's the cemetery located?" he asked.

"It's behind the house and the outbuildings. If there are lights on in the house, then we'll give this up for now."

Nappi looked up into the night sky. Toward the west we could see clouds begin to gather.

"I say we wait for an hour or so. By that time anyone in the house should be asleep, and I think we've got a storm moving in. Better cover for our work."

Anxious as I was to get on with it, I agreed. All that bright moonlight would be like shining a spotlight on us.

I saw lightning shoot from the clouds to the ground and heard thunder in the distance. The wind began to pick up, and I was reminded of the night I was attacked in my house. I shivered, although the night air was hot and muggy.

"Are you okay, Eve?" Nappi must have guessed the reason for my anxiety. "We can return another night, or better yet, come up with another plan to find out what we need to know."

"I'm fine."

Droplets of rain hit my face, and the trees along the fence line began to sway in the wind.

"Nobody's going to see us now," Nappi said.

We started our trek toward the house.

"I think we'd be better to come up on the graveyard from the back. That way it will be between us and the house." I led the way to circle the house and the small cemetery, entering the woods beyond them. I intended to come through the stand of palms, cypress, and strangler figs and into the rear of the graveyard. In the darkness of the woods, Nappi and I moved from tree to tree with our flashlights off. We both knew we ran the risk of disturbing some night creature slithering through the bed of leaves.

Suddenly I stumbled over an obstacle in my path and fell headfirst onto a raised mound of dirt. The white iron fence surrounding the graveyard loomed just in front of us. Another several inches and I would have fallen onto one of the pointed metal decorations that made up the posts of the fence.

"That was close." Nappi reached out and pulled me to my feet.

"What did I trip on?" I asked.

"Looks like someone recently dug a grave here." Nappi pointed to the mound of disturbed soil. "If we had the shovel you made me leave behind, we might be able to find out what's in there."

"I rethought the shovel. I don't want to disturb anything. I just want to look. Besides, we know what's in that grave." I pointed to a crudely fashioned wooden cross that had been placed near the mound of dirt. On the cross was the word "Brownie."

"The family dog," Nappi said.

"Uhm," I replied.

"Let's see what the cemetery holds."

I followed Nappi around the perimeter of the fence until we came to the gate. It opened easily, without a sound, not that anyone could have heard a creak with the gusts of wind and the thunder rolling in from the west.

As we entered the cemetery, lighting hit in front of us, illuminating the house, which was closer than I had realized.

"Someone looking out the window could have seen us," warned Nappi. "Maybe we should get out of here."

"Not yet. I just want to see how arrogant this family is."

"You really expect them to dig a grave for their son's remains and not try to hide it?" asked Nappi.

"Maybe. I don't know, but I need to find out."

Through the sheets of water, we looked for evidence of newly disturbed soil. We didn't find it, but we did find a marker.

"Albert Cypress, Beloved Son," it read.

The marker was old, and there was no sign of disturbed soil to indicate a grave had been dug there recently.

Were my suspicions wrong?

"Let's get out of here before anyone catches us." I grabbed Nappi's hand and pulled him toward the woods.

"WE GOT OFF lucky," said Nappi.

The two of us were back at my house, drying out our clothes and sipping tumblers of Scotch.

We spoke in whispers so we didn't awaken Max. Grandy was

already up when we arrived. She sat in the recliner, clucking her tongue at Nappi and me. Between clucks she told me what an idiot I was and informed Nappi she couldn't believe he didn't have the sense God gave a chicken. How could he justify aiding and abetting my crime?

"You're the adult," she said, as if I were a mere child.

He gave her a stern look. "I am also a mob guy, in case you've forgotten. This is stuff we do. We like it. We take chances, and if they don't pay off, we hire lawyers to get us off."

She waved her pudgy arms dismissively as if she held a magic wand to make him disappear.

I was certain I was right. It all made sense. It all fit, but how to prove it?

Nappi, reading my mind yet again, set his glass on the coffee table. "I know what I would do. I'd get my shovel and start digging up that graveyard, but that would be highly illegal."

"Where would you dig?" asked Grandy. "Eve said there were no new graves there. And that the marker for the son's grave or what would become his grave when they found him was not a new burial. You'd have to dig up the entire cemetery."

Suddenly it hit me. "There is a new grave there."

"A dog's grave behind the cemetery," said Nappi.

"Or so we've been led to believe."

I WAITED UNTIL morning to call Frida, asking if she could look at the tire molds the crime scene technicians had taken of the tire tracks in the dried mud behind the trees near the construction site. The forensics lab had identified the tires as those used on big trucks, information she had from day one. Until now those tracks seemed unimportant, but the foreman confirmed a truck had been parked in that location from the time the construction began. With the foreman's description of the man sitting in that truck in the stand of trees near the construction site and his indication that the logo on the side of the four-door white truck with dually wheels in the back was that of the Cypress Ranch, Frida might just have enough for a search warrant.

"Am I right? Do you have enough for a search warrant?" I asked her as we sat in a corner of Sabal Bay's favorite breakfast spot. It was an hour after most of the breakfast crowd gathered, so we had the place mostly to ourselves apart from a few men in suits—local bankers, I surmised, getting their usual late start on their money-managing day.

"It's a tricky case, but it fits together if you look at all the pieces as a whole. I would have bet my job that the truck hidden in those trees had to be from Gator Way. Weren't you surprised the foreman said it was a Cypress Ranch vehicle?"

"Well, a little, but once he did, everything seemed to fall into place. Am I going to get into trouble for trespassing on Cypress land last night?"

"It was a dark and stormy night. You just lost your way and wandered in there. Right?"

I nodded.

"Now I need to find a judge savvy enough to see the pattern, and willing to take a chance on offending one of the most powerful families in this town. I'd better get moving on this. Wish me luck." She got up and started for the door in a hurry.

"I'll get the bill," I yelled at her, but the door had already closed on her retreating form.

At noon, as I was about to go on a lunch run for Madeleine and me, Frida entered the shop with a smile on her face. "Got it." She waved a paper in my direction. "Want to see?"

I nodded, and Madeleine and I gathered around as Frida spread the search warrant out on the counter. We read it quickly.

"Carefully worded. I'm meeting my guys out there now. I've got to hurry."

"I wish I could come with you," I said.

Frida hesitated, tapping the warrant with her finger. "Well,

I've got no one to say otherwise, and I am short-handed as you know, so I guess I can call you one of the private investigators I took on for this case."

"I don't have a license."

"I'm sure Crusty McNabb will vouch for you as an apprentice, should anyone ask. Let's pop next door and see what he says."

McNabb was sitting with his feet up on his desk, the surface of which was littered with papers, sticky notes, and old coffee cups. One of his cigars burned in an overflowing ashtray.

"I thought you were coming back here to fill out some paperwork," said McNabb. "I guess you chickened out again. And here I thought Alex was right about your detecting skills."

Frida dismissed his remarks and launched into her story about how she needed his help. For once, I kept my mouth shut.

McNabb listened, reached in his desk drawer and drew out a sheet of paper. "Sign this," he said to me.

"Let me read it." I pulled the paper toward me.

Frida grabbed the paper, picked up a pen off the desk and shoved it into my hand. "I'm sure he knows what he's doing. It's his hide, you know, his business, his reputation. We need to get moving, Eve. Sign the damn thing."

So I did.

At the Cypress Ranch, the father met us at the front door, where Frida handed him the search warrant.

"What's she doing here?" he asked, pointing to me.

"One of the police's private investigators," said Frida. "Now let's get this over with." She tried to maneuver herself past Mr. Cypress, but he blocked her way.

"I need to call my lawyer, my son."

"I can wait, but he'll tell you to cooperate."

Cypress removed a cellphone from his pocket and turned away. I couldn't hear the conversation, but I assumed it was with Danny.

He turned to face us again. "My son will be here in five minutes. I'd like him to see the warrant."

"Certainly." Frida was being very patient with him, but then, she had him in her sights. There was no way he could tamper with what the warrant specified in the search.

A black Escalade sped up the drive and slammed on its brakes in front of the house. Danny Cypress jumped out.

"Let me see it." He held out his hand and Frida gave him the warrant. He read it over quickly. "This looks legitimate. Do your search." If he or his father was worried about the search, neither their body language or their faces betrayed any anxiety.

Danny turned to me. "I knew you were trouble the first time I saw you. I should never have invited you to my house."

"I thought the invitation was a mistake also, but it was your idea." I was being smug about my position here and I knew it, but I wasn't frightened, at least not until I saw the black looks on the two men's faces. If this search didn't yield what I hoped it would, I'd be looking over my shoulder for the rest of my life.

We proceeded to the cemetery. As we trekked through the field in front of the fenced-in graveyard, I looked back at the house and saw a face at one of the upstairs windows. It looked like that of Mrs. Cypress. This search would cause her more pain, regardless of how successful or unsuccessful it was.

Cypress Senior opened the gate to the cemetery and gestured for Frida, me and the other officers to go through.

"Not here," I said to Frida. "Back there." I pointed to the marker and freshly dug dog's grave on the other side of the cemetery.

"Wait a minute. The warrant specifies you'll be digging into a grave to find my son's bones. That's where we buried the dog. Here's where you're authorized to dig." Mr. Cypress pointed to the cemetery and placed himself in Frida's path.

"The warrant gives us the right to dig up graves, and that's where we want to begin." She pointed beyond the cemetery to the burial site of the dog. "Your son's bones were not moved to the cemetery, but to the dog's grave."

Mr. Cypress turned away and gazed out into the woods. Something had gone out of his face. His shoulders slumped as if in defeat.

Danny approached his father and touched his arm, but he said nothing.

"Go dig," said Mr. Cypress. "I'm going back into the house to be with my wife."

Danny turned as if to accompany his father, but he pushed his son away and shook his head.

"I'll accompany you," Danny said to Frida, "to make certain you do it right."

There was no fight left in the father, but Danny wasn't willing to admit defeat.

The officers began to execute the warrant, shovels biting into the black dirt of the lake basin, uncovering what I feared they would: dog bones. They removed the body of the animal and looked at me and Frida.

"Did deeper," said Frida.

They did. The dirt came out of the hole with ease, and I began to hope I had been right about my hunch. One of the shovels made a sound as if hitting an object more solid than loose soil.

"Got something here," the man said.

Frida and I approached the hole and peered in. A long gray bone emerged from the dirt. It looked like a man's femur.

Danny Cypress shook his head and walked off toward the trees. I followed him.

"Don't you think it's time for the truth to come out? Your father killed your brother, didn't he? What did he do to make a father do that to his own son?"

Danny said nothing.

"And what did he do to you to make you willing to kill Walter Egret to help cover up the murder?"

Danny spun around to face me. There was a murderous black look on his face as he reached out. I turned to run back to the newly uncovered grave, but Danny grabbed my arm and pulled me to him, moving his hand up to my neck and squeezing.

"Danny, you're hurting me." I choked the words out of my mouth. Frida saw Danny's stranglehold on me. She pulled her gun from her holster and ran toward us.

"Let her go, Danny." Frida leveled her gun at him.

I could smell the fear in the sweat that dampened his shirt front. He extracted a gun from his jacket pocket and pressed the barrel against my head. I tried to stomp on his instep with my heel, but he avoided my move and only tightened his hold on my neck.

Dead. I was dead.

Chapter 22

———

"I tried to defend you, Eve. I thought you were worth saving."

As the world began to turn black around me, my brain registered what I thought would be my final attempt to get the truth from Danny.

"Save me? How?" I managed to squeak out.

"I sent Connie Russo to warn you away from this case, to keep you out of it, to keep you away from tracking down these bones. It was our family secret and meant to stay that way." There was a note of pride in his voice, as if his actions had been those of a knight coming to the rescue of his damsel.

His grip on me loosened for a moment, allowing me to speak. "Then, of course, you had to tie up loose ends. You killed Connie."

"He was a slug, a piece of garbage. After I took out the backhoe operator, he stole that watch off his body. He was told not to take anything. *Anything!*"

By now Danny was yelling. Saliva flew from his mouth onto my face.

"I think you intended to lay the blame on Connie for Walter's hit-and-run, and then get rid of him, but you used him one last time when you sent him after me."

"Father told me that wasn't smart."

"Was it your father's idea to kill him or yours?" I asked.

He didn't answer, only pressed the gun tighter against my head.

"Don't do it, Danny," Frida warned, coming closer, her weapon aimed at him.

Then I felt his arm loosen, and I realized the wetness I felt on my face was no longer his spit, but his tears.

He shoved me away and inserted the barrel of the gun into his own mouth.

"Drop the gun, Danny. It's not worth it." Frida continued to advance on him.

I looked at Danny and then back at the house.

"Danny, your mother is here. You don't want to cause her any more pain, do you? Hasn't she suffered enough?"

Danny's eyes shifted from Frida to the sight of his mother being wheeled by his sister across the field to the cemetery. Mother and daughter were close enough to hear Danny and me as well as Frida.

"Don't kill my boy," said Mrs. Cypress. "Please don't."

Danny's gaze locked with his mother's. He lowered his arm, and Frida swept in to take his gun away. She signaled her men, who cuffed him and walked him toward the police cars in front of the house.

Mr. Cypress had been only a few steps behind his wife and daughter. He placed his hand on his wife's shoulder and squeezed it gently. She turned her face up to his, and he bent down to place a kiss on her lips. He looked across the small cemetery, toward the mound of dirt that once held his son's bones. "I killed him. I did it." His voice broke with strangled emotion, and he looked at Frida, who nodded and placed the cuffs on his wrists. I watched Frida and Cypress follow his son to the police cars and caught a few words as she read him his rights.

THAT NIGHT, AFTER Grandy, Max, and I finished a later supper, Frida came to my door looking as bone tired as if she had been dragged by an alligator through the swamp. She showed no sign of exhilaration or relief that the case was closed. Her eyes were dull with resignation and her jaw was tight with strain.

I handed her a snifter of brandy and she sank into my couch with a groan.

"Tell us what happened." I took the seat next to her while Grandy and Max sat across the room.

We had to sit forward in our chairs to hear her, as her voice was uncharacteristically low and flat. "Mr. Cypress, the Senior, asked for a lawyer once we booked him."

"And you got the confession from him on tape?" I asked.

"No. On the advice of his lawyer, he refuses to answer our questions. I'm sure the bones will be identified as his son's and we'll be able to place them at the original burial site near the lake, but there's still a lot of forensic work to be done. Cause of death, for example."

"What about Danny? He said he killed Russo."

Frida took a gulp of brandy and shook her head. "He lawyered up too, and he's following the man's advice to remain silent. I'm sure he took the car from the company lot, picked up Russo and ran down Walter Egret. Russo took the watch without letting Danny Cypress know. We'll get him for either Russo's murder or Egret's. Somehow. The whole thing is a mess though." Frida finished her brandy and set the glass on the coffee table.

"Do you think Danny was involved in his older brother's death somehow?" I asked.

Frida shook her head. "He had to have been, what, only five or so when the brother was killed. If he was an eyewitness, that must have traumatized him. And I don't think it was his idea to kill Walter. I think Danny was doing his father's bidding. The father must have been the watcher at the construction site, fearing what would happen if the bones were unearthed. He saw Walter get close to the body and couldn't take the chance that he'd seen or taken something incriminating." Frida yawned, sank back into the sofa cushions, and closed her eyes.

I decided not to ask her any more questions about the case tonight. "Your mom taking care of your kids tonight?"

She nodded, her chin dropped to her chest, and I could hear her breaths even out. She was sound asleep.

Fetching a blanket from my bedroom closet, I tucked it around her. I knew she wouldn't sleep there for long before heading home to her kids, but for now she needed the rest. We all headed for our beds, but I was certain I wouldn't get much sleep.

I'd just rolled over for at least the fifth time when my phone rang. I glanced at my bedside clock, which read one a.m. Who could be calling at this hour? My heart began to race as I picked up the phone. Could it be Sammy?

It was Amanda Cypress. "My mother wants to talk with you and your detective friend."

"When?" I was curious what could be so important she would call at this hour.

"Now. Can you get ahold of the detective? I don't want to call the station. Can you talk the detective into keeping this visit just among us for now?"

I thought I could talk Frida into it.

When I entered the living room to wake Frida, she was already up and moving around the kitchen making a pot of coffee.

"I heard the phone ring. A call at this hour of the morning can't be anything good, so I thought you might need a jolt of caffeine."

"You'll need it too." I explained our errand.

* * *

Only a light in the central hallway and one to the left of the door shone when we pulled into the drive. Amanda met us at the door and showed us into her father's study, where Mrs. Cypress sat waiting for us in her chair. Although the look of overwhelming sadness still shadowed her face, I could see something else in her expression, a look of determination and of even greater pain than before. It was as if she had made a decision she knew would make things worse for her family.

I was surprised at her voice when she spoke. She had said little when Shelley and I brought the dress selections to the house, and I hadn't taken notice of her speech earlier when she begged Frida not to shoot her son. I guess I expected her voice to match the sorrow on her face, that I would have to strain to hear it. I expected her accent to be heavy, since she came from Guatemala. Instead she spoke clear, unaccented English that carried easily across the room to where Frida and I had taken seats.

"I've kept this story to myself for too long, and I need you to hear it."

Amanda interrupted. "I told Mother she shouldn't be speaking to you, but she insisted. She thinks the secrets in this family are devouring our souls." Amanda sighed. "She may be right."

Mrs. Cypress didn't address her words to us. Instead her gaze wandered to the window, and she spoke while looking out across the field, as if talking to the grave where we had uncovered her son's bones. "I came from Guatemala many years ago, sent here by my family using human traffickers. My family were poor farmers, most of their land stolen by the government. I paid my way to this country with my body, something Danny Cypress was aware of because he met me in a brothel in El Paso. What I had done to save myself was of no importance to him. We were in love, so he bought my freedom and brought me back here to his home. Life seemed good. First we had a son. No other children followed, and we thought we should feel blessed with just one, but we felt overjoyed when Danny Junior was born some years later. It was almost a miracle. But as our first son moved into his teen years, he took up with a crowd of no-good boys—racing cars, smoking dope, drinking, stealing. His father bailed him out of trouble many times and finally told him he would not rescue him anymore. We knew he had stolen merchandise from a pawn shop in town. I think he took many items, but one of them was a beautiful pocket watch with a water bird engraved on the front cover. I saw him with it and asked him where he got it. He told me to mind my own business and stormed out of the room.

"Then I did a foolish thing. I had to know what else he had taken, so I went into his room and started to go through his drawers. He caught me and flew into a rage. He grabbed me and pushed me down onto the bed, tore off my clothes and assaulted me. In the doorway, I saw young Danny watching. I was horrified and ashamed of what my son was doing to me and even more ashamed that my youngest son was watching. Suddenly Danny ran from the doorway, and for a moment, I was relieved he was no longer a witness to his brother's depravity and my shame, but then I worried he had gone to get his father. I did not want my husband to see what his son was doing. I knew his anger would have been overwhelming and that he could not control himself. My oldest boy continued his assault of me, calling me names.

" 'Whore. You're nothing but a whore. Isn't this what whores do?' he yelled.

"And then he was silent. His blood spilled over my body. I looked up to find my husband standing over us.

" 'I'll take care of this,' he said.

"He pulled the boy's body off mine, carried him off and told me later he had buried him out at the lake. I have visited him every day since then, for more than thirty years. When his bones were moved here, I continued to visit the grave. My husband lied to me and told me he moved the bones to the cemetery. He didn't tell me he buried them with the dog's body, but maybe that's a fitting resting place for a son so filled with anger and hatred for his mother." Her gaze fell to her hands, clenched tightly in her lap.

Frida got up from her chair and crossed the room to place her hand gently on the woman's shoulder. "I understand. That's the reason your husband wouldn't talk about how he came to kill his son. He was too ashamed of what the boy did to you. He wanted to protect you, didn't he?"

Mrs. Cypress' head jerked up, and she met Frida's gaze. "You do not understand. He didn't shoot our son. I did."

AMANDA AND HER mother sat in the back of Frida's cruiser. Neither Frida nor I doubted Mrs. Cypress' version of the shooting. It all made some kind of tragic sense. I knew Frida's question now would be what Mr. Cypress would say about the shooting. I suspected he would want to cover for his wife by signing a confession.

At the house, Frida had pointed out to Mrs. Cypress that her actions were in self-defense. She nodded in agreement. "I know."

"So I don't understand why you wouldn't report what happened," Frida said, her voice sympathetic. The words were barely out of her mouth when the expression on Frida's face revealed she suddenly realized the truth, but I voiced it for her.

"Because her son's act was so shameful. No parent wants to admit that a mother had to defend herself from a child's assault, especially a sexual assault," I said.

Mrs. Cypress added, "There's more. I was married in Guatemala, and there was no divorce. Danny Cypress and I never married. We couldn't. I'm here illegally."

The story of the assault and the reasons for covering it up continued to race through my mind as Frida drove us to police headquarters. No one spoke. Frida escorted Mrs. Cypress into an interrogation room and asked Amanda and me to remain outside.

"What will happen to my mother?" asked Amanda.

"I don't know." I steered her toward a chair in the hallway. "I'm certain Frida will be kind, and she will sort this out."

But would she? Could she? Mr. Cypress had told us he was responsible, then refused to say more, but knowing how protective he was of his wife, he would not want her story to stand. I was certain his wife was repeating what she had said at the house and would be signing a formal admission of responsibility after Frida questioned her. I slipped my arm around Amanda's shoulders.

"I guess the real question is what will happen to my family."

"Do you think you should call your brothers at their homes? I know they don't live with you and your parents. Shouldn't they know what's happened?"

Amanda replied in a barely audible whisper, "I guess so."

I handed my cell to her. She took it from my hand, and I walked away to give her privacy, something I was certain no one in the family would have from now on.

She returned in a few minutes, wiping tears from her cheeks. I didn't want to ask her this question, and I wasn't certain whether Frida would be angry if I did, but I felt I should prepare her for what might come.

"Did Danny see your mother shoot his brother?"

"I think so."

What a traumatic end to an already horrible event for a small child to witness. It didn't make me like Danny Cypress Junior any better, but it gave me some insight into the troubled life he had led.

Amanda resumed her seat in the chair next to mine. "And before you need to ask, we all knew most of the story. Well, we knew my mother had killed our oldest brother. We didn't know why she did it, but we were told not to reveal what she did or she would be sent back to Guatemala. It was something we never discussed until a few weeks ago, when the bones came back to rest at the ranch."

What a troubling mess this all was, emotionally and legally. Frida wouldn't be able to sort this out on her own. I assumed the district attorney's office would wrestle with the case for some time until they determined what charges to press and against whom.

There was a commotion at the end of the hall, and Amanda's two older brothers, looks of rage on their faces, barged through the door and down the hallway. The two men clasped their sister in their arms.

Just then Frida left the interview room. When they spotted her, the brothers turned their anger on her.

"What the hell is happening?" the oldest brother yelled.

The other brother pushed his way past Amanda and me and confronted Frida, who didn't retreat a foot.

"You can't go in there now. You'll have a chance later to see your mother, but for now, you need to back off." Frida directed her next comments to all of them. "And once this is sorted out, I'm sure you'll be hearing from the authorities. I'm sorry, but that's all I can say for now."

I left Amanda in the arms of her brothers and exited police headquarters. Grandy and Max sat in their car in the parking lot. I was so happy to see them that I burst into tears and scared my Grandy half to death.

"I've never been so happy to see family as I am now. You don't know how wonderfully uncomplicated you look to me."

"I'll make pancakes and bacon." Grandy tucked me into the backseat of the car. Comfort in the form of family and food. What could be better?

CHAPTER 23

—

ONCE WE WERE home I was too tired to eat, so I fell into bed and slept without dreams until I awoke to the smell of swamp water and vegetation. Early morning light penetrated the sliding glass door and moved across to my dresser, where I caught sight of something familiar. My amulet lay on top of the bureau, and my heart gave a flutter of anticipation.

Was I imagining this?

I could hear the shower running in my bathroom. On my way across the room, I stumbled over a pile of clothing in front of the bathroom door. I kicked the clothes out of my way and opened the door. Steam rose from behind the shower curtain, then the shower stopped and a lean brown hand moved the curtain aside. Sammy stood there, droplets of water streaming down his body. He gave me a slow smile and reached out. I slipped my nightgown over my head and stepped in. He turned the water back on and pulled me into him.

"My Sammy," was all he allowed me to say before he pressed his full lips against mine. If the heat of the water didn't melt me, then Sammy's love would.

Later, as the sun rose higher in a cloudless cerulean sky, we talked.

"I know this will be difficult for you, my sweet impatient Eve, but I need time to think over my journey into the swamps and what I learned there. It was not quite what I expected. Can you give me that?"

Of course, I could. I would give Sammy whatever he needed.

"You take the time you need to understand that journey. When you do, you'll help me and the boys understand too. I know you, Sammy Egret. You are like all the Egrets, not given to impulse. I can tell this journey is not complete. Your brain needs time to process what you found. I can wait."

"Is Eve Appel developing patience?" Sammy expressed his disbelief with a soft snort.

"Following your example." I gave him a playful punch on his arm and changed the subject. "I assume Grandfather knows you're home?"

He laughed. "Because of some Miccosukee sixth sense?"

"How else?"

"Maybe he heard me start my truck when I beached my canoe to come here to see you."

There was that possibility also, but I preferred the sixth sense explanation.

"How are our boys?" he asked.

"They missed you."

"Did they say that?"

"No, but I could see it in their eyes. They'll be glad you're back."

"And are you glad?" He moved his fingers over my face as if he was comparing its physical presence to what was in his memories.

"Our shower wasn't evidence of how I feel?"

He smiled.

"You were pretty stinky, and you left your clothes on my bedroom floor. Now it smells like a gator hole."

"So you're saying you wouldn't have expressed your appreciation for my return quite as enthusiastically if I hadn't jumped in the shower first?'

"I wouldn't have come within twenty feet of you."

Sammy got out of bed, crossed the room and grabbed his clothing, which remained where he'd dropped it. He sniffed and wrinkled his nose.

I patted the bed. "We can wash them later. Come here. I want to make certain you understand how happy I am you're back, regardless of the smell."

Sammy grinned, opened the slider to my yard and tossed the clothes out the door. He jumped back in bed and put his arms around me, then stopped and sniffed again.

"What's that I smell now?" he asked.

I had smelled it too. "Grandy promised me pancakes and bacon last night, but I was too tired to eat. I think she's making good on her promise this morning."

"I'm starving," he said.

"Me too, but you can't go out there. You don't have any clothes to wear. You just tossed them."

"Hey, you're the wardrobe mistress. There must be something in your closet for me."

Grandy yelled from the kitchen. "Come on, you two. The food's getting cold." Now how did she know Sammy was here and that we were awake? Was I the only one who didn't have the sight?

I grabbed my nightgown and threw the matching robe over it.

Sammy came to the breakfast table in my red silk kimono. He looked really fine in it.

WE CHOSE TO be married by a justice of the peace at the county courthouse and then to celebrate at Grandfather's house, where tribal members brought their good wishes for our happiness and traditional food for the feast. Grandfather had purchased a pig from a local farmer and had begun cooking it in a metal box buried in the ground, coals surrounding it, a process he had learned from some of his Cuban friends. He started the roasting early in the morning, and by the time we arrived at his house, the pig was done and being removed from the container. I loved the crackly skin and ate too much.

All my family and friends attended, contributing to the feast: Nappi's lasagna, Grandy's rice pudding, Madeleine's garlic bread, and other dishes too numerous to mention and too tasty not to overindulge in. Frida appeared only for a short time, looking exhausted but happy for Sammy and me. Drawing me to one side, she confessed she was still elbow-deep in the Cypress case and probably would be for some time because the charges were so complicated. The evidence to bring the guilty to court had to be laid out clearly, the deaths of Egret and Russo untangled from the murder thirty years earlier.

"Mrs. Cypress hasn't changed her story?" I asked.

"No, and now her husband has signed a confession of his own. The man loves her and wants to protect her, but no one can make him see that his story won't help anyone." Frida gazed off across the yard and into the canal beyond. "This case makes me wonder if I should even be a cop."

"You're a good cop. You know that. You just need some rest."

"That I do." She ran her hands through her hair. "Well, I didn't come here to bring you down, only to wish both of you well. I've got to get back to the station, but first I wanted to give you this." She handed me an envelope. "It's not really a wedding gift, more of a shower gift for you. I know we already gave you a shower. I wanted to add this."

"If there's a sexy negligee in here, it's mighty small." I tapped the card against my leg.

"Open it and see if you like it. I can always return it. Actually, it's from both of us."

Both of whom? Before I could ask, Sammy came up to Frida, gave her a hug, and steered her toward the food. Our three boys grabbed my hand and insisted I come down to the canal and join them in sailing the small wooden boats Grandfather had made for them. I tucked the envelope in my pocket.

"Did you eat?" I asked them.

They nodded, and we launched the crafts along the canal, running after them into the shallow water before they could sail away.

Jeremy leaned against my leg as we watched the tiny boats catch the breeze and take off.

"Better catch yours now before it's lost," I told him.

"I want it to go out there, out into the swamps. Someday it might come back to me. Wouldn't that be great?"

I looked down into my youngest son's face and thought how like his great grandfather he was. I hugged him to me, and he wrapped his arms around my legs.

"Can I call you Mommy?"

SAMMY AND I decided our honeymoon would be a long weekend at the shack in the swamp, the place we had shared so many wonderful times. It seemed only fitting that our marriage should begin where we first suspected there was something between us. We knew the wedding festivities would run late into the night, but we were eager to be off to our hideaway, so we sneaked away after dark to the canoe and pushed it into the still waters. We glided by an object bobbing in the water, and I realized it was one of the wooden boats belonging to the boys. I pointed it out to Sammy. He had reached over the side of the canoe and was about to pick it up when I stopped him.

"Let it go. Jeremy wants it to travel the swamps in hopes it will someday return home to him."

Sammy nodded and we continued on our way, leaving the little craft bobbing on the water's surface. A breeze came up and caught it, pushing it down a smaller side channel. It was lost to our sight.

Sammy's paddle cut into the smooth surface of the canal, and we glided toward the landing area where we knew the resident mama gator would be watching. You don't make friends with gators, but this one had become accustomed to our presence and must know we were no threat. When she had a nest of babies, that might change, but tonight, when we beached the canoe, we saw no sign of her.

We picked our way up the path to the shack and zipped our two sleeping bags together. Before we climbed in, I reached down to remove the boots I had worn to the ceremony and party. They were a gift from Sammy, a designer brand I'd never worn before, never come across in any of my shopping trips, never knew I'd find so lovely. I caressed the soft rawhide leather of the knee-high boots. There was no three-inch heel on them, only a sole like a moccasin's. I found them particularly comfortable and loved Sammy for having them made especially for me. They were my Sammy designer boots.

"I know you won't switch from your signature footwear. I understand stilettos are you, Eve, but you might like these as an alternative."

I did. I loved them.

"I have a present for you, too." I reached into my pocket, extracted a soft rawhide drawstring bag, and handed it to him.

He pulled the top open and tilted the contents into his hand. The moon shone off the bird etching on the face of the gold watch.

His eyes glistened as he looked at me in wonder. "Where did you find this? I thought it had been destroyed in Connie Russo's fire."

"Somehow I couldn't believe it could be destroyed that way, not after over thirty years resting in the dirt of the lake basin. You know what Grandfather says about the swamp returning what it takes. Perhaps the lake was the same. And I also figured Connie Russo wouldn't keep it. I hoped he'd pawned it before he was killed. It took some hunting through pawn shops up and down the coast, but I found it. I knew I would. I took it to a jeweler to be cleaned and repaired, but it works."

"You are one patient woman," said Sammy.

"No, I'm not. I'm just stubborn. I don't like to give up."

As we settled in our sleeping bags and I shifted to face Sammy, something poked me in the side.

"What the ...?" Then I remembered the envelope from Frida.

"Turn on the lantern, would you?" I explained to Sammy about Frida giving me the gift earlier tonight.

"What is it?" Sammy shined the light on the card as I withdrew it from the envelope.

"Unfinished business," I said. "It's from Crusty McNabb and Frida."

I showed him the card, which read:

"Flirting with Sammy Egret leads to marriage, but flirting with bad guys can be lethal."

"It's a gift card for the shooting range." I wasn't certain whether to be amused or angry.

"What are you going to do with it?"

I turned to him and kissed his cheek. "You are such a good man. You could have told me what you thought I should do with it, but instead you're going to let me make up my own mind."

"I'm not only good, but I know you. Telling Eve Appel what to do is like wrestling a fifteen-foot gator. I'm not that dumb."

"I'm not certain what I'm going to do with it yet."

"Uhm," was all Sammy said, then he rolled over and pulled me to him. "Later." He extinguished the lantern.

"Later," I said, meeting his embrace.

SEVERAL DAYS AFTER we returned from our honeymoon, I tried to find Frida at police headquarters, but the duty officer there said she'd taken vacation time to get some rest. I knew better than to disturb her. She needed time away from the case. Instead I decided to stop by Crusty McNabb's office. It was early enough in the morning that I had thirty minutes before I opened the shop.

Crusty looked up from his messy desk as I entered his office. The only difference between the desktop this morning and when I had last visited was an increase in the number of coffee, fast-food bags, cups, and stacks of papers added to the already overflowing piles.

He grinned and offered me coffee. "I was wondering when you'd stop by. You signed a contract, you know."

I glanced over at the coffeemaker sitting on a TV table under the window. The sludge in there looked like the bluish-black color of the dirt in a sugarcane field. "Frida showed the paper to me. It's a good thing the authorities didn't want to see proof I was your apprentice. The contract was from the rental center for a new compact fridge."

"And I expect you to honor it. I had the old one carted off to the dump yesterday." He propped his foot up on the desk and one of the stacks of paper slipped to one side, teetered for a moment, then fell onto the floor. I started to pick up the papers.

"Leave it."

"Some more contracts from the rental place? Maybe for a desk chair." I pointed to the one he was tilted back in. "That one looks as if it might fall apart any minute."

"Have a seat." He signaled to an equally rickety chair in front of the desk, then unwrapped a large cigar, cut off the tip, and lit it. Smoke wafted around his head and across to me. I coughed, but decided to ignore the smell. For now.

I slid into the chair and laid the wedding/shower gift in front of him. "Explain this."

"You've been in here several times circling around the idea of becoming a PI. Detective Martinez and I just thought you'd like to see how you felt about handling a weapon. It's usually part of the job, you know."

"Is it a necessary requirement?" I'd seen too many times

what firing a gun could do, and I wasn't eager to put myself in a position where I might have to do it.

"Nope, but lookie here. I think people should make decisions based upon information, not their own prejudices or whatever. You can't decide whether or not you'll carry if you haven't tried shooting a gun, and I'm betting you haven't fired one." He blew some more smoke across the desk. I waved it away.

"It's not as if I tackle the bad guys unarmed."

Crusty looked curious. "You carry a knife or something?"

"Nope. Don't you remember? We had this discussion before. These are lethal." I lifted one of my stiletto, three-inch Manolo Blahnik slave-strap sandals to show him, then plopped it down on his desk to join his boots there.

He waved them away as if they were as insubstantial as his cigar smoke. "Do the gun range and see if you think your sandals can hold up to a .45 or a .38. And remove your shoe from my desk."

"You've got yours up there."

"Yeah, but it's my desk."

"Okay." I shifted my foot back to the floor. "But here's the deal. I sign a contract with you to become your apprentice— and I mean a real contract—I do the gun range, and then I decide how I feel about a gun."

He smiled and held out his hand.

I ignored it. "One more thing, however."

"Name it."

"No smoking in the office. It's not good for you, I hate it, and I'm certain your clients have complained."

"Damn, you're a hard woman."

"So I've been told."

We stood and shook hands.

Eve Appel, I asked myself, *what are you getting into?* Was I really ready to be a pistol-packin' fashionista?

Epilogue

In Miami, after the two gang bangers were brought up on charges and before they were led away by the bailiffs, they signaled to their gang members in the courtroom. The gang needed to find the young man they had coerced and threatened into firing the shot that killed Alex Montgomery and make certain that boy could not testify against them when they came to trial. But in the days afterwards, no sign of the young man or his sister and mother could be found at their apartment or with any of the family's relatives and friends. They had vanished from the city. It was rumored that a mob boss along with his street-smart lawyer had hidden the family out of town and would return the young man only when he was needed to appear in court. In the meantime, most of the gang members disappeared from their usual haunts. They grew suspicious of one another, and the number of members decreased, taken out by rival gangs or arrested by the police for various crimes in the area. Again, rumors were circulating that the mob boss had used his sources to discover and feed vital information about the gang to the authorities, information that finally took them off the streets and put them in jail or moved them into hiding. One less gang preyed upon the city's residents.

Although Sammy Egret's journey into the swamp to look for his father was over, he wasn't certain his search would ever be. On a summer night not long after he and Eve were married, he paddled his family, wife, and three boys into the swamp. It was cool for July and the weeks of rain had left the fields green and the swamp lush. On this night, however, the sky was clear. The family decided it was a good night to spend in the shack Sammy and Eve had claimed as theirs. The boys were excited at the prospect of staying overnight there. Eve was also, perhaps because she felt this trip would reveal something important about the swamp, something Sammy had not yet shared with her.

Sammy cautioned the children not to stray from the path once they landed the canoe, warning them that the mama gator who resided there was tolerant of their passage to the shack but perhaps unwilling to allow wandering around her territory. He built a fire in the area where the shack's roof had collapsed and the sparks and flames could reach into the night. The family huddled around it, the boys chattering happily about being able to help their great grandfather with the airboat business and their father at David Wilson's game ranch. Sammy and Eve talked about selling her house and building a new one on Grandfather's property.

The fire died down, and the boys' eyes began to close. Sammy scooted over to be closer to his wife, and Eve rested her head on his shoulder. Quiet descended on the little shack in the clearing of palm trees.

A branch cracked, and everyone was on alert, worrying that the gator had decided they had intruded into her place too long. Eve pulled the boys to her, but Sammy stood up and walked beyond the dying embers to the edge of the trees. He stood there for a moment. Beyond him, moving through the trees, Eve could see a figure of a man. She watched Sammy hesitate, then move forward. She rose and pulled the boys close, concerned that the intruder meant to do them harm. When the two men stood together, they grabbed each other's forearms and embraced.

"Sammy, who is it?" Eve asked.

Sammy turned back to his family, his hand on the man's shoulder.

"This is my father."

Creations in Fotografia by Rafael Pacheco

LESLEY A. DIEHL retired from her life as a professor of psychology and reclaimed her country roots by moving to a small cottage in the Butternut River Valley in Upstate New York. In the winter, she migrates to old Florida—cowboys, scrub palmetto, and open fields of grazing cattle, a place where spurs still jingle in the post office, and gators make golf a contact sport. Back north, the shy ghost inhabiting the cottage serves as her literary muse. When not writing, she gardens, cooks and renovates the 1874 cottage with the help of her husband, two cats and, of course, Fred the ghost, who gives artistic direction to their work.

She is the author of a number of mystery series and mysteries as well as short stories. *Old Bones Never Die* follows the first four books in the Eve Appel mystery series, *A Secondhand Murder*, *Dead in the Water*, *A Sporting Murder*, and *Mud Bog Murder*.

Visit her on her website: www.lesleyadiehl.com.

Now catch up on the first three Eve Appel Mysteries

Spunky Eve Appel moves from Connecticut to rural Florida intent on starting a new life as the owner of a consignment store. But Eve's life, and her business with it, is turned upside down when a wealthy customer is found stabbed to death in a fitting room. As accusations fly and business slows, Eve takes matters into her own hands.

During an airboat trip in the Florida swamps, Eve's Uncle Winston is shot in the head. Eve soon discovers that Winston was "connected," although this was no simple mob hit. The Sabal Bay consignment shop owner vows to find his killer, even after her car is wrecked, she is left to the mercy of the alligators, and her best friend is kidnapped.

Madeleine's new beau, David, has been framed for murder. Who's the real culprit? What about his nasty neighbor Blake, whose rival hunting lodge features illegal exotic animals? Who kidnapped the nephew of Eve's Miccosukee Indian friend Sammy? Can Eve and Madeleine rescue their consignment shop from Blake's horrid wife Elvira? Gators are not the only predators stalking rural Florida.

When Eve Appel catches an airborne head while protesting a mud bog race in her adopted home of Sabal Bay, Florida, she recognizes it as belonging to one of her consignment shop customers. Jenny leased her property to the racing company. So who killed her? Her ex-fiancé, an environmentalist? Her daughter's thuggish boyfriend? In solving the crime, Eve enlists her usual crew of friends and family.

Also check out three short stories featuring Eve and Madeleine.

Wondering how it all began? Here's the opening
of book 1 of the series,

A Secondhand Murder

CHAPTER 1

━━━

I JERKED THE dressing room curtains closed, swallowed, then
swallowed again. The lump in my throat wouldn't go away.
I opened my mouth to speak, but I was at a loss for one of my
usual, Eve Appel, sassy gal retorts—the ones I generally have
on hand to fend off difficult situations. What's the protocol for
a dead body showing up on the opening day of business? I took
a deep breath and punched 9-1-1 into my cell and managed to
tell the dispatcher about the emergency. Not bad. The lump was
gone. I made my voice as cool as the breeze wafting from the
window air conditioner. I didn't want to alarm our customers.
"Madeleine, could you help me a minute? I think we've got a
problem with Mrs. Sanders." I might be able to fool others with
my calmness, but Madeleine, my business partner and lifelong
friend, would know better.

She poked her head of bouncy red curls around the hallway
corner. "I told you the damn dress would be too tight. I was
right, wasn't I?" she whispered.

"C'mere." I signaled her. "You don't have to whisper. Mrs.
Sanders can't hear you." I shoved the curtain to one side and
pointed, my red nail polish making a bloody colored blur as

my finger shook. I stuffed my hand into my pocket.

Madeleine's ivory skin turned an even whiter shade of pale. "Gads."

Mrs. Sanders lay face up on the dressing room floor, a knife protruding from her chest.

"The dress is way too tight," Madeleine said with a nervous giggle, a sure sign she was in anxiety overload.

"Madeleine, get a hold of yourself." I grabbed her hand and leaned in to get a better look at the body. "The knife ... I think it's from that cutlery consignment we took in on Monday."

"She was looking at them earlier before she spied the cocktail dress." Madeleine said as she turned her head away from the body.

"I just called the police." I held up my cell.

"Thank goodness. You know I fall apart in crises." She pulled the curtain closed and leaned against the wall, her tiny freckled hand over her heart.

"Buck up, girl. You just make certain no one comes back here."

"Did I hear something about the police?" A woman appeared at the end of the hallway.

Oh, no. It was Mavis Worthington. She was the writer for *About Town*, a new monthly magazine that offers in-depth coverage on people, charity events and business enterprises in the area.. She wrote the "What'Sup in Town" column. If she couldn't find anything 'sup, she made it 'sup. On any other day, she wouldn't have even been in the store, but today was the grand opening of our consignment shop, Second to None. Madeleine and I had sent her a personal invitation and a Ten Percent Off coupon to entice her to cover the event.

"No, no." I steered her out of the hallway, back into the main part of the store, which was filled with customers. "Did you see the lovely selection of Capris we got in, some in more statuesque sizes?" Enormous sizes was what I meant. Mavis was an abundantly proportioned woman, whose ample body seemed to quiver when she walked.

She nabbed several pairs off the rack.

"I'll need to use a dressing room." She nodded her head toward the cubicles.

"Uhm. No."

"No? You can't expect me to buy these without trying them on first."

I wrung my hands and twisted my body in the direction of the dressing rooms, then back to confront Mavis. I must have looked like Gumby. Dressing room? Definitely off limits, especially to the town's professional gossip.

"We've had a bit of an accident. You can't use the dressing rooms."

"What kind of accident?"

"Ah, well, you see ..." I was stumbling around like a teenager whose mother had found her birth control pills. I couldn't tell her the truth—that we were keeping a dead woman in the dressing room next to the one she wanted to use.

"Well?" She held up the teal and coral pants and shook the hanger at me.

"We've had a leak, and the only unoccupied dressing room has a wet floor." I smiled. Close enough to the truth.

"Too bad, but I'm certainly not going to buy these without trying them on." She made an impatient gesture toward the sign displayed behind the cash register that said: "All sales are final."

"For you, Mavis, this sale is not only twenty, rather than ten percent off, but it's not final. You can bring them back if you don't like them, or if they don't fit right."

"Great. Then I'll grab a few more things while I'm at it." She headed toward the dress rack near the front windows. I hadn't intended to offer her the entire store at a reduced rate, but I had more important things to do than worry about how much merchandise Mavis hauled out the door. Getting her to peruse more clothes would keep her around until the cops showed up while also steering her away from "What'Sup" in the rear of the store.

Madeleine stuck her head around the corner of the dressing room hallway. "Where are the cops?"

I rushed up to her. "They should be on their way." I motioned toward Mavis, who was loading yet another dress onto the growing pile in her arms.

"Maybe we should close the store and tell the customers to come back tomorrow," Madeleine said.

"No! The police will want to interview everyone."

"People have been going in and out, and Mrs. Gaulfield looks like she's ready to leave."

Mrs. Gaulfield didn't look like a killer, but I wasn't going to pass judgment. I rushed past Mavis and threw myself in front of the door. "You don't want to leave."

"Why not?" The tall, thin woman shifted her purse to her other arm. "You're charging mighty stiff prices for secondhand stuff."

"Classy, designer quality, secondhand stuff, gently worn by women of excellent taste," said Madeleine, barely keeping her temper in check.

"Go back to the hallway," I hissed in her ear.

She smiled at Mrs. Gaulfield and nodded. "The most discerning women of impeccable taste." She fled to the back of the store where I hoped she was retaking her post in the dressing room hallway.

I placed a gentle restraining hand on Mrs. Gaulfield's arm and whispered in her ear, "We're having an unannounced thirty percent-off sale in several minutes. Stick around and you can get that silk blouse for fifteen dollars."

Her eyes lit up, and she spun on her heel, making tracks to the blouse round where she pulled a filmy turquoise item off the rack. Hugging the material to her, she said, "I'll look for a skirt to match."

Made in the USA
Charleston, SC
13 February 2017